Venero Armanno is the author of *Jumping at the Moon*, a short story collection, and many critically acclaimed novels, including *The Dirty Beat*, *Romeo of the Underworld*, *Firehead*, *The Volcano* and *Candle Life*. *Firehead* was shortlisted for the Best Fiction Book Award in the 1999 Queensland Premier's Literary Awards; *The Volcano* won the award in 2002. His books have been published in the US, France, Germany, Switzerland, Austria, Holland, Israel and South Korea. *Black Mountain* is Armanno's tenth work of fiction. He lives and writes in Brisbane.

VENERO ARMANNO

Black Mountain

UQP

First published 2012 by University of Queensland Press
PO Box 6042, St Lucia Queensland 4067, Australia
Reprinted 2012

www.uqp.com.au

Cover design by Blue Cork
Author photograph by Letchford Photography
Cover photographs © Karen Ingham/Millennium Images; iStock Photo
Typeset in 12.5/16pt Bembo by Post Pre-press Group, Brisbane
Printed in Australia by McPherson's Printing Group

National Library of Australia cataloguing-in-publication data
is available at http://catalogue.nla.gov.au

Black Mountain / Venero Armanno
ISBN   978 0 7022 3915 1 (pbk)
        978 0 7022 4768 2 (pdf)
        978 0 7022 4769 9 (epub)
        978 0 7022 4770 5 (kindle)

University of Queensland Press uses papers that are natural, renewable and
recyclable products made from wood grown in sustainable forests. The logging
and manufacturing processes conform to the environmental regulations of the
country of origin.

Black Mountain

Prologue

THE DREAM ALWAYS GOES LIKE this: a man in a pale blue shirt and pale blue trousers is standing in a small bare room. A creature with no face is with him. This creature, something like a man, shuffles across the cold hard floor and reaches out to him.

The way it puts its hand out is clearly not a threat, only a supplication. If the creature had the ability to speak through the small red gash that is its mouth, it looks for all the world as if it would make a plea for help.

Its palm is unlined and perfectly white. Like its face, it too has no features.

The creature feels blindly around with its hand until it finds the man's wrist and pulls it hard to its own throat. The man snatches his hand away, but the thing uses all its strength to press his hand back to its throat, holding the fingers around its delicate windpipe.

Begging.

The man's face is full of horror, which changes to terrible pity as the creature's eyes fill with tears.

Then a change comes.

As the man's hand is held locked to the creature's milky throat, human features slowly take shape. A face forms.

It's his own. The creature acquires *his* face.

And soon the man is looking at himself, is strangling his own image.

★

Mark Alter had been having the same dream for as long as he could remember, a scene so vivid and perfectly played out it was as if he was always stumbling into a cinema mid screening, with no information about how he'd got there or what kind of movie was showing. The scene confused him, never failed to wake him with a roaring of blood in his temples, but what was immeasurably worse was that sometimes in his waking hours he would turn a corner and see the creature. Or perhaps out of the corner of his eye, yet in an indefinite space, he'd catch a glimpse of the thing that had been the undercurrent to everything he'd thought or done for more years than he could say.

He didn't know what or who it was supposed to be. Mark wondered if it was a monster from deep in his psyche, or – and this was what he'd believed as a child – some brief encounter with a space alien that had seared itself into the depths of his mind and refused to go away. By the age of thirteen that particular idea was pushed aside.

The creature, however, never was.

Something started late one evening when he couldn't sleep and the television reception was particularly poor.

He'd only just turned twenty-two years of age, a dropout from university with no prospects ahead and no one else to blame for this fact. For the past year he'd been living alone in a rundown rental shack outside a tiny beach town called Prospect Point; the solitude was one of the only things that felt right to him. A very bright student at school, to the pride of the parents who'd adopted him at the age of five, he'd entered law, only to abandon it all just two and a half years later. Study and campus life and other students seemed somehow irrelevant. He moved away, disappointing Joe and Maria Alter, who'd given him their name and hearts. After months of aimless travel and itinerant work, he ended up settling in the quietest and most peaceful area he could imagine.

In Prospect Point he knew life was passing him by, or had already roared past him, but he also knew that the absence of friends, of a lover, even of a purpose, didn't seem to mean all that much to him. There were mornings he woke with blank thoughts in his mind; there were other times he opened his eyes thinking, *One day I will find myself.*

Find myself?

It was one of those rare nights when he felt particularly lost, when he wished he had somewhere to go and people to talk to. Outside it was wintry. An ocean storm sent giant waves thundering into shore. Mark could hear the dull reverberations. He wanted to brave the weather, but it was too miserable for him to take one of his long night-time coastline walks. Yet inside the shack every book he had was already digested. The television offered nothing.

He decided to brave the cold in a different way. He'd ride his bicycle to the local picture house, snuggle up in his heaviest coat, and take in whatever was going.

It turned out to be a horror movie. A cheap slasher film. The ten or twelve other patrons, all well under the minimum classification age of eighteen years, laughed at the blood and the gore and threw popcorn at the screen whenever young naked bodies were featured. Which was often.

Mark sat in a back-row corner, alone. Then, unbidden, certainly without any expectation that something like this might happen, a purpose grew in his mind. The idea sharpened. Later, he could hardly sleep for excitement.

The next day brought sunnier weather. He called in sick at the café where he worked in order to pay his rent, feed himself and buy second-hand books off internet sites, and rode his bicycle to the nearest big town's library. Even though Edgecliff was thirty kilometres away, the library staff knew him well; he was a regular patron.

Mark found and withdrew all the 'How To' texts they held on screenwriting. There were six. In the following days he absorbed each book as carefully as he could, returning again and again to that small theatre in order to watch whatever movie was showing, and to test out the sorts of things he was learning. He didn't mind if he saw the same film two or three times; in fact he preferred it.

Plot, structure, character and theme.

Dialogue, setting, turning points, climax.

Mark Alter absorbed those books, all those second- and third-rate films, then on his creaking computer, purchased two years back at a day market for seventy-three dollars, he opened a new document and finally typed his title. The title was the easiest thing of all because it had been with him all his life.

'No-Face.'

This thing, No-Face, is hidden away in a foetid cell somewhere. It has one hairless arm, a bald and pallid head with tiny tributaries of blue veins tracing beneath the raw scalp, and no facial features at all, except for what could be its mouth. There's no real possibility of expression in that bland white absence.

It is dressed in what could have once been a hospital gown. Soiled bandages reveal a stump where the left arm should be; for some reason it's been hewn away.

Who would have done this? Why? The dream never supplied the information.

The man standing alone in the room with the creature is not a friend. Not someone to offer succour. *Maybe he's a trainee doctor of some sort, a novitiate to the sciences. What do his pale blue clothes signify?*

And the story from Mark's dream, of the white, slim and milky creature dressed in rags, pours out onto his screenplay's pages.

The telephone was ringing, a dull burr on the landline he kept only by need of his work at the café. He'd never had a mobile telephone, barely used email, and didn't actually like the computer on his kitchen table. A young woman who'd spent a rare three nights in his bed had called him a luddite on her permanent way out. She'd been right.

'Hello?'

'This is Justin Blackmore.'

Mark Alter's heart actually skipped a beat. Justin Blackmore was a perennial of film and television, a man who'd directed and produced small screen series and big screen movies over an almost fifty-year career. When Mark had completed the fifth and final draft of his screenplay, 'No-Face', a slasher movie about a shape-shifting demon from the Id, set in a small beach-side town resembling a cross between Prospect Point and Edgecliff, he'd looked up all the film directories he could find. Discovering a listing for the famous Justin Blackmore and his production company, Blackbird Films, Mark had packaged up his best draft and mailed it to the post box address with a small note: *I hope you like my movie.* He remembered to include his contact details.

'Is this Mark Alter?'

'Yes it is.'

'Hello.'

'Hi . . . Well, uhm, hello, Mr Blackmore.'

There was no immediate reply. Mark wasn't sure if he should say something to break the ice. He was wearing a pair of pyjama bottoms and nothing else. His shack was cold but the winter's day outside was bright and blue. He stood at a dirty, sea- and sand-smudged windowpane and looked at a crooked dead tree, once a flourishing palm, in the backyard.

'You received my script?' Mark ventured.

'I did,' the voice replied. There seemed to be an edge to it. 'And I read your script. That's why I'm calling.'

'Okay.'

'Tell me something.'

'Yes?'

'How old are you?'

It was a strange question and Mark couldn't imagine what it could mean.

'I'm twenty-two.'

'*Twenty-two.* A youngster. And you're educated. I can tell that from your writing.'

'Yes.'

'You have some sophisticated ideas and quite a sophisticated way of getting them across. Even for a little horror film.'

'Yes,' Mark repeated, not knowing what else to say.

'Well, I've got bad news for you, and an educated young man like yourself should have seen it coming. I'll allow you a free pass on account of your relatively tender years, and that's the only reason I'm taking the time to call you. I think one serious and tough warning early in your career might scare you straight. Do you understand?'

'Ye-es,' Mark said yet again, though now he really had no idea what the man was talking about.

'You mustn't plagiarise. Ever. Never help yourself to other people's ideas. It is *stealing.* There is no lower or more contempt-ible act in the mind of creative people. I can see that you haven't completely stolen *all* his ideas, but this "No-Face" creature, that's not yours to play with. It has no right to be in this film you've put your name to. Disgusting. A disgusting act of thievery. Do you hear me?'

'I think . . . I think there's been some kind of misunderstanding.'

'Really? Cesare Montenero gave you free access to his work?'

'I don't know who Cesare —'

'And if he did, where is the copyright notice? There isn't one. There is no agreement, is there?'

'But I want to say—'

'Let me tell you this, young *Mark Alter*,' Justin Blackmore spoke, his voice nakedly contemptuous, 'do not try to squirm your way out of the hole you've put yourself in. Do not try to fast talk me. I've been around too long and I've seen your type come and go. You're a thief and that's flat. Now I'm here to tell you that I'll give you a let-off because it's early in your career. No other reason. This *is* a first screenplay I take it? Well, here is your one chance to learn and move on. Hear me?'

'Yes.'

'Do not do it again. Do not even *try* to finesse your way out of having been discovered. Consider it a blessing that you were caught by me and not by someone who might have decided to take more punitive action.'

Mark swallowed hard. He knew there was no way to make this Justin Blackmore believe he was innocent of whatever crime he was supposed to be guilty of.

'What should I do, Mr Blackmore?'

'Good. Good question. Now you're thinking. The answer is simple. Start afresh. Burn this garbage you've written. Delete it from your computer and apply your talent to a worthier project.'

'It's that bad?'

'*Bury* it.'

Mark had to breathe hard. Had to remind himself to breathe.

'Okay.'

'Or . . . if you sincerely love the source material so much, do the right thing. Go through the right channels. Organise yourself to work on a proper adaptation of the book. Though I'd wager you'd never get permission or the rights. Not an inexperienced kid like you.'

'Rights?'

'Of course. The writer Montenero, or his estate if he's already dead, would have to sign proper contracts on *Black Mountain*. Even a novice like you ought to be able to figure that out.'

His screenplay was delivered back to him in a brown envelope several days later. It had clearly been read. Pages were crumpled, some were torn, and a blue pen slashed innumerable sections in angry strokes. Mark felt ashamed without understanding why he ought to feel ashamed. *Plagiarism?* When 'No-Face' was all about the no-face creature he'd been seeing in his dreams and nightmares, and out of the corner of his own eye?

As it turned out, the Edgecliff library needed eleven weeks to source a copy of the novel *Black Mountain* by one Cesare Montenero. The length of the delay was due to the fact that the book had been published five years previously and was now out of print. Second-hand copies were difficult to source; none were for sale through the usual online sites Mark used. He had almost toyed with the idea of contacting Mr Blackmore for his copy.

In the meantime, Mark did some research. He would have liked to have done more, but very little information seemed to be available. Despite innumerable library and internet searches, Mark Alter could only glean the following information about a writer named Montenero.

He was Italian, from the region of Sicily.

He'd published two notable novels in the pre-Second World War period. These were in Italian, of course, and there was no record that they'd ever been translated. From one of the Italian cooks at the café, Mark was able to learn that Montenero's titles in English would have gone something like *God is a Young Man* and *A Life of Disappearances*.

Two prestigious awards for the first book, nothing for the second. Then zero information after that.

No more books were listed, no writings of any sort, no details about the writer himself. It was as if the man had looked at the title of his second novel and taken it literally: he'd disappeared from the face of the earth.

Then, out of nowhere, *Black Mountain*. Published in English.

'Cesare Montenero's first novel in more than fifty years,' announced the publisher's web page, which had been archived and was no longer active.

'A sensation,' went their old marketing blurb.

No sensation at all.

The book seemed to have garnered few, if any reviews, and sales-wise had sunk like a stone. The publishing house in question, a private company called 'The Living Press', had gone out of the business of fiction and non-fiction, and now produced only glossy cookbooks and maps, and the odd large-format coffee table tome about fabulous cities and extraordinary holiday locations.

It would take Mark Alter some time to understand what he had done that was so wrong.

And so right.

He felt a twin burst of dread and excitement when the librarian crooked her finger at him and called him over. The book that had ruined his screenplay's chances, and that had impelled as legendary a figure as Justin Blackmore to call him and accuse him of being a cheat, was held shut with elastic bands. The library call note was still attached. If Mark hadn't been perspiring from the long bicycle ride he would have now from the sight of the book.

He forced himself not to look at it until he was home again. He rode fast, his treasure safely held in his backpack, then he showered, dressed in fresh clothes, pulled all the blinds down over the windows, lay in his bed propped up with pillows, and nervously snapped off the elastic bands.

Maybe Blackmore was wrong. He had to be a man in his seventies, at the very least. Maybe he'd gone soft in the head and was inclined to read things into a novel and a screenplay that simply didn't exist. Mark's palms had dampened. He found it hard to understand the line between his own trepidation and anticipation.

He hoped, really, that this *Black Mountain* might speak for itself.

At first glance the book's cover was a pure, plain black, but turning it in his hands he felt its texturing and looked again. Etched into the dark gloss was the outline of a mountain exhaling a line of smoke. A volcano. For some reason that touched him, touched him somewhere deep. Mark thought about that but couldn't draw any conclusions. There was only this: he knew Cesare Montenero was an Italian writer, in fact a Sicilian writer, so the volcano was most probably the island of Sicily's famous Mount Etna.

How could Justin Blackmore see a connection between *that* and his screenplay?

And why did Mark already feel a sort of affinity for the slim volume in his hands?

He soon learned.

Black Mountain was a short novel about rebirth. A little fantasy about growing young. It turned on the hope of a second chance. Even, it seemed, of a chance at eternal life.

In it, an octogenarian living alone in a mansion at the top of a secluded hill is haunted by a figure, a *no-face* figure. This thing, so spooky and terrifying, also holds a sort of promise: to transform into the old man, to be him, fresh and new. Circumstances, however, take a turn. The creature becomes sick even as the old man himself withers; the disease of one is reflected in the other. All hope seems to fade.

With a sort of thudding in his head Mark could see that the creature was the thing from the corner of his eye, the monster so carefully described in his screenplay. Mark forced himself to read on carefully, to not jump pages ahead in an attempt to discover some secret key to his own inner world.

Then, there it was, only a short chapter later. The definitive cause for Justin Blackmore's infuriated telephone call: a scene that was the direct echo of Mark Alter's screenplay.

Or vice versa.

The no-face creature is in a cold cell, begging without speaking, wanting death, and the man in blue is there, hands tightening around its throat.

Mark Alter pushed himself from his bed and staggered to the bathroom. He felt as if an unseen fist had punched him in the belly and a great hand had slammed his head against a wall. It wasn't possible. It simply *was not possible*.

How? How?

He didn't know and he couldn't imagine what the scene in Cesare Montenero's novel would lead to. In his screenplay, after that scene in the cell, the no-faced creature did not die but instead went on a murderous rampage. A product of some failed government scientific experiment – which explained the man in the blue coat – all the monster knew or desired was to maim and to kill. The twist was that in each murderee's last moments, No-Face acquired *their* face, so that, in effect, each person was being murdered by a version of themselves.

He threw up hard, three times into the bowl of the toilet.

Yes, he had plagiarised. Yes, he had stolen. He was a thief. But was it stealing to do so completely unintentionally? For one more time in his life of aloneness he wished someone else was there with him, someone he could talk to and ask questions. Mark thought of calling his father and mother, but their relationship had never been marked by communication. The fault wasn't so much that of those good folk; Mark blamed himself. They'd tried to love him but year by year he'd drifted further from their care. Joe and Maria Alter might have brought him into their lives at the age of five, when all seemed good and promising, but even by the age of fifteen he'd been certain he wasn't like them, or like any of their relatives, or of any other friends.

One day I will find myself.

But what if I don't?

All twisted up inside, Mark read into the evening. When the small book was finished he returned to the first page and started again. From that scene in the cell, with the terrible one-armed creature begging for assistance, Montenero's story and Mark's story diverged. The book's little fantasy played out towards an unexpectedly happy ending. The old man transfers his life into yet another blank and milky creature, and so starts again. Mark's screenplay, by complete contrast, moved quickly into a sort of comic book celebration of murder. No-Face's rampage is vicious, cruel, completely without remorse, and promises to continue without end.

Mr Blackmore had been correct in one aspect, at least: Mark Alter was guilty of stealing a basic idea and a complete scene, but not an entire storyline. Yet how could any of this have happened?

Mark took a clean sheet of paper and composed a hand-written letter.

Dear Editors,

I would like to contact the author of the novel Black Mountain. *I have read the book and greatly enjoyed it. I would like to communicate with its author. In fact, I would like to meet him. Maybe Mr Montenero would be interested in someone writing a screenplay adaptation of his novel? If so, I'd be very interested in the job.*
Yours sincerely,
Mark Alter

From there, he had no idea what might happen. All he was certain of was that he shared *something* with some forgotten writer. And just how *old* was the man, anyway, if his first books were published before the war?

A reply to his letter came within ten days.

Dear Mark Alter,

We are not a contact agency for Mr Montenero, however, in this instance, we have passed along your message. He advises that he doesn't receive guests and has no interest in film.
Regards,
Laura Bird
Publishing Editor, The Living Press

There were full contact details, so, undeterred, Mark wrote an email to this Laura Bird.

Hi Ms Bird, Mark Alter again. Thanks so much for your letter. Could you let Mr Montenero know that I'm a scriptwriter, and pretty good, and that I still think his book would make a really, really great film? He doesn't have to be involved, but I'd just like to talk to him about how we might go about it. Could you ask him if it's okay for you to pass me his contact information please? All the best, MA

The reply? It came the next day:

I tried him again. He still says no.

Mark tried to sleep on it. Somehow he had to find a way to see this man. He'd already looked up telephone books, but the few Monteneros listed had never heard of someone called 'Cesare' and didn't appreciate being bothered.

At the café, the Italian cook looked at the slim novel Mark had taken to carrying around with him, and said during a coffee break, 'You know what? That book's writer's name is the same as the title.'

'Huh?'

'Montenero, get it? "Nero" and "negro" translate as the same thing, which is the colour black. And what's a "monte"? It's a mountain. So you get "Black Mountain" out of his surname and in a couple of languages too. Italian, but maybe Spanish and Portuguese as well, I'm no expert. So it's an autobiography or something?'

'Not unless the old man's planning on living forever,' Mark replied, and something cold seemed to slide down into his spleen.

Mark decided there was only one way forward: the truth. He emailed Laura Bird one more time, promising himself that if things didn't work out he'd force himself to forget about an old writer and some forgotten book.

Hello Laura, I know I can't ask you to keep doing this for me but there's one thing that's sort of important. If you could get this message to Mr Montenero then it'd really mean something. Could you just tell him that I understand what he means about the creature? I've seen it too. I know all about it.
That's all. Mark

There was no email reply. Two days passed, three, four, a week and then two weeks. Mark took the book back to the library. He tried to deny its very existence. He deleted every one of his screenplay's files from his computer's hard drive and he physically destroyed the backup thumb. One day he was looking out his grimy window, at the dead crooked tree in the backyard, and he remembered the other thing Mr Justin Blackmore, famous producer and director, had admonished him to do.

Bury it.

Why not?

Mark took the hard copies of 'No-Face', and an old shovel from the small store of tools under the shack, and buried his various screenplay drafts in a box deep, deep, deep into the ground by the roots of the dead palm tree.

Posterity could have his film. Or ants and worms.

The telephone was ringing and when he answered it a husky voice asked, with an accent, 'Do you feel pain?'

Mark experienced the same leap of his heart that he'd felt when Justin Blackmore had called him. He knew, instantly, without doubt, that this was Cesare Montenero.

'Why would I?' he replied. 'Of course not.'

'Then what do you think you know?'

Mark swallowed hard. Somehow tears sprang into his eyes. It choked him to speak.

'Only that . . . only that I see it too. What you wrote in your book.'

'A creature?'

'Yes.'

'So you put it into a film script?'

'How do you know that?'

'Blackmore told me. We go back. Don't have dealings with the man. Don't trust him.'

'This is Mr Montenero, right?'

Mark was stalling for time, trying to get his thoughts straight. Why was the old writer telephoning him now? And now that he had him on the line, what ought he ask him?

'Am I the person you've been looking for? You know the answer.'

'I do.'

'And no pain, you're certain?'

'None at all.'

'You're too young. Twenty-two.'

There was a sharp intake of breath on those last words. Mark heard it.

'You're – you mean, you're in pain?'

'I don't know,' the old man spoke, and Mark could tell it was an honest answer. There was quiet breathing, then: 'I don't know what it is. I don't know what to call it.'

'I want to come and see you.'

'It's more realistic to think that I might not be here much longer.'

There was another intake of that breath.

Mark imagined an elderly gentleman sitting in some chair somewhere, and an old-style telephone receiver, probably Bakelite, pressed to his ear, his torso doubling over as something that hurt went through him. Trying to suppress it. Trying not to reveal too much of it to the person on the other end of the line.

But breath doesn't lie.

'Then let me come now,' Mark said quickly, afraid the old man would die before he ever had the chance to properly speak with him. 'Tell me where you are, I'll get moving.'

'No. It's too soon.'

'Too soon?'

Silence. No breath. No nothing. Then: 'What did you do with it?'

'With what?'

'The screenplay Blackmore told me about.'

'I got rid of everything. All the drafts. Deleted them. I'm going to trash my computer too. And the paper copies, well, I buried them. Under a dead tree.'

'You buried them under a dead tree?'

Now there was a hint of amusement in the old man's softly accented voice. Amusement in a man who sounded as if he was just this side of death.

'But I can tell you all about that when I meet you. When I come see you.'

'Are you certain you buried those things under a tree?'

Amusement and – was it a sort of longing?

'That's what I said.'

A pause. Breath in. Breath slow on the way out.

'What do you think you'll find by coming to see me?'

Mark wanted to reply with the clear and absolute truth – *I want to find myself* – but he knew how foolish, how *young*, that would sound.

'I don't know. But please let me.'

'I already said I might not be here.'

'Then I'll come now. This minute.'

'No.'

There was a longer pause. A ragged sigh. Mark wondered if the old man might not expire on this very line.

'Then when? Somehow I'll find you. I will, Mr Montenero, I promise you that. So you might as well tell me where you live.' Mark swallowed. With his sleeve he wiped those tears away. 'Please?'

The old man was clearly thinking it over. His voice was softer: 'Two weeks. A fortnight. Then you can come.'

'What if . . . what if you're not there?'

'Once you're here you'll know where you are.'

'What does that mean?'

'You'll know.'

'Where do I come? Where do you live?'

Instead of giving the answer, Cesare Montenero whispered, 'You think you want to live forever?'

'Live forever?' Mark's brow was furrowed. Such a thing had never crossed his mind. 'No.'

Then he stopped.

Had it never crossed his mind? Really? Who wouldn't want to live forever? The question snapped at him, confused him, then, somehow, he knew exactly how he had to answer the old writer. Mark had to answer with his own question.

'Do you want to live forever, Mr Montenero?'

'Huh.' A pause. A reflection. Then the husky voice. 'I never used to.'

And the line went dead.

In the following two weeks Mark Alter felt more alive than he'd ever felt before. He was nervous and sleepless with anticipation, but was also wracked by anxiety, by anguish. He would meet this old man who saw the same thing inside his mind that he saw, he would find some real answers. Yet how would Montenero let him know his address? When would Mark be contacted again?

The telephone didn't ring except for calls from the café to confirm his roster. Worse thoughts crept into Mark's mind. What if Montenero has passed away since the telephone call? What if I never have the chance to find out what binds us?

Exactly fourteen days after the telephone conversation, an email appeared in the electronic in-box he so rarely used.

Here is the address.

It was from Laura Bird.

As if liberated from chains, Mark immediately readied his backpack. He used a red pen to work out the route on a fold-out map and he checked bus and train timetables. No need to fly; a day and a half would get him there.

Without calling the café to say he wouldn't be back for some time, perhaps a very long time, he rushed out of his home and started his life's journey.

The road in both directions was hot and dusty, heavy traffic lumbering past in the monotony of midday. More than twenty-four hours had passed, too many bus and train connections had been taken, but he knew he was almost there.

Where?

Cesare Montenero's address was somewhere deep in the country. Mark had arrived into the sort of outlying area that should have been rural but was now very obviously on its way to becoming thoroughly suburban. Construction vehicles rumbled past him. Billboards advertised farmland sell-outs and subdivisions.

At the next turn marked on his map things changed, and for the better.

Along Greatrock Road, Mark found that the vista was different. There were tall trees thick and full of birdlife. Insects were chirruping and lizards and other creatures scuttled through the undergrowth. The sweat dried on his face and in his shirt, and the road narrowed until it became a nice, cool country laneway. Few cars passed. Cattle and horses grazed behind country fencing. The region was marked on his map as 'Godbless'.

Mark hiked on and a good half century melted away.

★

The place he was after seemed to be at the peak of the hill in front of him. It was no black mountain, but there was a steep gradient to the top. Empty paddocks and swaying grass were the only neighbours. A driveway cut upwards and a splintered wooden post box was nailed to a stump. The number was the same as the one on his scrawl of paper.

A large handprinted sign read, *No Visitors.*

Then, going higher, Mark saw what must have been Cesare Montenero's house, an absolute oddity sitting in the centre of a huge hilltop parkland.

It was a red-brick mansion with arches, gables and a pair of chimney stacks that weren't smoking. More than anything the great home resembled a kind of dilapidated European manor, something that should have resided in the green meadows of provincial France or Italy. The house was nestled amid five, maybe ten manicured acres on which were mature jacaranda trees and scores of hoop pines, giants every one of them – Mark thought they must have been fifty, a hundred years old.

Further back, the land started to dip to the natural curve of the terrain, and a green perimeter marked the start of thousands of acres of state forest. In all, this place was built for seclusion; if you liked privacy and solitude, he thought, here was your paradise.

No bell, buzzer or intercom. The long, swing-open gate had a reminder of the sign down in the lane: *Private Property, Keep Out, This Means You.*

Making sure to shut the gate behind him, Mark started up the drive toward a large circular courtyard. Before he was halfway there three dogs appeared from around the side of the house.

They came so fast across the jade lawns that he didn't have time to make a run for safety. Their heavy paws pounded the ground. At the last moment, with a gasp of horror, he turned his face and body away, expecting to be mauled like meat.

Instead, all three dogs circled his legs, panting hard, tails wagging.

A black, a white and a red-brown. Breathing again, Mark continued to the house, three dogs at his heel.

The front door was heavy and hand-carved, with an iron knocker in the shape of a snake consuming itself. He rapped hard.

Thirty seconds, sixty. No one came. Mark walked carefully around the side of this peculiar manor, past four locked garage doors and a thriving vegetable garden.

Another door in the back. He knocked on it and called out.

'Anyone home? Hello?'

No answer and not a single sound from inside.

Then Mark saw something extraordinary: a large wild and overgrown patch of forest that had been fenced off, constituting maybe an acre of the virgin woodlands the entire Godbless region must have been generations back. It was a private jungle, preserved perfectly. Flowering flame trees gave the illusion of fire and movement. The treetops were full of the blues, reds and greens of budgerigars and parakeets; a great squawking wave of white cockatoos passed over Mark's bemused head.

He turned back to the house. 'Someone home?' he yelled at the top of his lungs.

No answer.

He went and sat on a steel bench near the driveway. The dogs curled around him.

As evening descended, Cesare Montenero's little world at the top of the hill started to move towards stillness and silence. Even the birds disappeared. Grey clouds passed overhead and a deep chill set in. Without a coat or jumper, Mark started to shiver. The dogs grew unhappy and restless. They rose to their feet, stretched, then started to whine and scratch at the back door.

He went to that door and tried it. The thing was unlocked.

Mark called inside, knowing there would be no answer. 'Hello?'

Then in a hallway: 'Mr Montenero?'

The dogs had rushed in ahead of him. Their claws scuttled over a polished floor scarred by plenty of dog activity, and they huddled into a comfortable downstairs lounge room. It was full of deep chairs, dark couches, a four-seat sofa, a sideboard and an enormous fireplace. There was no sign of life.

Not wanting to, feeling the trepidation growing inside him, Mark slowly walked through every downstairs room. He discovered a large country kitchen in need of paint and new utensils and appliances. There was a walk-in pantry as big as his bedroom at home, a formal dining room, the living room, a sunroom like a ballroom, and small, quaint sitting areas. A black Bakelite telephone was on a squat mahogany table by an upright chair, almost exactly as he'd pictured it.

Mark could see the old man named Cesare Montenero sitting there, speaking to him, his breath coming hard with inexplicable physical distress.

Shaking, he went up the carpeted internal staircase and found a vast study lined with bookshelves. They were heavy with books. Many different languages. There were two desks for working at. For *writing at*, Mark corrected himself. No computer. Another sofa, more soft lounge chairs, walls that were a deep red colour, and a black carpet. The room ought to have looked funereal but didn't. Not in the slightest.

The top floor, the third.

Two glistening bathrooms and many bedrooms, all of them large, built for an extended family, for visiting relatives, for guests. None of these rooms looked as if they had ever been occupied. The beds and the furniture were dusty. There was little light. Mark didn't count how many bedrooms, for he soon found what was clearly the owner of the manor's own room.

It was a well-appointed master bedroom with an ensuite. This place had been lived in, very well lived in, perhaps in preference to the rest of the house. Mark checked Cesare Montenero's closets, thought he could even smell the old man on all the clothes hanging there. Rows of shoes. Nothing gaudy or expensive. Mostly apparel for the property, for farming land. The dressers held undershirts and underwear, socks and belts. There were bottles of prescription medications, but only a few.

A lint brush; a mirror; a clean hairbrush.

Mark slipped out of the bedroom, not wanting to intrude further. He couldn't help wondering, *How many people live in this house?* The answer came to him.

One old man. Three dogs.

Or, perhaps now, simply three dogs.

He shivered again.

Mark returned to the living room and tried to make himself comfortable as night started to creep through the house. The fireplace was cold. There were gas heaters but he didn't touch them. They weren't his. He oughtn't even to have been inside this place. Where was the old writer?

You think you want to live forever?

I never used to.

The cold turned deep and strong but the longer Mark was in the house, the better he felt. He was hungry, but tired too. Soon he curled up in the deep sofa. The dogs snored softly. There was nothing to see outside now, only an inky black. And it was quiet. An absolute and utter quiet. No wind either.

What was going on?

Once you're here you'll know where you are.

Mark didn't know.

He wondered how an image of a blank-faced thing with no eyes and pasty, gelatinous skin had got him here.

He slept.

The night passed and the cold didn't get inside him.

★

In the morning little had changed, except that the new day filled the house with light and the dogs needed to go outside.

They also wanted to be fed. So did Mark.

He opened the back door and the animals immediately scooted down the atrium and into the garden at the back. They urinated and defecated, poked around, sniffing at whatever life had gone on during the night. Mark let down his zip and urinated against the side of a tree. The blue sky caught his eye. He listened to birdsong nearby. He took in Mr Montenero's patch of forest.

The dogs came to his side and rubbed against him, licked at his hands. They were begging. Mark returned to the kitchen and opened Montenero's refrigerator. There wasn't much, and nothing for dogs. Then he remembered the pantry: he'd seen an older fridge in there. He took a look and had guessed correctly. There were plastic-wrapped packs of meat and bones from some produce store. Their labels read 'Pooch Cuts' and 'Doggie Treats'. Mark took several packs outside, unwrapped them, and let the dogs have the lot. They ate heartily, and after they'd finished and had drunk plenty of fresh water from the bowls near an outside tap, they wouldn't leave his side.

He stood with them, eating cheese and slices of wholemeal bread.

Mark wondered if he ought to look for a neighbour and find out if they knew anything about the old man and where he'd gone. He traversed the property, liking the day, the view, the terrain, the ambience. Across smooth paddocks of grass and in the towering branches of Chinese elms and hoop pines, white cockatoos feasted on nuts and seedlings, and tore off shreds and strips of tree bark.

Nothing else. No one. No neighbours at all.

He walked back to the house, looked down the driveway for an approaching vehicle.

Empty.

Once you're here you'll know where you are.
Oh yeah?

The dogs went playing in the patch of forest. They'd heard something in the undergrowth and wanted to investigate. Maybe a hare, Mark thought, or some kind of lizard. He followed in through the first thick line of trees. The dogs emerged from the brush onto a path, eyes bright, tails wagging. They hadn't found anything but were happy enough. Mark looked around.

So many trees, a heavy canopy, mottled sunlight.

Mark had the place entirely to himself, yet he wasn't at all lonely or sorrowful. It only felt right, to be so alone.

He walked further into the jungle, going around eucalyptus and jacarandas, the wide trunks of the hoop pines. There was an ocean of foliage and he found that the leaf- and mulch-covered pathway lead to an old wooden picnic table and benches. Here the air wasn't simply fresh and clear, it vibrated.

Mark wished the owner of this place, the owner of that hoarse, gruffly accented voice that had spoken to him on the telephone, was there with him.

Then he stopped breathing.

Someone *was* here.

No. He saw some*thing*. In the corner of his eye.

Mark spun around. The dogs looked at him. Studied him. They sensed his apprehension. Mark tried to make sense of whatever it was that he'd glimpsed from the corner of his eye.

The creature.

There.

Then he looked again.

No – he'd been startled by something perfectly commonplace: the thick, abbreviated trunk of a dead eucalyptus deep in the undergrowth. It had one short branch. In the shadows of the forest canopy, in this indistinct light, it had looked for all the world like a monstrous one-armed *thing*.

Still curious, Mark made his way through the brush, leaving the path. Lorikeets moved in the branches overhead.

He found that the dead trunk had been cut by human hands and stood a little taller than chest-height. Mark saw that any other trees that had been chopped down over the years were simply stumps close to the ground – it would have taken ten times the effort for someone, especially an old man, if indeed it had been Montenero, to swing an axe to that sort of elevation. No downward motion to give the axe head greater swing and heft.

And there, by the rotted trunk were abandoned tools. An axe, a mattock, a shovel.

Slightly overgrown with weeds and thorny creepers.

Mark contemplated this. *Been laying there a while, then.*

The dogs waited patiently for whatever this young stranger might do next.

Mark remembered the old writer asking him what he'd done with his screenplay, with him replying that he'd got rid of everything, was going to trash his computer too, and had buried the paper copies in a box under a dead tree.

You buried them under a dead tree?

The hint of amusement in the old man's voice, and a sort of longing.

Mark's heart thumped again. *No way.*

He started in with the mattock first.

The sun had climbed high into the sky, then had moved on, starting to sink. Just as the tip of the shovel Mark was using struck deep down into something that was clearly not a tree root or a rock, the dogs stiffened and tore away. It took Mark a moment to realise that someone had arrived.

He heard an engine, a door slamming.

A voice cried out, 'Hello! Anyone home? It's Peter!'

Mark climbed out of the hole he'd dug, legs and arms aching, his soft palms long-since covered in the ragged remnants of blisters that had burst and bled.

Filthy face running with sweat, Mark made his way from the jungle. A brightly painted van was in the driveway and a white-haired strutting cock of a man played with the dogs.

At least now I'll get some answers.

As he came closer he saw the van was some kind of pet pickup and delivery service. 'Godbless Pet Motel', read its gaudily painted side panels.

'Hey, hello, Peter here for the dogs. You working for Monty now?'

'I'm doing some digging,' Mark said, wanting to remain noncommittal.

Peter slammed open a side door and the three dogs immediately jumped into the metal cages waiting for their transport. They clearly had done this many times before, and liked it.

'The old fellow's gone travelling, huh?'

'I don't know. What did he say?'

'Not sure. He's paid six months. Don't you worry about the dogs, they'll be fine with us. But funny someone Monty's age makes plans so far ahead. I said to him, "What do I do if you don't come back?" You know what he said?'

'What?'

'"It'll be clear by then."' Peter laughed. 'Yeah? Will it?'

Mark thought about this. 'Did he tell you anything else?'

'Nuh.' Peter rolled the side door shut. Mark was almost sorry to see the dogs leave him. 'You gonna be a caretaker or something?'

'No, just finishing a job.'

'Well, have a good one. Guess I'll be back in half a year. Me and these dogs are going to become *very* friendly.'

Mark wanted to ask more questions, get some clearer idea of what was happening, but, he thought, really, now he had everything he needed to know. Old Montenero had decided to leave, had gone somewhere, and had arranged for his dogs to be looked after. Maybe things like utilities to the house had also been arranged, would be switched off soon enough.

Then why had he agreed to let Mark visit?

The van circled and then headed back down the driveway. Mark wiped his face of perspiration, gently rubbed his painful hands against his ruined shirt.

Nothing made sense.

Then he remembered the stroke of the shovel's blade against something hard.

It was a locked metal box and he extracted it from the dirt and broken shale. Kneeling on the leaf-covered forest floor, Mark used the tip of the mattock to carefully snap the latch. He thought his discovery's contents might be precious and fragile, or they might be underwear and accounting pages.

Old newspapers protected neatly bundled loose-leaf manuscripts. These were held together with twine. Written in Italian, the manuscripts seemed to be novels. Each had a title page and a date, and were all of course by Cesare Montenero. The titles were also in Italian, and perfectly similar: *Monte Nero. Black Mountain.*

Same book, over and over.

The dates showed the diligence with which Mr Montenero had kept at his craft all the way through the decades. There was no let-up, but the writing seemed to start around 1950. Nothing before that. Some of the random pages Mark tried to make sense of were mottled and water stained, but most were unspoiled, perfectly preserved.

Beneath these bundles were a collection of quarto-sized notebooks with covers of different colours. Unlike the typed manuscripts, the bound notebooks were filled with steady handwriting in a blue fountain pen. From the very first page the script was neat and assured. The notebooks were numbered one to eight and the pages were hand-paginated so that by the end of the last book there were three hundred and seventy-three pages.

A title was written small and neat on the facing page of number One, which was a black notebook. It wasn't called *Monte Nero*. The title was *Sulphur*.

It took Mark a moment to realise that all the handwriting was in English. Astonished, he turned the page. Its first words were addressed to someone.

So you've found me.

The air in the jungle seemed to shiver.

Mark Alter slammed the black book shut.

Then he waited for his thoughts to make a straight line.

They did make a straight line, and the line went from Mr Cesare Montenero, once only a hoarse voice on a telephone line, directly to himself.

Because those words were addressed to him. They had to be.

Mark took the metal box and all its contents into the house. He couldn't do anything about the Italian manuscripts, but the notebooks . . .

Before he started reading he had to calm down. Occupy himself a little.

It wasn't easy.

Mark ate some of the old writer's food. He had a glass of wine from a corked bottle in the refrigerator. He took his time building a wood fire in the living room's fireplace and getting it ablaze.

Then and only then did young Mark Alter trust himself to sit down with the first volume. The black book. His hands were cold and his heartbeat was irregular, but from the very first words he felt an affinity with everything that was written.

In fact, the old man said it himself:

So you've found me.
And that means you've found yourself.
Please don't look away.

sulphur

By
Cesare Montenero

so you've found me.
And that means you've found yourself.
Please don't look away.

Black Book (i)

I DON'T KNOW WHO YOU are, friend, your name, your age.

I don't know what you know, what you might suspect, what you imagine you are.

It's a mystery to me how you think of yourself and how you perceive the world and its souls. I can only tell you my story. Perhaps it will turn out to be our story combined, perhaps not.

If these first pages sing somewhere inside you, then we're on the right track. If they leave you cold, we're wrong. You're free to burn these pages and to never have to turn your thoughts towards one lost old man.

This is how it starts.

A long time ago, in another place, I had a different name. Now I know that it was the name I had when the bastards gave up on me: *Sette*, which means 'Seven'.

So, at the start, there were at least six others like me.

There must have been many more who came later, children nicely labelled *Otto*, *Nove*, *Dieci*.

They got rid of me young, sold me, I believe, at maybe four or five years of age. There's no town or village that I was born into, and I don't remember the faces of any people who surrounded and studied me. I do recall a mood, however, a permeating sense of failure and disappointment. I don't know why this has stayed with me over so many scores of years, but I do know they started getting rid of us, the ones who hadn't already died or gone mad.

There's an unclear picture in my mind of a man delivering me to another man, and a transfer to a place that in my innocence must have looked both beautiful and strange. I learned that this would be the start of my new life. I was sold and this was a perfect act of subterfuge. In that era the Sicilian poor usually lived with a plentiful supply of children, and the strongest males could be sold young in order to bring the family some small but much-needed income. Not to mention fewer mouths to feed. It wasn't called slavery, though that's what it was.

The subterfuge was that I was supposed to be one of these pressed boys, dumped here from some tiny village, from some worthless family. So now who would be able to trace my true antecedents?

For the first thirteen years of my life I was in Caltagirone, famous for the production of pottery, terracotta and ceramics. The principal feature of the town remains its decorated Staircase of Santa Maria del Monte, with its one hundred and forty-two steps, on which construction had started in 1602 in the old part of the town. Each of those steps is lovingly and painstakingly hand-decorated. Go see them, friend. Once a year they're lit by candles in veneration of Saint James, the city's patron saint, and when our master was happy with us – which was not a common occurrence – the luckier boys would be brought out to the ceremony in order to appreciate the sort of fine work that had been in the Gozzi family business for centuries.

Caltagirone is in the province of Catania, and I was housed with many other children who were mostly older than me. Our master was Aldo Gozzi. He and his family business created and manufactured tiles for the great houses of Italy and Europe.

Using boys for labour was an easy enterprise for a man like

Gozzi. We were beaten into working hard, and we ate little and died frequently. His command was everything. Whenever a boy collapsed for a last time under the weight of the clay he was carrying, his corpse was bundled into a sack and transported away in a cart. If coughs and fevers commenced, the onset of influenza, asthma or tuberculosis, the individual in question was quickly moved to the so-called 'medical quarters' and was deemed very lucky indeed if he was ever seen again.

One day Gozzi had acquired a group of new boys of particular ruddy health, so he decided to prune his existing workforce of bony children. He picked me out, plus six others, and without ceremony and in the rags we were wearing he made us stand in front of a gathering of prospective new masters. Gozzi's overseer recorded transactions in a ledger as the other six boys were purchased almost immediately. My sin, apparently, was to be the most emaciated of all.

A door swung wide and a latecomer entered. Gozzi looked up: 'Giovanni?'

This man, who was in his late thirties or early forties, replied, 'Signore.' He looked at me, a skeleton standing there. 'Is this a joke?'

'It doesn't pay not to be punctual,' Gozzi said without interest.

I saw a frown deepen in Giovanni's forehead. He looked around. 'It's tough work where we're going. Get him to lift that barrel and bring it here.'

It was half-full and would have tested any man. I went and grunted and strained until I had it in my arms, then I delivered it to his feet, water sloshing.

Half-impressed, he stepped around it and came close to me. 'Are you obedient?'

I replied, 'What sort of work am I supposed to do?'

Giovanni raised his hand and slapped the side of my face.

I said, 'I am obedient, sir.'

'Cut your asking price in two, Don Gozzi. It looks like you're trying to sell me your problems.'

The men started to sign the necessary papers.

My life in the world of making beautiful and desirable tiles, ceramics and porcelain, was already over.

So there is a hell on earth, friend, and Giovanni took me there in his horse-drawn cart with another boy he'd purchased.

It was the sulphur mines thirty or forty kilometres from Caltanissetta, past the hilly region by the Salso River. For as far as the eye could see, the natural vegetation of the area had been burned into black stick and charcoal. I learned that the poisonous, billowing smoke and vapour from the smelters were responsible for this abomination, and the ground and undulating hills looked as if they had all been scorched by some great fire-breathing beast.

The boy with me was named Natale, and he'd been working with a gravedigger for so long that he was confused as to whether that was his first or family name. On that day we rode into the sulphur fields and watched the spread of our new home and workplace with the dawning realisation of what we were in for.

Natale was maybe a year or two younger than me, and said he'd been sold after he turned seven. His grave-digging mentor disliked him so much that he often threatened to inter the boy alive with the corpses they buried. One day Natale had the pleasure of burying his master himself – he dropped dead of a heart attack – but freedom hadn't followed. Instead, through a local agent and proxy, his family simply had the boy onsold, and he'd arrived here.

We were given bowls of tepid water with what might have been pieces of potato in it for our evening meal, then shown the shed where we would sleep. It was a night of a full moon. We heard the padlock in the door snap shut as Giovanni locked us in for the night. I scrambled to a window to watch the light bathing the devastated earth of our home. The vista was almost beautiful in its macabre way, but Natale was silently weeping. Tears glistened on his thin and dirty cheeks.

'I want to go home, I want to see my mother,' he repeated. 'You'll come with me, we'll run away.' Then he huddled in his cot, pulling the empty sacks that were meant to be bedclothes over him.

I didn't shed any tears. The difference between us was that I knew no better, and he'd been sold after living a childhood in his family home. Eight brothers and sisters, he told me: far too many mouths to feed when a father and mother received almost no income from whatever type of unskilled peasant labour they performed.

Natale and I, and all the *carusi* – the boys in the mines – we were minute cogs in a system that was a slave trade in all but name. I was fortunate in a way. I had no memories to make me yearn for home and family. Natale never stopped weeping, he never stopped longing for the family that had seen fit to profit from his tears.

Giovanni worked a single tunnel and I never heard what happened to his previous helpers.

The tunnel was a sulphurous hole in the earth, and it twisted and burrowed into the dark hot depths. The burn in the atmosphere stung our eyes and noses, even our skin. At every step it felt as if suffocation would come next. This particularly affected Natale, whose eyes never stopped coursing with tears that were now involuntary, and whose nostrils dripped constantly. Even his skin developed red, raw rashes. He itched and he scratched and he bled.

On the other hand, except for the strain of the heat and the pungent stinging in my eyes, I found I could complete the work

Giovanni demanded without my body wanting to collapse. Whenever we were away from our master, when we were hauling sacks and cane baskets of ore up through the tunnel, I often accounted for Natale's load as well. We managed to make progress like this, me acting as the pack mule and Natale leading as the guide, squinting through the water in his eyes.

In the hut where we slept we tried to get rid of any signs of Giovanni's previous boys. We had two beds out of ten. Most of these looked as if they'd never been used, or hadn't been needed for a long time, but there were etchings and scratches in the walls; days counted off, abandoned, taken up again; stick figures.

Natale and I spoke about how our predecessors must now be enjoying a wonderful freedom off somewhere with their families, and we painted pretty pictures of clear fields and open plains, and pure fresh air to breathe. But at night when we lay falling into the sleep that always came quickly, I was certain that Natale and I shared the same vision: of boys suffocating in the tunnel, or of falling dead under a load, or of having the life beaten out of them for infractions we couldn't imagine. The emptiness of those extra beds in our shed spoke the most eloquent truth of all, and though we tried we couldn't quite fool ourselves about what our real prospects were.

As a miner Giovanni worked the depths, digging out ore that was transported to the smelter at the edge of this vast plain of desolation. There, the sulphur was extracted and he was paid by the amount of crude he could bring to the surface. Sometimes he had us dig and scrape away at the rock walls with him, using a variety of handheld tools such as chisels, picks and shovels, or the brute force of a hammer, but mostly our job was to carry his valuable rubble through the baking twists and turns up to the surface, where we deposited it all into large neat mounds.

Every four or five days the carrier from the smelter came by in his cart, which was drawn by a single, sad mule. The carrier would record the breadth and depth of the pile we made, then Natale and I would shovel and haul the rock onto the cart before descending back into hell in order to start the process all over again. At least out in the open there was some respite; Natale's eyes and nose would dry, the cooler temperature would make us feel half alive; but there was nothing around worth looking at, nothing that lifted the spirit, and the air itself remained as acrid as ever.

At night we spoke about escaping. We thought that if we could somehow break out of the shed soon after Giovanni locked us in for the night then we would have all the hours until dawn before he'd discover we were gone. Not that Natale or I had very much idea about where we could escape to – we thought we could lose ourselves in some big city, though we'd never even been in one and had no idea how to get to one or how we'd survive there. Or maybe we'd stow away on a ship or ferry bound for the mainland. This was an even greater fantasy, for what was 'the mainland'? What were the people there *like*?

Each night we were too deadened by our exertions to follow our thoughts to some logical conclusion. The word simply went through our heads like an idiot's prayer: *Escape. Escape. Escape.*

Giovanni's tunnel wasn't the only hole into the pits of hell. There must have been another twenty or thirty just like ours, and in each of them there worked one or two miners with their own *carusi* to help them. The number of these boys varied depending on how productive the site was, and the miners kept mostly to themselves and the boys never mixed. The only contact Natale and I had with someone other than Giovanni was the cart driver from the smelter. His name was Pino and his mule was Luisa, and that long-faced, sad-eyed creature was often more friendly than anyone or anything we'd ever known, standing waiting with her head bowed, receiving out pats and neck rubs, her eyes closing gratefully at the small kindnesses we offered.

As Pino measured the quantity of ore piled up, we would offer Luisa a pail of water, which her rough tongue lapped with a gentility and grace at odds with the harsh service expected of her. Sometimes Pino would laugh at the fruit of our labours and tell us things that turned our blood cold: 'Giacomo and his brother over there have only got one boy, and he gets twice your haul'; 'Last week Pasquale up at number five got tired of his *carusi* eating too much and he put a pick into the biggest one's eye'; 'Keep this sort of work up and pretty soon Giovanni will realise how useless you two are'; and finally, 'A cry-baby and a skeleton, you know your master must be mad?'

We couldn't know if the things he said were true or if he was merely satisfying a sadistic streak, but the words had their effect: we worked as hard as we possibly could, and Giovanni seemed satisfied enough with our progress that he never beat us, not even once.

There were women in these sulphur fields too, and they must have been the wives or the concubines of the luckier miners, though we rarely saw their faces and had never witnessed their hair flowing free. They covered themselves with coats, shawls and scarves, trying to keep the heat and pestilent odours at bay, but probably also understanding just how lonely and desperate most of these single men and boys were. Worse, they probably knew all about the all-pervading lawlessness in this place, and would have heard the same rumours we did: of fights that ended with knives and blood; of bare-knuckle contests that didn't end when an opponent was knocked down; of men's bodies dumped into forgotten tunnels, their goods and chattels looted and anything that remained being burned in rusted barrels or dumped into the smelter itself.

Natale and I daydreamed about Giovanni one day taking a wife, about what it would be like to have a woman who could act as a mother to us, who would cook us decent meals and wash and darn our clothes. We wondered if one day a woman's face might bestow us with kindly smiles, if she would caress our cheeks and make our daily descent into hell just that little bit easier to swallow.

On occasion, Giovanni had to leave us to work the tunnel on our own. These were the times when he went into Caltanissetta or some other town on an errand or for supplies. Often we'd see him returning across the wasteland, a wisp of a figure taking shape out of the smoke and steam, pushing his cart loaded with another week or two's necessities. Then we'd pray that among his chattels was something entirely new, a bride, but it never happened.

During his daytime excursions we were free to do our work unsupervised, and though we usually hauled a little more lacka-daisically, and dug half-heartedly, we never took these occasions as opportunities to escape. For all the others were in the fields; two boys scurrying across the scorched plains would be immediately recognised for what they were. We'd be dragged back, our only gain the ritualised beating we'd seen from afar being meted out on other *carusi* who attempted escape. To his credit, however, Giovanni never complained about our slower pace when he was away and, as I mentioned, he never beat us – then again, he never needed to, for we followed his every word like obedient dogs. After that first time in Gozzi's warehouse when he'd struck me across the face, Giovanni didn't show the slightest inclination to strike me again. Sometimes I even thought that, at heart, he might be a kind man, a good soul.

A good soul in hell.

The biggest problem he had was that his seam into the earth was dwindling in its usefulness, and much less sulphur-producing ore was capable of being extracted. As his fortunes decreased, his drinking increased. Every night we continued to be padlocked in our shed, and we began to overhear Giovanni in his quarters drunkenly ranting about the paucity of the earth's providence and his overall bad luck in life. Other times he simply howled wordlessly like some beast looking down into damnation.

Then we learned just what sort of damnation we ourselves were in, and the price of escape.

We were dead asleep when there was a commotion outside. Soon we heard men coming to our shed and the padlock being fumbled open. The door swung wide to the wintry chill of approaching winter. Giovanni swayed in the doorway, his mouth rotten with cheap wine, and behind him was a group of men carrying oil lanterns.

'The boy Angelino who works for Don Salvatore here has run away. You two know anything about it?'

Natale huddled to me and whimpered, believing he was about to suffer for something he was completely ignorant of. Not only did we know nothing about this escape, but we didn't even know who some boy named Angelino was. As for this miner we were confronted with, the one called 'Salvatore', we'd never seen him before either.

Giovanni seemed to have forgotten how closely he'd guarded us against contact with others, and Salvatore himself now stepped into our shed. Holding his lamp high, he seemed to fill the space. The man had great bushy red moustaches and bulging eyes. His boots were very fine indeed, and very clean, and his trousers and shirt were neat and without holes. This man had a woman, no doubt about it, and she must have been a good one. He must also have had a lease on a very productive tunnel, or tunnels, because not one ghost of the death in our master's face was in his.

'What do you know?' Salvatore demanded. 'Tell me. If there

was a conspiracy to free Angelino then speak. If you do then I'll buy your freedom tonight. If you don't speak, well, it can only go badly.'

I wished that I did know something. I would have spoken up immediately and grabbed the slightest chance to get away from this place. Instead I could only tell him the truth.

'We don't know him. We don't know you. We don't even know which mine is yours. The only person we know other than our master is Pino with the smelter's cart.'

Pino was standing there in the group. I could see his long face in the flickering light. Funny, but every day he seemed to more and more resemble his mule. It was one of the few things that Natale and I could tell each other to keep ourselves amused.

Our master Giovanni shook off his stupor. 'He's telling the truth.'

'Then get your shotgun and bring your boys,' he told our master. 'Let them learn what happens.'

Salvatore strode out of the shed and the other men gathered around him outside. Giovanni looked none too pleased to be pressed into their service. I thought that had less to do with the expedition and its nature, and more to do with the wintry cold, the loss of bedtime, and the subsequent loss of a day's digging or more.

'You heard him,' Giovanni said. 'Get dressed. And better wrap your feet as well as you can.'

There were three groups that went hunting beyond the black plains into the hills, and our group came upon the boy Angelino as an orange dawn bled through the sky. The best thing about the hunt was that for a few hours Natale and I travelled out of that sulphur mine into land that was as beautiful as any that God has handed His children. The air was sweet, the hills were green, and vibrant meadows filled the valley. Even with winter's terrible cold only weeks away, here the world was as new as on the first day. We saw deer running. Our master raised his *lupara* – the traditional sawn-off shotgun used by Sicilian hunters – to bring a hare home for the pot, but Salvatore stopped him. Why let the running boy know where we were?

Our particular group was Giovanni, Salvatore, Pino and his mule, and Natale and me. I thought we would have to trek over and through these hills for days, if not weeks, which was a heartening thought. Keep running and hiding, Angelino, I prayed, I'll do my best not to find you. The journey filled me with a vitality I hadn't felt before. Natale's cheeks were red, his face full of colour instead of its usual grey. Even poor Luisa came to life. I was amazed by the way her hoofs trotted so adroitly over the rocks, her tail swishing as it had never done before, ears straight and alert.

Then came the worst thing: Pino spied the boy coming down the side of a treacherous hill. It looked as if Angelino had decided to go off in the sort of direction any tracker might least have expected, which was a good idea, but his route must have proved to be impassable. He was struggling to get back down onto a reasonable track. The boy was far away and hadn't seen us, but it was clearly going to take him some time to negotiate that hill.

'Let's get closer,' Salvatore said, his voice flat. The thrill of the hunt was already over and what lay ahead was the brutal necessity of what had to come next. I knew the boy would be captured, chained, punished without mercy, then he would just go back into the pits, probably to haul even greater weights and quantities than before.

When he was satisfied that we'd come close enough, Salvatore stopped the group.

Now I saw the terrible, straining expression in Angelino's face.

The air was cold, he hardly wore anything, and he had no shoes or sandals. The rocks would have been cutting the soles of his feet to shreds. And it looked like his descent had only brought him into even more troublesome terrain.

Salvatore pulled off his gloves and put the index finger of each hand to his tongue. His whistle was long and almost friendly, like a country hiker who sees a *paisan*, a countryman, in the distance. It took a moment for the whistle to reach Angelino's ears, then the boy looked up and around, startled out of his concentration. Salvatore raised his arm and waved in a grandiloquent gesture. Angelino spied us. What would he do? Surprisingly, even comically, he waved back. But he redoubled his efforts, scrambling along a treacherous decline of stones and gravel, much of which tumbled away. Larger rocks gathered speed and crashed to the flat ground below.

I could sense Angelino's terror. How, with so much open terrain all around, such hillsides and meadows, and those mountains that looked so perfect to escape into, had this frightened boy gone so completely wrong?

'Go on, Giovanni,' Salvatore said to my master. 'See what you can do.'

Giovanni hesitated, then he looked at his shotgun. It was loaded and ready for shooting but quite useless at this distance. He made sure the safety catch was set, cracked it in two and unloaded its two bright red cartridges. He slipped these into the pocket of his overcoat, then handed the gun to me.

Salvatore passed him the rifle, and Giovanni looked around then sighted across Luisa's back for support. He concentrated hard, but as he fired I saw my master shut both eyes. Just as Angelino had no heart for being shot, Giovanni had no heart for being a murderer. In that moment, in all ridiculousness, I felt a strange welling of love for the man. He was a miner, a tough, unhappy, unlucky rodent of the earth, with little knowledge of or interest in caring for two boys like Natale and me, but he wasn't a killer. He acted the tough-guy role for the men around him, just as he'd done in front of Gozzi, but now I understood he was cut from finer cloth than any of them.

My master's shot missed by some considerable margin. We saw a puff of dust raise up. For Angelino of course the miss was little comfort. He was still out in the open with nowhere to escape and nothing to hide behind. I thought it would take him at least another five or six minutes to get down off that terrible hillside and into cover.

Salvatore half-laughed and half-sighed. 'Goddamit but I forgot my glasses, so there's no point me trying to shoot him from here. Let's get closer. But we better not waste any more of the day chasing him.'

Pino let go of Luisa's reins and he proffered his open palms. '*Permesso*?' he said. 'With your permission?'

A little surprised, Salvatore now offered the rifle to him. Pino spat onto his right thumb, then wiped the end sight with it. He raised the rifle to his eye and drew aim, not needing Luisa's back for guidance. He kept perfectly still then eased the trigger. With a terrible crack, Angelino half spun to the right then tumbled away.

As Pino returned the rifle, Salvatore said, 'Giovanni, do you mind if we send your boys? My stomach's rumbling.'

'All right,' my master nodded. 'Go get him and bring him back,' he said to Natale and me.

We set out as Salvatore was making himself comfortable and unpacking smoked, dried meats.

The boy was broken across some rocks. There was no life in him; the way he was lying made it look as if there'd never been any life in him to start with. We stood over his body and took him in. In many ways he looked just like us, though an even more decrepit version. The boy was a smaller skeleton than Natale and me, and when we rolled him over we saw that he had the wizened face of a one hundred-year-old man. His existence with Salvatore must have been much worse than ours with Giovanni, though it was hard to understand how that could have been possible.

The bullet had hit Angelino in the neck, going in one side and coming out the other, taking a thick lump of flesh with it. There was a great deal of blood. I don't know why I did it, but despite the freezing cold I took off my outer shirt and bandaged the torn flesh, then I helped Natale get the body onto his back. He carried him a short distance then I carried the still-warm body the rest of the way.

We set Angelino down gently by the group. No one had lit a fire. They didn't intend to camp. The men were eating the thick, dry meat from Salvatore's pack and as our reward for being good hunting dogs, Salvatore threw Natale and me half a salami, which we shared, the best food we'd had in months. Giovanni was sitting a little further away, almost alone.

Salvatore and Pino were smoking. Our master stood, stretched, then went and crouched beside the corpse. He unwrapped the shirt, putting it aside for me, bloody as it was. Then he said to Salvatore, 'Well, you've lost one boy. I guess I can let you have my two for the price of one.'

'Don't give up heart,' Salvatore told him.

'It's not a case of giving up heart,' Giovanni replied, though the expression in his face said that this was exactly the situation. 'My lease isn't any good. I can't afford to try a new one. It's like my life is cursed.' He continued to look at the dead boy as Salvatore turned his gaze toward me.

'How strong is he, really?'

'You saw him carrying this poor beggar,' Giovanni gave my defence. 'He gets the job done. Half price.'

And so again I was sold, and yet again it was at a discounted rate.

★

It took Giovanni less than two days to organise his affairs and clear out. He sold his tools to the other miners and our last errands for him were to deliver these odds and ends to workers at their mine camps. It was the first time we'd been allowed to range so far and wide on our own, and it was liberating, even if what we traversed were burning circles of hell.

As Natale and I returned to Giovanni's camp, where we'd now lived and slaved for more than a year, I knew what the chances were of either of us ever leaving. We mined what must have been one of the most horrible substances in the world, sulphur. Used for the gunpowder that kills, it was once called brimstone, which – more than appropriately enough – fed the eternal fires of Hades. We'd been told that most of the sulphur mines in Sicily had been closed before the start of our century, putting tens of thousands of men and boys out of work, but ours was still a prof-itable enterprise and might well go on for decades. This was the life we'd been sold into, and we had to accept the fact. The only logical escape route was by way of Father Death – and that grim master's presence was always very close indeed.

Our sulphur was also meant for the better tasks of smelting copper and making bronze, but these fine substances meant noth-ing to boys like Natale and me, who tried to live in the fumes and felt it setting fire to our lungs, our eyes, even the spit in our mouths. Distributing Giovanni's tools gave us our first real con-tact with the other miners and their boys camped in this scorched valley. We discovered that everyone looked and sounded the same as we did. The boys were just as pale, thin and dead-eyed, and over us all worked the smelter, which belched poison into the world.

Seeing all of this close-up and firsthand, I prepared questions that I wanted to ask Giovanni before he disappeared: What do we have to do to earn our freedom? Why don't you take us with you and we'll be your willing servants and errand boys?

But when we returned to our camp it was already deserted.

Giovanni had used the cash from the sale of his chattels, including Natale and me, to purchase an old nag with very few hiking and riding days left in her. Away he'd galloped, without sentiment for the boys he left behind. Or maybe stealing away like that made it easier on his conscience: he knew exactly who and what he was leaving us to.

We stared across the plains. Clouds of dust and smoke shrouded the encampments. Both Natale and I must have been wondering the same thing: if we were to take off now, how long would it be before our new master Salvatore set out after us, how far would we get? But wouldn't it be preferable to run right now, to run for kilometres into the sweet scents of meadows and trees, even if it meant stopping a bullet there? At least our last gasps would be of good clean forest air, untainted by smoke and sulphur.

Natale looked at me and I looked at him.

We didn't run. We didn't even discuss the possibility. Instead we turned and left this place we'd called our home, and trudged toward Salvatore's camp before he decided to give us a hiding for being so tardy.

At first it was as if the luck that had eluded us all our young lives had finally arrived, because Salvatore's wife was in the kitchen of their large wooden and corrugated iron hut, and she was making herself very useful indeed. Salvatore had us sit outside on a rough-hewn bench beneath the kitchen window, and as she cooked and hummed our bellies grumbled and growled with the ache of near starvation. We were moved to tears at how beautiful the scents from her stove were.

Soon she passed out two bowls of soup, her mannish hands through those windows looking like those of an angel reaching out to us. The soup was rich and red, and there was tender meat in it, and soft sweet potato, and greens that looked like string bean and broccoli. She also gave us chunks of sour bread she had baked herself. We ate quickly. No more came. It didn't matter. With food like that in our bellies we decided we could haul and dig each shift without tiring, and finally sleep soundly – some nights it wasn't so much the exhaustion and aching bones and the sound of wintry winds that awakened us, but hunger itself, the sheer need for sustenance to quell the never-ending ache in our bellies.

So yes, if food like this was going to come out of our new master's kitchen, we felt as if there'd be nothing we couldn't do for him, and probably with songs in our hearts too. What had Angelino had to complain about? Why had his body been so emaciated, his face so wizened? Our spirits lifted and we were full of renewed hope. We started working for Salvatore at the same dawn hour we were so used to with Giovanni, but this new miner was more powerful, and picks and shovels and chisels looked like toys in his meaty palms, and his tunnel was deeper and more dangerous than the last.

The bushy-headed, red-bearded, goggle-eyed Salvatore was easily twice the worker of our previous master, and it was so hot in his mine that we had to work almost naked. Natale's skinny frame and my stronger back were constantly bowed under the enormous weights Salvatore had us carry to the surface. His dark skin gleaming with sweat, his broad, long back and buttocks rippling with thick muscle, the man was like the engine of a train, ceaselessly driving forward with unimaginable reserves of power. His arms and shoulders looked like they could have uprooted and snapped trees, and his mood was infinitely fouler than Giovanni's had ever been, for he gave us great clouts and kicks whenever he was displeased or whenever he felt like it, which was often.

He grunted and cursed as he attacked this rock he needed to dominate, and we grunted and cursed with the exertion of carrying his product out of that unforgiving hole in the ground. On the third day in our new workplace Natale fell with exhaustion and was asleep before he hit the ground. Salvatore put the spike of his pick hard between the boy's exposed ribs. The boy let out a long sigh of pain but didn't move. Our master picked up an oil lantern and pressed it to the sole of Natale's bare foot. He screamed and moved. We resumed our labours.

In no better mood the next day, Salvatore kicked me hard for not moving quickly enough when he told me to bring him the iron file for sharpening his axe head. Unluckily for me, I was standing at the crest of a long rocky downward passageway that would have benefitted from a stepladder. The kick tumbled me backwards into space. I landed heavily on my side, but the ground gave way and I fell to the rocky level below, and felt my right leg snap and crack beneath me. Pain of a quality I'd never experienced seared through my body and into my skull.

Salvatore came down screaming curses: the Virgin's a whore; what a beast our Lord is; to hell with all the saints and their stupid faces. None of these curses were new of course, but I'd never heard them uttered with such murderous vehemence, as if he would literally strangle me for my utter stupidity.

Blood stained the hot stones around me: my head was cracked. Salvatore lifted me up like a rag doll and my ruined leg untwisted. I didn't pass out, which was a pity. A white bone protruded from the torn skin and meat just below the knee, and another one had split the ankle. I was faint, swooning. When I pressed my hand to my mouth it came away with more blood. I realised my nose was also bleeding; so were my tongue and lips.

Salvatore dragged me to the surface and to this day I am certain that he meant to drag me to the smelter and simply fling my useless body into the great fire. However, his wife was at the mouth of the tunnel, dutifully delivering food and wine for his lunch. She must have read what was in this man's mind because she spoke with even more authority than he ever did. I was to be deposited at their hut, she would do the rest.

And she did.

Only not so well.

There was no inclination to take me to a hospital or even to call someone with real medical experience. Salvatore's wife, whom I discovered was named Annunziata, did her best, but she proved she was no nurse. The woman attended to my broken bones and straightened and stitched my leg herself. She bandaged me from ankle to hip and made sure the wrapping was always clean. Pain never ceased, and week after week was a red haze spent mostly in a daze or unconscious.

I spent my time on a pallet under the kitchen window and, when the weather was foul, which was ninety percent of the time, she either dragged it herself, or had her husband drag it, into shelter. All this time of course, Natale had to contend with Salvatore's demands without me. I rarely saw him; often I was convinced my only companion was already dead. Then he'd appear out of nowhere, white as a sheet, exhausted and aged horribly, a mirror-image of the one hundred-year-old-face of the dead boy, Angelino.

When I could finally walk a little my left leg seemed as strong as ever, but the right remained bent and wouldn't straighten. I limped, I shuffled, I held back tears and knew I was useless. There was still no reason for Salvatore not to throw me into a fire. I was surprised he hadn't already made a journey to find a replacement. It could only be a matter of time before my master decided to take things into his own hands, no matter the protestations of his wife.

That day finally came. I lay on my pallet and watched a litter dragged by two beautiful chestnut-coloured mares come and collect La Signora Annunziata, and take her away, take away the source of the only hope I or Natale had known in this place.

As soon as she was gone, Salvatore appeared around a corner and looked at me.

'Stand up,' he ordered, as if I was God's greatest criminal and malingerer.

I found my feet as quickly as I could. The bandages were gone and the long, thick, puckered scar ran the length of my right leg. The wound was ugly as sin, but it had healed remarkably quickly and there was no more pain, all of which was baffling. Even Annunziata had seemed taken aback at her skills.

'Your beautiful holiday is over,' my master said, and he shoved me towards the mine by the back of my neck. I hobbled as quickly as I could and Natale met us at the mouth of the tunnel. The boy wept with relief to see me, though it appeared his eyes could no longer produce tears. He hugged me and held me hard. I whispered that everything would be all right, he could count on me to do the hardest work again.

Annoyed by all this sentiment, Salvatore boxed our ears and sent us downward.

While his wife had been in attendance she'd kept the workers' quarters clean and had even hooked a stained mirror onto the wall. Natale had been there all by himself during my recuperation and I discovered that Annunziata had even persuaded her husband to repair a spout operated by a hand pump. So that gave us running water. That water was tainted with sulphur and therefore not good for drinking, but to have water to wash with actually inside our hut was a luxury almost beyond comprehension.

The next day, Salvatore gave us leftover stew to eat for breakfast, but that was as good as things were to be because we received no more food at all, not even the slightest scrap into nightfall when we were unceremoniously locked into our hut. My right leg had been holding up surprisingly well and even though Salvatore meted out his usual slaps and kicks, he had no particular need to admonish me for my shuffling limp. A shuffle was the best any of us could achieve in those tunnels anyway, especially when weighed down by sacks or baskets of ore and tools, not to mention the stifling heat. So I was back to work in almost the same condition as before, but now as a crooked boy with a crooked leg.

A long and bleak winter had set in, and the days were spent alternating between the sweltering heat deep down inside Salvatore's slice of hell, and the swirling cold drafts whistling through the mouth and upper reaches of the tunnel. There, the sweat that normally dripped off our bodies turned to ice and made us shiver uncontrollably. Outside the winds might have been freezing, yet down in the hole we still worked almost naked. The only result of all this privation, as far as I could see, would have to be sickness – pneumonia, tuberculosis or the simple loss of will. Whichever it would be, Father Death was on hand.

Subsequent weeks proved no better, and Don Salvatore often didn't remember to give us food until the afternoons, by which time Natale and I would be faint with hunger and alternately chilled to the bone or cooked like meat. We trembled and shivered with distress while our master, who had suddenly struck a richer vein, took to singing loudly and with gusto, his voice a baritone that boomed along the tunnels like some tuneless angelsong sent to make our labours sweeter.

It's hard for me now to believe we actually survived that first period of work for this mad master, but Salvatore was satisfied with the results and he gave us a Saturday and Sunday to do nothing but what we pleased. What pleased us was to lie in our beds with the windows and the door sealed against the wind. We slept endless hours under as many filthy covers as we could find, and when we raised ourselves up we were allowed to enter the main house and help ourselves to food from the kitchen. Sometimes Salvatore was there, huddled in a great coat or in a blanket, sitting at his kitchen table tallying his accounts, writing letters, or chopping vegetables for the evening's stew. Other times he was absent, his home completely empty.

On those occasions we moved meek as mice and touched only those things we absolutely needed to. We didn't go near his stack of ledgers, didn't breathe upon the vat of whisky, and didn't look into the rows of hessian sacks we knew contained nuts, chickpeas, lentils, dried beans and dried fruits. We barely helped ourselves to anything more than the bare necessities, always terrified of his whip and thick leather belt. Not to mention his hands like bear paws. Mice would have eaten more crumbs, would have lapped at more goat's milk. Always we withdrew with the respect boys would have accorded God's own secret rooms, and then we'd go outside and make-up a simple game until our master returned.

The truth of exactly where we were and who was holding us, and the real reason for Angelino's sad attempt at escape, plus the fact of his one hundred-year-old face, made itself known on the Sunday night before we were to resume our labour in the mine.

Hours after we'd gone to sleep the hut's door slammed open.

I was instantly awake. Salvatore's great bulk was framed in the archway, the wintry wind blowing his bushy hair. He came inside with a clump and a clatter. The man had been drinking, and heavily. He had a swaying list as if this was a boat and the waves were tossing. I could smell the whisky on him. Unlike our previous master, Giovanni, who sang and screamed while he was drunk, Salvatore was completely silent. He went to Natale's bunk and looked down, then his heavy step came to my bedside and he looked down at me. My eyes met his veined, bulging eyes and beneath his red moustache his fat lips were wet. Though I had no idea what thoughts were in his head or why he was here like this, some instinct told me to maintain the eye contact, to not look away, to not blink or allow myself to reveal the slightest trepidation.

Salvatore decided he didn't like what he saw, and he swayed back toward Natale's bunk. He shoved him until he was awake. It was like rousing a corpse. He made the boy get up and pushed him outside, then locked the quarters as he left. I didn't quite understand why but I was relieved to be still incarcerated there.

By morning Natale hadn't returned. Salvatore unlocked my door at roughly the usual hour and this time he threw me a chunk of sour bread with a wedge of hard cheese. I drank a quart of goat's milk as I followed him to the mine. My master was in good enough spirits, though his head was obviously sore, but I felt that all it would take was one awkward or impertinent question or comment from me for those spirits to darken. We worked that day at the usual rate or, if anything, at perhaps one fraction more slowly, and at the middle of the day Salvatore even remembered to feed me a little more. It was the same repast – sour bread and hard cheese, delicious.

Later, as I came in for the evening, Natale was there curled up in his cot. He wouldn't speak. He couldn't utter a word or sound, and kept his head under the covers. I don't know if he slept or not. I did, like the dead, thoroughly spent. In the morning as we prepared for our work day, Natale still wouldn't meet my eye and refused to utter even the most basic conversation. I did notice him glancing at himself in the stained mirror *la signora* had left us. Salvatore unlocked the front door but he didn't want Natale in the mine. He took him by the shirt and shoved him toward the larger cabin.

'Get it all clean and arrange things so it's not a pigpen. Sweep, dust, shake everything out. And make some food for tonight.'

With eyes downcast Natale tottered away. In the space of only two days Salvatore had turned Natale into his woman. I was glad to be working down in the sulphurous hole.

Evening came and there was something warm and disgusting to eat that the boy had concocted. I choked it down but murmured how tasty it was. Salvatore slapped the back of my head and sent me on my way. Later, Natale didn't return to his bunk. I slept alone another night, then another, then a week passed, then Natale vanished completely. Salvatore burst into the room in the morning.

'Have you seen that little prick?' He was already checking his rifle and arranging his ammunition strip over his shoulder. 'If he told you which way he was headed, now's the time to speak or I'll put a hole in your stupid skull, too.'

He pushed me out into the morning's ice and I fell onto my knees. I had the feeling he was going to shoot me in the back of the head anyway. The wind had picked up and scattered flakes and flurries of snow. Even I knew the boy wouldn't get very far. At least the previous runaway, Angelino, had sense enough to try to leave in pleasant weather.

'Well?'

'He didn't tell me anything.'

Instead of a gunshot he gave me a kick in the back that sent me sprawling forward, my face hitting the cold, hard-packed earth. Salvatore was already striding away.

'Let me come with you! You can't hurt him!'

Infuriated, Salvatore returned and dragged me up and bodily threw me back inside the cabin. He put his boot into my right leg, making me howl. Then he locked me in, but not before I saw the ice that had formed at his nostrils and in the corners of his mouth. Specks of frost nestled in his plentiful eyebrows too. I didn't know who would constitute the hunting party, but it was clear Natale's fate was decided. The boy didn't stand a chance: the elements or the bullet.

★

It was the elements.

Salvatore returned as darkness fell. He hadn't found Natale. It was too cold for him to camp out and he'd left unprepared anyway. When he unlocked my door and let me out I went to break the covering of ice in the trough outside, which had stopped me being able to pump running water all day. There the boy was, sitting beside the wooden trough, huddled into himself, frozen into his own block of ice.

Only one eye was open and it had the flinty quality of the dull ore we'd hauled out of the mine. Shaking, I sat by him. Natale was like some sculpture made by the cold and snow, and when I put my hand over his all I sensed was the same empty contact you receive from rock. As with Angelino before him, there was no life left, but worse, no sense that there'd ever been life in him at all.

Salvatore came around the corner to see what was taking me so long. When he saw Natale's frozen body his thick lips pursed but it wasn't with sadness, only annoyance. My master picked Natale's body up and bore him to the cart. He found some sacks and swathed the frozen corpse. As Salvatore lifted the cart by the handles and made to push off, I said, 'You'll bury him?'

'Of course.'

Salvatore shoved off into the wind and I noticed that there wasn't a shovel or a pick in the cart with the body. There was no graveyard that I knew of anywhere in this place. Natale and I had often suspected that dead *carusi* were thrown into the smelter's main furnace. Better-connected miners who came to a sudden end were sent back to their families, but the poorer men, and of course we chattels, suffered the fate of dead animals and broken tools.

Blue Book

WITHOUT NATALE'S HELP THE WORK was more arduous than ever. It would always be backbreaking, but now the danger was double. The boy wasn't there to guide me along, to hold me steady when my bad leg faltered in those twisting tunnels. Now when the footing moved beneath me, I sometimes lost balance and fell backwards, losing the load and tumbling helplessly down irregular stone steps, risking more broken bones.

At least Salvatore's digging revealed brighter prospects, and so his mood was improved. Some days he was positively buoyant. The giant would sing and whistle, completely ignoring me, and despite my problems I managed to keep up. Pino would come by with Luisa and his cart, take note of the quantity, then nod his head, almost impressed.

'A leg like a chicken's and look what you can do.' He'd inspect my palms and hands to see how much I was tearing them up, then look into my eyes and ask me to open my mouth to show him my tongue and teeth. 'Clean your teeth once a week. Keep to good hygiene. Make him feed you more and use your spare time to sleep.'

Meanwhile I'd caress Luisa's fur and stroke her head. She always made an appreciative lowing grumble and would press her forehead into my chest. The beast was as close to a friend as I had – and, I thought, might ever have.

Pino was correct in what he said about sleep. I wouldn't have believed it possible, but as the weeks bled on and I continued to serve my master on my own, my exhaustion deepened until there were days I couldn't differentiate sleep from wakefulness. I hauled ore with my eyes open and my eyes shut, while awake and while daydreaming and while snuffling in my bunk. I yearned for longer sleep more than I yearned for food, more than I yearned for the drafts to stop whistling through the tunnel to freeze me every time I came up dripping sweat from the furnace below.

Some nights I was certain Salvatore stood drunkenly swaying at the door, those bulging eyes taking in my huddled shape in the bunk, but I was always too tired to raise my head. Then he'd leave, something unresolved twisting through his head, and I wouldn't care, just so long as I could keep my eyes closed.

Things took a turn for the worse when my master stopped whistling and singing during his labours. I don't think he was unhappy with what we were producing, it was simply that he'd pushed himself hard on this very plentiful and profitable seam, and even his own powerful body was reaching its point of exhaustion. He should have employed another miner or two to help him, and of course more *carusi* like me, but it was clear that he didn't want to make the expenditure – his intention was to accumulate as much money as he could for the smallest possible outlay, and return to his wife in whatever part of the country they came from.

I was on my last legs, and it was hotter than ever in the mine. A breaking point seemed to loom when Salvatore decided to shift his vat of whisky down into the pit with him. He sat it on top of the barrel of water all miners keep close at hand during their digging, and as he took a deep draught from the water he would follow it with a quick swallow from the vat. He sweated more, his breathing came in gasps, and by the afternoons he would swing his pick with less accuracy. Sometimes he inadvertently broke the axe handle and would need me to go up to get a new one, or try to find a way to repair an older one.

It wasn't long before he broke his last remaining pick handle by smashing blindly at a new face of ore and missing completely. The handle cracked clean in two. None of his older stocks were in any condition to be repaired one more time. Shouting in anger, he called me to run to the next mine and beg, borrow or steal a replacement. By the fury in his eyes I knew that if I came back empty-handed I would pay dearly. I shuffled up through the tunnel as quickly as I could and climbed out of the stinking hole. Pino was there with Luisa and the cart.

When I explained the problem to him he pointed to a site about a kilometre away. 'That's Franco. He's a friend of your master's, better try him first.'

I limped and trotted through the sulphurous mist, and here out of the tunnel I understood what a cripple I'd truly become. My gait was awkward and I traversed the scorched ground far more slowly than I wanted. Even though it was deep in the worst days of this Sicilian winter, one that seemed never-ending, the sweat poured off my face. When I found Franco I made sure to keep my eyes downturned, the only way someone of my standing could speak to someone of his. My bad leg was burning in a way I hadn't felt for some time. Though it had healed, I'd noticed that a certain pain had started to creep back during my labours, and, strangely, it was becoming harder than ever to straighten.

'Tell him to be more careful. And tell him to stop drinking.'

Franco gave me three new pick handles and I hurried back across the burned terrain, though this time I didn't run. The sky had already darkened in the early afternoon, and eddies of snow swirled to the whipping wind. In the distance, the smelter poured black death into the day and scores of fires were burning around it. My face was frozen, but my lungs were filled with acrid, hot ash. It was almost a relief to find our tunnel and descend once more, getting away from the sleet and cold. The deeper I descended the more the heat intensified. It thawed me quickly, and not in a pleasant way. A coughing fit wracked through my chest and I had to lean against a wall of rock. That wall seared my back and shoulders, but the coughing burned far worse. A great wave of nausea rose up from my belly and I felt myself starting to tumble forward.

Splayed on the ground, the temperature was unbearable, but the trembling of my limbs only increased, as if a spell had been cast over me, one made to shake a boy's arms and legs from his body.

I knew it had to be the start of some sickness. My face burned, this time from the inside. My vision lost focus, blurred completely. The pick handles had clattered out of my reach. I kept telling myself, *Get up, don't let him find you now, just get up*. If Salvatore saw me like this he would likely decide I'd reached the end of my usefulness, bludgeon me with one of those very handles, and pitch my body into the smelter.

I didn't know much about the symptoms of pneumonia or tuberculosis, but on Gozzi's property I'd witnessed boys dying while spitting blood or thrashing with fever. Still, whatever the disease, it hardly mattered. The result would soon be the same.

So this is how I finish, I thought.

So.

Something remarkable then occurred. My vision cleared and the worst of the illness passed, almost as quickly as it had hit me. A new strength surged through my body, as if some important reserve of energy had been discovered. The change happened more quickly than a turn in the weather. I picked myself up and stood uncertainly for a moment, but my legs were quite strong and my head wasn't spinning. The fire in my chest had been replaced by a warmth that was almost pleasant.

Of course I didn't know what to make of this, but had no

time to think about it either. I continued down and down and down, the three new pick handles over my shoulder, and found my master slumped where he should have been digging. He'd taken the vat of whisky off the water barrel and was holding it in his lap. His chin rested against his chest. Even though he was completely naked, he was propped with his back against a wall. He didn't seem to feel the pain, but I knew his tough hide would have to be burning.

'Help me up,' he grumbled, uninterested in the fact that I'd completed my errand. Despite being weak and helpless as a kitten only moments before, I placed my shoulder under his arm. Lifting him was like trying to raise a fallen oak tree. My master stank of old sweat and sour alcohol. His lips were wet and there was dirt and perspiration in his moustache and eyebrows. I managed to get him to his feet.

'My clothes.'

I found a tattered pair of shorts and a checked shirt that was torn all over. He pulled them on, sometimes swaying, as if he couldn't decide what part of his clothes to put his foot or hand through next. I turned away, not wanting to be compelled to dress him, and when I turned back he had a heavy gaze upon me.

We took his lantern, but left everything else, and I helped him make a staggering journey to the surface of his burning world.

In his cabin, Salvatore dragged on more and more clothes against the cold. Everything was in disarray, and I couldn't help remembering how neatly turned out he'd been in the days when his wife had been here. He eased himself down into a chair at the table with some wine, which he poured straight into his mouth from a dirty bottle. I stoked the fire and added lumps of wood, and put water into a pot to boil on the stove. I thought he needed something warm to drink. I did too. I found some chicory, but as

I broke it into the water I heard my master's chair pushed backwards abruptly, then he came to me, his heavy hands hard on my shoulders and his wet mouth pressed to my neck.

'Don't fight,' he grunted, and pushed my face down onto the kitchen bench in front of me. One hand tore the trousers down from my legs and tried to spread them apart. The saucepan was on the stove beside me, and then I had its handle in my fist and the heavy pot bounced off the side of Salvatore's head, warm water spraying around the room.

His thick matted hair absorbed and blunted the blow, so I lifted the pot again and hit him as hard as I could. His head rocked backward but he was still standing, and a third blow opened a jagged seam across his forehead and down his brow. Salvatore dropped as if the bones had been taken out of his legs. His skull bounced off the floor and he was still as a rock. For a minute I stood over him, frozen as surely as Natale had been, and I thought I'd killed him. Then he gasped.

Salvatore's chest rose and fell, but his eyes didn't open. He coughed up a gob of dirty green mucous. Blood was over his face and in his hair and on the floor. I turned and looked out the window, breathing hard. Through the frosted panes I could see that even though there wasn't a thick snowfall, sporadic flurries were being whipped by the wind.

There couldn't be any turning back; I had to run if I wanted to survive. But look where running had gotten Angelino, look what escape had done to Natale. My hands were trembling. My face had gone dead cold. That great lump of a man on the floor had the power of life and death over me, so I opened a drawer and found a serrated blade, and for the long minutes I sat on the floor and watched him I tried to tell myself that I had the power of life and death too.

As soon as he started to mutter I tore open Salvatore's shirt and pressed the point of the blade into the thick red hair over his heart, and pressed down, ready to stab him all the way through. At the first bubble of blood I stopped and flung the blade away and thought, *You bastard, I'll show you what I'm made of, I'll show you what I can do.*

There was plenty of rope and twine in the cabin, so I found good lengths of both and rolled his heavy body over, tying his hands at the wrists behind his back, then tying his feet together and lashing them to the stubby legs of the heavy iron stove. I dragged him and sat him up, and ran another rope under his bushy, foetid armpits and around and around his chest, then tied him upright to a timber post in the middle of the room. I lifted his chin and used an old shirt to make a gag that went into his mouth and was tied tight and firm behind his head. Blood still dripped from the deep wound in his skull. I picked up a rag and started to dab at it, but another lever seemed to be pulled inside me, and just like that the cold outside was in my bones.

With a shudder I felt myself drop to the floor.

When I opened my eyes the cabin was dark. The fire in the belly of the stove had almost expired. The room was cold and Salvatore was staring at me, a glaze in his eyes. I picked myself up and added wood to the stove, stirring the somnolent ashes with the metal poker. They started to flare. My chest was too hot inside, and even my good leg was weak. My miraculous recovery must have been only a slight reprieve. I thought my master was in much better condition than me, and couldn't help wondering if Father Death was going to get me long before Salvatore did.

Once the fire was roaring I shut the metal grate. It would take some time before this room was warmer. My stomach grumbled but I was used to that. Much worse was how thirsty I was. I drank draught after draught of water, and when I looked at Salvatore I saw that he must have been as hungry and thirsty as me.

Well, he could wait, the gag was going to stay where it was. Instead I took some clean rags and a bowl of water and found some ointments in his medicine drawer. I went onto my knees and wiped and cleaned his wounds. There was a lump like an egg in his hair. Another just above his temple was much larger. Salvatore didn't wince or reveal the slightest flicker of pain, though I was certain his terrible drunkenness had passed. I put plaster over his wound. His eyes burned into me. He must have thought I was attending to him in order to beg his mercy, but that wasn't the case. I knew exactly what my prospects were. Instead, I wanted him to see what I could do, what I was made of, and that his world of cruelty and contempt had failed to enter me.

When I was done I sat back and looked at him. Now Salvatore tried to speak through the gag. Nothing was intelligible but I thought I knew what he wanted to say: *Untie me and we'll forget this ever happened*; *Set me free and guess what, I'll give you your freedom*. His eyes, however, said other things.

'Are you hungry?' I asked. He nodded once. 'Thirsty?' He nodded twice.

I retrieved the serrated blade I'd thrown aside. We were in near darkness now, the only light the glow from the fire in the stove, and this was the way I wanted it. Salvatore didn't like the blade in my hand and he barely relaxed even as I cut him a piece of bread and a hunk of *pepato* cheese. The wind whistled outside, the doors and walls creaked. Something rattled loose out in the dark and wouldn't stop. I reached behind Salvatore's head and undid the shirt that gagged him. As soon as he was free he spat twice onto the ground and moved his mouth and tongue, trying to get them back to life. He took deep gasps, getting air into his lungs.

'Water first,' he said.

'Yes, *master*,' I replied, and he understood the heavy sarcasm in my voice. Even so, he probably still believed he had the upper hand, and that in a moment I'd be begging for mercy. I ladled some water into his mouth and he lapped at it like a great cat. Then I fed him some of the bread and cheese, but carefully, so that he wouldn't choke.

While he was chewing we both heard a heavy footfall on the step outside and the quick rap against the door. His mouth stopped moving and hung open, full of half-masticated food. His gaze was on me but now I had the blade up. I held the point at one of his bulging eyes. The sharp tip was a hair's-breadth from his eyeball. He knew not to make a sound. There was another knock and a man's voice called out.

Everything was just about over for me. The door was unlocked, if this visitor wanted to try it. The windowpanes were bare, if he wanted to look inside. But I held the point of that blade to Salvatore's eye and didn't waver. My face was still dead cold and a sort of nausea hadn't stopped rippling through me. My chest was hot but at least my hand was steady. Then there was another footfall, and whoever it was went away. Maybe the cold made him hurry off; maybe it had been Franco wanting his money for the three axe handles.

I didn't relax for sixty seconds. When I finally took the blade away Salvatore slowly started to chew the bread and cheese in his mouth again. He swallowed and asked for more water and I gave him more water, then he said, 'With your leg the way it is, and the weather outside, why should I bother trying to do what nature will do for me?'

The man was painfully correct. What he didn't know was that I had an even worse impediment: this sickness in me. I tried to imagine what sort of a taste of freedom I'd have before my own body consumed me.

'Got any ideas?' I asked my master.

He almost wanted to smile. 'I don't want you here anymore. Let me go and I'll pass you on to another miner. I'll say we're incompatible. That's the best I can do.'

I shook my head.

Salvatore said, 'You think you deserve your freedom after doing this? You're a boy who doesn't even have a family or a family name. God made you for the mines and nothing else. If God wanted a better life for you, he would have given you opportunities.'

I came a little closer to him. 'God is the shit up your backside. There's nothing over us. Nothing.'

Now he did smile. 'You see why there's no road for you? You think that because you're empty, the entire universe must be the same.'

Salvatore shook his head. That glaze had gone out of his eyes and now they seemed to glitter with delight. Perhaps with even a little anticipation. I made that stop by stuffing my own mouth with the last of the bread and cheese, and retying his gag. Hard and tight.

He hadn't expected that.

What I expected was that sooner or later someone else would come to the cabin, or that the person who'd knocked at the door would return. Maybe Salvatore spent some evenings like this with other miners, drinking, playing cards, I couldn't know for sure. I stuffed my mouth with food and made sure to lock the door and latch tight all the windows. Snow was now falling hard. The only good thing about that was that it would quickly cover my tracks.

It was time to go if I was going to have any chance of surviving much past the next few minutes or hours, and it was strange that despite the terminal sentence of the sickness growing so quickly inside me, no part of me wanted to give up, to die. There was only one thing in my mind, only one reasonable objective, and it was this: to be allowed to face Father Death my own way. Even by my own hand, if it came to that. I didn't want to give Salvatore or any of the other men in this hell the ultimate authority, the power of being the ones to end my life.

It wasn't much to hang on to, but it was all I had to keep me going. It was time to try to trick Salvatore so that he'd never guess what sort of a plan I had in mind.

I pretended to start to lose my nerve, making my actions and movements more frantic, more agitated. I mumbled to myself ridiculous non sequiturs he could attribute to someone coming apart. I let him see my trembling hands. I let him see me moving around the kitchen as if with nowhere to go.

'You say I don't have a family, but I do, I know where they are, I know all of them and I know my name,' I babbled, the words coming out of me a lot more freely than I liked to acknowledge. 'If I stay here you'll kill me, I know what you do to boys like me, I know it because you let me see it with my own eyes. Angelino, you shot him like a dog, and poor Natale, you let him freeze to death out there —'

I tried to get tears into my eyes. I think my sickness made them all watery anyway. Then I threw myself at Salvatore and grabbed his hairy face.

'You won't catch me, you've got no idea how fast I can run.'

Despite the way I was laying it on so thick, his expression told me that for the first time he was becoming afraid. If my mind was unhinged then I might decide to do something really desperate – but all I wanted him to believe was that I was going to run and run and run, as far and as fast as I could, consumed by terror, the way Angelino and countless other boys must have done.

Still moving frantically, I found two sacks and started to fill them with as much of Salvatore's food I could find. I threw his larder open and took cheeses and salamis, preserved meats and dried fruits, nuts, raisins, anything. Soon, of course, those two sacks held more than it was smart to carry, but I needed them, or else I couldn't see how my plan would succeed.

When I reached behind his head to loosen the gag so that he wouldn't choke, my hands were trembling without the need to pretend. Maybe the act was the real part of me after all. Then I went into the small room where Salvatore slept and found heavy clothes to wear. I tried to pick things that didn't carry too much of his stink. With extra pairs of socks, his boots were a reasonable fit. I pulled an overcoat over my new attire, all of it loose because he was so big.

When I emerged dressed in his clothes, Salvatore's eyes filled with impotent fury. I pulled a woollen cap down over my ears. Maybe this ruined my entire performance, the fact that I would have enough presence of mind to dress as warmly as I could, and to protect my face and ears. I didn't know, I couldn't think straight anymore. I found gloves and pulled them on, then hefted the heavy sacks and placed them near the door. I looked at Salvatore but now I'd lost the facility for words. The serrated knife was on the floor. I went over and picked it up. My escape really would be much easier if I ran that blade across his throat. It might take days or a week before anyone discovered him and raised the alarm. He must have known what I was thinking. I put the knife into one of the sacks, left him where he was, trussed like an animal but safe, and carefully unlocked the door and edged it open. I hefted the sacks over my shoulder, gripping them with one hand.

At first it was almost impossible to see through the snow flurries, but the swirling winds actually helped. It scattered the snow as it fell, so that as my eyes adjusted I could see a way ahead. The entire ravaged landscape was white. There were fires in the distance and a great glow that was the smelter. Tonight it looked like some shimmering doorway. Winter had turned our immense graveyard into a sort of fairy paradise.

I set out, striding quickly, my right leg already burning and the food sacks too cumbersome. At least the work in the mines had taught me how to endure, how to go on doggedly when my body and mind wanted to collapse. I trudged through the snow, almost certain that no one was out, but keeping away from all the other mines and cabins anyway, leaving this wasteland behind and travelling by instinct in the direction I decided I didn't want to go, which was north-east. Let them think I had family somewhere in a place like Palermo, and that I actually believed I could traverse more than a hundred kilometres overland in order to get there.

The snow on the ground wasn't thick enough to slow me down, but in a way I wished there was more of it, so that when a party set out after me they'd have incontrovertible proof of the direction I'd taken. Still, I doubted anyone would find Salvatore until at least tomorrow, if that, and maybe all my tracks would be gone by then anyway. My plan would have to work even without the tracks. I hoped I had acted my role well enough with Salvatore. And, anyway, the miners tended to keep to themselves, or kept at least to their own camps and the teams who lived there. What made me wonder was that knock at the door. Maybe whoever had come would return the next night and discover Salvatore. Or perhaps Salvatore would never be found and would simply die in his bonds of thirst and hunger. I tried not to think about him or the possibilities, because whenever I did, the strongest picture in my mind was this one: Salvatore catching up to me and raising his rifle, a satisfied look in his bulging eyes as he shot me through the head.

It was difficult to measure time. What I knew was that it had to have been well before midnight when I set out, and I'd already been walking for hours. I was probably safe to keep going another hour or two before dropping one of the food sacks as a marker for trackers to be certain of my direction, then to double back, retracing my steps. I had to return to the sulphur camps before the first gleaming of dawn; if I didn't all would be lost.

My plan was simple: from the haphazard way we'd tried to track Angelino down, I'd learned that the miners were not very good at manhunts and no one was likely to recognise one set of footsteps made inside another set. I'd retrace my steps as perfectly as I could, hoping the snow would cover any disparity, then I'd hide in the sulphur camp itself.

There were obvious flaws to this plan. Not only was it virtually impossible that I'd be able to retrace myself step-by-step, but once I was back Salvatore's camp wasn't my final destination. The old one of Giovanni's was. So somewhere along the way a fresh trail would have to start, and it would lead straight to Giovanni's abandoned mine. Well, I'd just have to try my best to cover those tracks behind me, and hope for good luck and bad weather. I couldn't think of anything else. Trying to escape in a straight line was simply a shorter route to the grave.

I started to cough. It came so hard my legs went weak, and I fell into the soft snow. Things were going dark inside my head. For a long time I had the sensation I wasn't out in the open at all, but was in my bunk, asleep and dreaming, then the tightness and the wheezing and the inability to breathe brought me back to my senses. I picked myself up and saw that my wish had come true: the snow fell much harder. It would cover all telltale signs of travel within hours, offering a complete cloak of invisibility.

This was my chance. I had to go back now. I had to trust the snowfall would continue through the night, maybe even into the next day. I had to trust that Salvatore hadn't already been found and wasn't on his way. The hunt had to start as late as possible, that way there'd be no inconsistencies in the tracks left. Otherwise Salvatore and his cronies would only need to walk down into Giovanni's mine and string me up at their leisure.

I opened the sacks and tried to reduce my haul, keeping the

best and most useful food items for the single sack that I'd take with me – but my hands had lost their feeling and my vision was doubling and it was becoming harder and harder to breathe. The air itself was like ice, but inside my throat and lungs every intake burned like hot coals. I knew there wasn't much strength left in me. I dropped the heaviest sack with whatever precious commodities it held. The men would find it and hopefully it would encourage them to continue into the north-east.

I turned back. I hurried. Giovanni's mine was my only hope at survival.

This part of the journey was a blur. Sometimes I thought I was wandering aimlessly, the arrow in my head pointed in no particular direction. Other times I thought I was going in a circle and would soon meet myself here in the snow. And for long stretches I floated far above my body, as if my spirit was already out, free to observe the mechanics of a doomed boy's final hour. I thought of the masters I'd had and felt no particular hatred or recrimination. Instead I was happy that I now knew the worth of being my own master; for these precious hours, for the first time, I belonged to myself and no one else.

Then I saw the orange glow of the smelter and understood that, improbable as it was, whatever muddled plan I'd had in my head was close to being executed. I hung back at the perimeter of the sulphur plains and looked around as carefully as I could. There wasn't much to see other than driving snow. I forced myself to stay where I was and scan the entire area, and do it again and again.

The shivering grew uncontrollable. My face was entirely wrapped except for the slit-holes I'd made for my eyes. My cheeks and forehead burned. Perspiration dampened the cloth. My body was numb. I kept looking, searching, scanning.

There were no winter animals and no men. Reaching into the sack, I took out a handful of almonds, cold as ice, moved the wrap down from my lips, and put them into my mouth. I forced myself to keep chewing. Whatever floating spirit was above my physical self moved on ahead, and in the cold wet darkness it showed me the way. I lost track of time, trudging and chewing, sweating and shivering, mumbling to myself and hearing voices in the snow. I kept away from terrain that I thought would be easy for men to read. Then by the most circuitous route possible, I was at the opening to the shaft that I remembered so well. I looked behind me. The tumbling snow was going to cover my tracks, and very quickly at that. As I faced the tunnel I felt relief flood like blood through my veins, and my legs decided enough was enough, and I plunged down into my old familiar hell.

This tunnel was not as deep as Salvatore's, but it was a long way away from anyone else's. I knew every twisting turn as if they were a part of me, of my nature, which in a way they now were. I'd travelled up and down these subterranean passages for Giovanni hundreds, probably thousands of times. I was so weak that I could barely pick myself up or drag the sack of provisions after me. My muscles had turned to water.

I stumbled downward, the walls holding me up, the hot rocky ground always ready to greet my knees and the palms of my hands when I fell. I crawled down into the steaming pit of the earth as if crawling back to the womb. The womb of a woman I never knew, and who had never wanted me. *Who was she? Where did she live?*

Down here it was easy to understand that there was no God. If God did exist, what crimes did He think I'd committed that I should be made to suffer for? Angelino, Natale, why did they deserve to be dead? And all those *carusi,* only half alive or already killed because of this shit of a life in the sulphur mines, why would an omnipotent being want to bring them into this world

74

just to make them toys and chattels of men whose only real god was money?

Skin on fire and hands trembling, in this place it was far easier to believe in the devil. As I continued downward, into this darkness that I had no need to light, I thought, *Take me into your house, merciful Satan, you know how happy I am to be with you again.*

The fever lasted a span of time I can't measure. Even after it passed I was still cooking alive. My hallucinations and vile thoughts had evaporated, but the heat in this pit went through my clothes and inside my body. My blood felt like treacle. I couldn't move at any speed.

Slowly I eased off Salvatore's coat, which now felt as heavy as an animal. Then I opened the first shirt and took it off, and the next, and Salvatore's undershirt too. His pungent odour was married to mine. I fumbled with the laces of the boots and they felt as if they'd melted themselves to me. Taking them off was like taking off great weights. Now my feet wanted to float away. I rolled off the thick pairs of socks and the exertion of all that made me have to lie flat on my back, lifeless as a corpse.

Soon I knew I was still wearing too much. I struggled with the belt that kept me in Salvatore's oversized trousers, and finally I was naked and sweating. The pain in my chest wasn't as sharp anymore. Instead it was a dull ache that occupied my entire torso. My face was hot but this seemed more a product of the heat in the cave, rather than fever. I was in darkness deep underground, a wonderful black tomb, and I felt safer and more protected than I had in years. No one knew I was here. Maybe no one ever would. I was finally my own master.

I felt around for the sack of provisions, unsure that I hadn't dropped it somewhere along the way, but my fingers soon found its rough fabric. Very calmly I let one hand explore the contents inside. I prayed I'd had the presence of mind to bring the one with the sticks of pinewood matches in it, and the prayer was answered because I found the wide wooden carton. At Gozzi's property they'd still used the old white phosphorus friction matches that spread sparks and that were dangerous to use, but most of the miners had these newer and more reliable types. When I struck a first safety match the fizzing blaze dazzled me, but then revealed exactly where I was. Some instinct for survival had led me all the way down to the very end of the mine, the last seam Giovanni had attempted to work, the place which had broken his spirit.

Striking a new match, I saw all the items he'd left behind. The oil lamps on the wall were still almost completely full, waiting to be lit. A broken toolbox was on the ground, but best of all, his water barrel was elevated in the centre of the tunnel, sitting high on a pile of rocks. That was meant to keep it at its coolest. I lifted the wooden lid and, though the water was almost as hot as the walls, there was plenty of it. The lid prevented evaporation. When I had a little more strength I'd do the trick Giovanni and all the sulphur miners performed in these bleak winters: I'd take the hessian sack to the surface outside, fill it with snow, then pile that snow into the barrel to cool the water and create more.

For now I slaked my thirst as best I could, and though I wasn't hungry I forced myself to eat some of the more perishable items. The baking heat would spoil these quickly. The almonds and strips of bitter jerky were better saved for later.

I felt as if I had everything I needed – in fact I possessed much more than I ever had in my life – even if I was going to be dead long before hunger became a problem. I tried to remember how quickly boys with tuberculosis or pneumonia had perished. It had always seemed to vary, depending on how strong they were in the body and in the heart.

Better to enjoy the time I had. I staggered to my feet and went into another rock chamber and relieved myself. There was a certain luxury to such privacy. I can even say that I was happy. A thought struck me: if I ever found permanent freedom, I might want to live like this. In my own space, away from others, alone and only answerable to myself. That, to me, seemed to be the truest freedom of all.

When I lay down to sleep I didn't feel the need to maintain a light. Better to conserve the oil in the lamps. So far underground, no one was going to come sneaking up on me, and if they did, what could I do?

The fevers came and went with the next days that passed. For hours and hours I'd feel perfectly well, then like a snap of the fingers I'd take a turn and collapse, hardly capable of movement. Whenever I felt well I went up and gathered mounds of snow for the barrel. The first time it was a night; for my next trip, daylight. I didn't venture far from the opening, even though both times the snow was falling and I didn't expect to meet anyone.

Another journey to the surface, and it was just turning dawn, cold but without snow or sleet. I watched streaks of light spreading through a perfectly clear and clean sky. When I slept it was dreamlessly and without trouble. I would close my eyes expecting they wouldn't open again, and when they did I felt well, though always parched by heat. Liberal intakes of water and snow soon fixed that. It was odd; in the winterland outside, even though the smelter kept on pouring its black smoke into the air and sky, the snow always tasted pure, the water it made becoming as clear as something from a forest stream.

My little paradise couldn't last much longer. I estimated that I'd already managed to live more than a week in that hole. The bread was finished. The hard cheeses and the dried meats had turned. The nuts were all right, and the dried fruit, but there weren't enough of them. When a day came that I realised I was rested and strong, and that the sickness seemed to have sweated itself out of me, there was no more snow to find outside the hole and only tiny flakes sprinkled down. That meant no more water and no possibility of getting any more. Now I had to ration what was left, and when the barrel was close to empty I'd have to be on my way.

Without the chance to haul down any more snow, I had to find another way to keep my remaining water cool. Very carefully I moved the barrel out of the deep pit and secreted it closer to the surface where the rocks weren't even warm. The oil in the lamps had expired so I lived the next few days and nights in darkness, and whenever the blackness seemed too much to take I went up and sat near the entrance, near the light. Sometimes deep at night, I went out in Salvatore's coat and boots and walked around the ruined world, but didn't venture far, didn't push my luck.

How long now since I'd left him trussed in his cabin? How much time had it taken before someone had found him?

There would have been an immediate manhunt, but it was impossible to know whether they'd travelled a long way and were still looking or if they'd already given up and returned to the mines. After all, for these men, every day away from their work was lost money; how dogged and determined would Salvatore and whatever group he put together really want to be?

Five centimetres of water. It was stagnant and putrid too.

During my time underground I'd hit on the idea of pressing hot rocks onto the aching, bad parts of my right leg, which gave comfort. Once I started trekking, I knew my step would suffer for these weeks spent in these tunnels without any real activity, but I wanted to give myself the best possible start.

There wasn't much left worth eating, and Giovanni's old goat-skin sack wouldn't hold more than a day's foul water – I had to hope for clear streams ahead. As for food, I wrapped up my remaining collection of almonds, cashews and other nuts, with no idea how long it would be before I'd find more to eat. Maybe I could have risked raiding a miner's cabin before setting off, but the only time to do that was in daylight hours when they'd be underground; I had no stomach for pushing my luck any further than it had already gone.

It was almost inconceivable to me that I was still alive. Now that I had my health back and was thoroughly rested, a renewed sense of hope made me wonder if somehow I might actually succeed in getting away from this hellhole and find a new life.

My objective was the Italian mainland, about which I'd tried to glean as much information as I could. In his rare talkative moments, Giovanni had said that there they had prosperity, wealth and more food than could fill people's bellies. True, he said, in Italian cities Sicilians are thought of as no better than Africans and no smarter than monkeys, and the mainland Italians speak a language that differentiated them completely from people like us, but he'd told me enough to make me think that, given the chance, I would find a way to get by. It was either hope for this or give up now.

To me, my biggest hurdle seemed to be the ferry he'd described, the one that carries travellers across the Straits of Messina. *How would I get on it? How would I pay for the trip?*

The night I set out I thought I knew the best direction to take and what I'd use as my beacon. It would be the volcano, Etna, almost exactly opposite to the direction in which I'd left tracks and clues for Salvatore's hunting party.

The snow hadn't returned, and now even the flurries had disappeared, though the winter's cold remained. I was dressed in Salvatore's heavy gear again, but this time I wore it lightly – nothing seemed to weigh me down. I put the extra shirt and undershirt into my hessian sack. My plan was to travel by night all the way to Etna, and from there make my way down to a city called Catania, where I could lose myself in the crowds. Somehow I'd find my way to the port city of Messina. I thought that once I was far enough away from the sulphur fields I could risk finding day work, make just enough money to feed and clothe myself and buy tickets for buses and trains, and not have to hike cross-country in the most obvious manner possible. Of course, the thought of using my own money to buy something as simple as a ticket filled me with trepidation. I'd never done such a thing in my life, but some of the older workers at Gozzi's factory, and even Natale, had said it was easy as pie.

Then I'd live in cheap rooms, and if people in bigger centres suspected I was some kind of a fugitive, what would they care? No one would know me. I'd be just another face and therefore invisible.

The possibilities seemed endless. I was full of optimism. I believed that if I could make it to the environs at the base of the volcano without Salvatore finding me, then I'd be free. No matter how furious he was, it simply could not be worth his while to keep wasting time looking for me.

It was a dark, clear night. I'd added my last remaining food and my stolen knife blade to the few things I would carry over my shoulder with me. In the snow's absence the entire landscape had returned to its vista of destruction, as if a war's monstrous weapons had been used to destroy everything resembling life. In the far distance were the pinpricks of light that signified miners' cabins, but these soon disappeared behind me and even the smelter's orange glow was fading. The next time I stopped and turned to look the pitted landscape was gone, a bad dream that, in the end, was easily left behind.

After what could only have been two or three hours of my

limp walking, I came to the first signs of nature and its renewal. There were shrubs, bushes, trees. These thickened until I was skirting a forest, and behind it were blue-edged mountain ranges. Off in the distance was a red glow in the clouds that could have been mistaken for dawn, but which I believed was Etna itself. This clear night was offering me every assistance, even immediately revealing my beacon.

I kept on, comfortable enough in these boots made soft by several pairs of socks, and two layers of clothes protecting me from the whipping winds. Still, it was nowhere as cold as it had been the night I'd first escaped from Salvatore. I was happy breathing this chill air. I felt alive, and now it was good to be out of the tunnel, no matter how safe it had been there. I thought it might take me three or four nights' good trek to get to the volcano – and from there I'd have to find a way to Catania. Others had told me that a city like that revealed itself; you didn't have to go looking for it. You stood on a ridge and there it was, great and glowing like heaven and hell combined.

That's what I thought I'd do: climb the volcano's slopes until I could see where I had to go next. Then a better idea grew on me. I'd been so secure in Giovanni's abandoned mine, and the pitch-black and rock hadn't bothered or frightened me, so if I made it safely to Etna mightn't it be wiser to find another good hiding place and lay low many more days? Maybe even a week or two, whatever amount of time I could hold out? There had to be innumerable caves and caverns in a place like that. Wouldn't it be safer to secure myself somewhere around there, rather than immediately entering more populated regions? The longer I held out the more certain it would be that Salvatore and whatever team or teams he'd put together had abandoned the hunt.

It seemed a good thought. I'd mull it over while I walked.

Gaining confidence, I was certain that even better ideas would soon come to me – and of course I had no idea that in setting out on my trek I'd already given myself away.

By following the outskirts of the forest, I came to arable land and the first patchwork of fields were in view. Not even one full night's journey and already the land had changed. Almost without noticing it my path had gone gradually uphill, and now, unexpectedly, I was on a hillside with the ground dropping away and a gorgeous valley of farmland and tiny villages spread out before me. I settled down on the grass and rested. My eyes were filled with the sort of beauty I'd only seen once before, on the hunt for the running boy Angelino.

I reached for my hessian sack, wanting to chew the last of the almonds and nuts I'd brought with me, and discovered they weren't there. Neither was the blade, the one I'd held to Salvatore's eyes. In the sack was the shirt and undershirt the slight change in weather meant I no longer needed to wear – and nothing else.

Breathing deeply, I investigated how this could be. There, a rent in the fabric. My things had worked themselves free.

But where had they fallen – somewhere across the sulphur fields? Or somewhere in the plains or in the forest? If so, mightn't they remain hidden forever?

A simple tear – and from a simple tear, perhaps a simple death lay ahead.

My thoughts raced. Eight or ten hours must have passed since I'd left the old mine. Maybe the wrapped almonds and nuts, plus the blade, had fallen out during my climb from the tunnels and were still underground. The fact of their disappearance didn't necessarily mean this escape was doomed, did it? Perhaps no one would find them anyway, regardless of where they were. And even if someone did – what would they care? How would they know what they signified, how would they even know to go tell Salvatore?

With a sinking feeling in my belly and head I watched the way the day was beginning to come to life. Nearby I could discern a creek or stream. That was a godsend. I set off again, but this time at a run, and by the time I'd found a route down to it and was near the running water, dawn had broken and there were spots of movement in the countryside: men on their own or leading livestock, a group of women moving toward a field, an immense black bull stomping in a spacious pen.

I felt as if I was in a great glass bowl and anyone who wanted to find me had only to peer inside. I longed to be back in the tunnel, back to the safety of being buried deep among the sulphurous rocks and darkness. But there was no turning back. I had to go forward, and expect the worst. Plan for the worst. I couldn't tell myself that by some providence I hadn't already given myself away.

Scuttling close to the ground like an animal, kneeling by the stream, I washed my face and hands, then drank the icy water. It bore no trace of sulphur or any other sort of contaminant. I closed my eyes at the wonder of it, of fresh running water and how good it could make me feel. But why had I allowed this dream of escape to turn sour so quickly? Why hadn't I simply left everything behind in the tunnel and trusted in what the land and forests might provide me?

Then I heard voices, but these came travelling along the surface of the stream, and so I still had time.

When the three men walked past, I was well-hidden in the crowded dark of the trees. With relief I saw that there were two younger men and one older, and they were wearing the peasant attire of field workers. Boots, long trousers, checked shirts with buttoned vests, cloth caps on their heads. The young men carried picks and shovels over their shoulders. The older man had a water sack and a tied hamper of what must have been their food for the day. One was smoking and the crisp smell of the cigarette was very clear. They were heading away to some labour but were completely devoid of the bent frames and dead-eyed demeanour of everyone I was so used to. Instead, these men talked in strong voices. Even though their dialect seemed quite strange to me, stranger still was their laughter – which was happy, and something else, companionable.

After they'd gone, I stole forward and doused my hair in the stream, washing my face and neck again, drinking more. To me the forest was as welcoming as this water, so I retreated far into it and found a spot where I thought no one and nothing would bother me. It was much colder in there, and I pulled my coat around me, then I tried to curl up on the bed of grass, my head cradled in my arms. There was no use trying to keep going in this broad daylight. Sooner or later someone was bound to see me. I would have to wait for the cover of darkness before setting off again. I didn't like the idea of staying put, but far worse was the possibility of giving myself away.

The forest ground cover wasn't as luxurious as I thought it would be, but within minutes I'd slipped into a fitful, anxious sleep.

The sound of a horse neighing woke me, then I could hear something coming through the undergrowth. My eyes were open, but I didn't sit up. Instead I forced myself to remain as immobile as possible. The horse was picking a careful way very close to me and I heard the rider giving encouragement with tongue clicks and soft whistles. When I thought it was safe I slithered slow and quiet behind the trunk of the tree that had sheltered me. I made sure that no fronds or bushes moved. Flat on my belly, brush and bushes covered me entirely.

Horse and rider passed perhaps ten metres ahead, and I was able to get a good look at the man's profile. Relief washed over me. He was a stranger. It wasn't Salvatore nor any of the other miners I'd seen in the fields. In fact, I was certain that of the many things he might have been, one of them wasn't a man who worked with sulphur and ore. His clothes were too tidy, his hair too neat, his skin too shiny. I didn't relax, however, because of the pistol at his waist and the bolt-action carbine hanging from a leather scabbard buckled to the saddle.

I didn't know who he was or what sort of beast he was hunting, and I didn't much care as long as it wasn't me. For long moments I'd feared that Salvatore had already managed to track me. I lay where I was, and didn't move until this man with his horse had gone and no more sounds disturbed the forest's silence. Then I waited longer and even longer again, just to be certain he hadn't dismounted and set up somewhere nearby.

As far as I knew, no one had laid eyes on me since I'd left Salvatore tied up in his cabin. It was best to keep it this way. The longer I remained invisible, the further I travelled from the sulphur fields, the better my chances had to be. It was possible no one would ever find what had fallen out of the hessian sack. The way that rider or hunter or whatever he was had passed so startlingly close helped decide my next actions. There was no way I could use country roads and trails either by day or by night. And if someone really was coming after me, I had little choice about hiding and sleeping by day and running by night. I would simply have to move at every available opportunity, whenever I thought it was safe. What was paramount was distance. I would have to stay to the forest and undulating countryside, and find ways to get food and water by methods that wouldn't reveal me. And my destination would certainly be the volcano and its peaks, where I was now determined to hole up for as long as was humanly possible.

Let Salvatore give up on me; let any notices he might have distributed fade from people's memories. Etna would be remote enough and bare enough to protect me – who would think a boy would escape from sulphurous plains only to disappear into a sulphurous mountain?

The local villages were nothing like the camps I was used to. When night fell all activity didn't cease and everyone didn't immediately retreat into their homes. I saw lanterns moving along narrow streets, in small courtyards and in winding laneways away from the houses and closer to fields and paddocks. People stayed out and enjoyed their evenings; there was nothing to fear in this particular darkness; for them the evening air was worth savouring.

I moved away from the clear stream where I drank, because it ran too close to a collection of neighbouring farms and homes, and soon I discovered a dry creek bed that gave all indications of travelling directly toward the glowering redness in the sky. All around me was an almost pure pitch-black. I stumbled on. There were sounds among the trees but nothing revealed itself. Animals – I was less afraid of them than I was of men, but I'd also heard stories of the great cats that lived in the hills, and how a wayward local or traveller could come to grief. I found a nice heavy branch for protection and carried it over my shoulder, having dug a careful hole with my hands and buried the useless sack and its meager contents.

More pressing was the state of my feet. At first the thick socks had been helpful, but gradually the ill-fitting boots and constant walking had taken their toll. I tried to put the swelling and pain out of my head because if these were going to be my worst problems then I didn't have any problems at all. I tried to keep myself feeling optimistic. Freedom itself had to be intoxicating enough to inure me to all discomfort.

Many hours later, along this creek bed I discerned a dark hillside rising up. There was a small house that overlooked fields, pens and barnyards. My stomach wouldn't quieten and I'd grown almost completely parched. There might be a well up there. In the neatly planted rows there were probably things I could pluck off the stems to munch on. Deciding to take the risk, I climbed over an embankment and started to cross an empty paddock toward what looked like some kind of animal enclosure. Two dogs appeared like wraiths and stood in my path. They weren't barking and they didn't bare their teeth, but no part of them moved either. They simply stared with eyes I couldn't see for the dark, waiting for me to decide what I would do. That's what would trigger an action in their brains: what I chose to do next.

I didn't move and I didn't try to call to them. Gradually my eyes adjusted and saw that their tails weren't wagging but were set dead straight. I slowly moved a foot backward, then the next. I didn't turn around but kept the dogs as much in sight as I could. Finally I climbed down the embankment and found my way to that dry creek bed once more. My clothes were drenched in sweat.

I didn't see the dogs again.

There was nothing else for hours. The bed was dry and full of flat, smooth rocks and stones. I wanted water. I didn't know why there was no water here, but I did know that my boots were making far too much noise. I couldn't take them off. Then again, maybe the scrunch of rocks and pebbles underfoot was keeping animals away . . . or attracting them. I imagined the dull appetite inside some hillside cat, how it would love to chew the meat and crunch the bones of a lonely traveller.

Much later I saw a sole structure standing close to the creek bed. I was exhausted. I climbed over a bank of dry, crackling reeds and weeds and went as close to the hut as I could. It was the size of a very small barn. One or two cows could have occupied it. There was a latch but no lock on the door. It clicked open, and there was a cluck inside: a chicken house. Some family's home was probably perched beyond the rise. The hut had been closed and latched, so someone would have to come in the morning to do the reverse. Dawn looked a long way off. I knew I ought to make use of these last hours of darkness but my feet and my belly and my head were in rebellion. I crawled down into the hay and sat amongst white and brown chickens that didn't mind my presence. They barely moved and didn't make much more sound than I did. I wondered what they made of me. I lifted one hen, who fluttered her wings but was otherwise docile, and felt the warm spot where she'd been laying on her eggs. There were three. I cracked an egg into my mouth, swallowed quickly and immediately retched.

The hen let herself be held in my lap. The owner of these chickens must have been a gentle soul. My hunger was greater than my disgust. I cracked another egg into my mouth and when I was able to keep that down I took the third. Then I lay back into the smell of hay and chicken droppings, and their warmth. They'd been closed in because of foxes, I guessed, but no one had considered the intrusion of a boy.

I was no good at lighting fires with sticks but I still had plenty of Salvatore's matches in the pockets of his coat, and in the late morning, at the base of a rocky hillside protected by a thick, encircling copse of trees, I built up a small fire that I thought would do the job. The hen whose eggs I'd eaten was plucked and I opened it with my hands, digging in with my thumbs, and pulled out its innards. An hour earlier I'd painstakingly cleaned the brown chicken by the side of a small tributary of a larger fast-running stream, my eyes darting to the left and to the right in case someone was about to come upon me.

Cleaning the chicken with cold water was murderous. I knew I needed a pot of boiling water to soften the feathers and skin.

At least the water had been pristine – I drank my fill and felt half-human again. Then I'd set to pulling the feathers out one by one and used gravel from the bottom of the stream to rub the puckered skin clean.

Hours and hours before that, I'd left the small hut after hiding the broken shells under a thick mound of hay, and had tried to smooth the surface so there'd be no sign of a visitor. Twelve hens. Now eleven. The owner shouldn't immediately notice one missing. I hoped some small child with other things on her or his mind would have the chore of letting the chickens out and collecting the eggs. But if it was a farmer or his wife they would likely notice the discrepancy in the number of fowl straightaway.

It was too much to worry about, but I kept wondering what the penalty for being a chicken thief was. Buckshot in the seat of the pants? Public hanging?

The bird's pieces were taking too long to cook and I was becoming agitated – agitated more by fear than hunger. A local farmer now had reason to come after me, or to complain to whatever authorities existed in this place. I closed my eyes and prayed for the meat to hurry up and cook. I'd hide all trace of the fire and bury the bones just the same way as I'd collected all the hen's wet feathers and stuck them in a hole. To speed things up I tried putting flat stones into the fire and placing the pieces on top of them. Then burning brush on top of that. But it didn't help, and a thin trail of smoke drifted into the day, sending up a signal to anyone who wanted to know where I was.

When I was finally eating, though, the taste sent me into a swoon. I'd never had anything quite like this before. I'd cooked myself the finest meal the world has known. I chewed quickly and forced myself to only eat half the bird. The other pieces I wrapped in clean green leaves and tied with stringy dry reed, slipping them into the overcoat's pockets for later. I poured dirt into the fire and stomped on any remaining embers with my boots until I was sure it was all out. Then I covered it with even more dirt and set brush and brambles over the area so that no passer-by would know what had gone on. Not that there should be any passer-by. The forest remained quiet as eternity. Nevertheless, I buried the leftover bones deep in the rich soil.

The water in the stream was as cool and welcoming as ever. I washed myself and drank my fill, then set out for the deepest part of the wood.

Without my stomach grumbling and that constant thirst itching at my throat, I slept heavily, in a deep exhaustion.

Then the call went off in my mind, the remembrance of all the early starts at Gozzi's factory and the mine, but instead of waking at nightfall I discovered I'd slept all the way through to the next morning. An aura of light was touching the horizon. I rubbed my cheeks and shivered. What luxury to sleep so long, and what a relief. My feet throbbed in Salvatore's boots, but I didn't dare slip them off to see what sort of state they were in. Instead I allowed myself to enjoy the rare pleasure of coming awake without the feeling that I'd already been robbed of hours of sleep.

Mist drifted like smoke as I stretched and yawned. My hair and face and hands were damp, the overcoat wet and heavy. My thoughts were clear and sharp. I knew exactly where I was and what I needed to do. Pushing aside the brush I'd covered myself with, I stood and stretched some more, patting myself down. The stream was a hundred metres ahead, invisible now for the thick press of trees, yet I could almost smell its coursing flow. I tramped quietly along then kneeled on the bank and drank the icy water down, splashing my face and neck. As I was drying myself, my breath misted in the frosty air.

The world here was silent; I could risk travelling among the thickening trees.

The volcano billowed smoke in the distance. I knew the direction to take.

Close to evening, I saw the rider again and this time he wasn't alone.

There was a rifle crack, followed by another, then two men on horses rode hard towards a clearing near the eastern edge of the forest. I didn't know what they were hunting, but as they rode across a short plain into the woods I recognised the first rider as the man who'd come so close when I'd been sleeping in the forest. I didn't know the second man. Maybe they were local farmers ridding the hills of marauding cats.

Even though the trees protected me and I was safe at this vantage point, I knew I ought to leave fast, head as far away in the opposite direction to the two men with guns as I could possibly go. But for a moment curiosity had the better of me. Wouldn't it be better to make certain their presence didn't have anything to do with me?

The light was fading as I made a careful way down a thickly treed hill, moving as silently as I could. I knew I was safe enough, because near the plain below both men were very busy. They pulled a deer out into the open. The compact animal's powerful legs were splayed but still quivering. It must have been one of the last of its kind; as I understood it, hunters had all but emptied Etna's forests of larger prey such as deer, wolves and boar.

One man tethered the horses and started to make camp while the other dispatched the poor animal and set to preparing their kill. This was the man I'd first seen, and he knew how to use a knife. I thought he was the leader of these two, but as the second man built up the fire, he stretched and took off his coat and hat, and I saw it was big Salvatore. His face was clean-shaved and his bushy red hair had been cut right back to his skull so that he was almost completely bald. His trademark moustaches were gone but it was him, definitely him, and I knew then he'd hired an expert tracker and hunter so they could come collect me.

How? The nuts and knife blade had given me away? Or had they been prowling these forests and this landscape ever since Salvatore had been freed of his bonds?

Rolling onto my back, I faced the darkening sky. My mouth was open and I pressed my fists into my eyes, silently shouting with rage and frustration, berating myself for not having moved faster, for having left some kind of trail that men could follow, and for lying here now with nothing in my head but anger and terror.

It was as if I was locked to the earth by unseen hands. I was too scared to stay where I was and too scared to try and slip away. Biting my lip hard I tasted blood, then that's what revived me and got me going again, the taste of my own blood and the picture it conjured: the holes in Angelino's neck, one neat and the other torn out with a mound of flesh. I rolled onto my belly and crept forward so that I could see what Salvatore and his tracker would do next.

The first waves of blind panic passed and I steeled myself to not scamper away like a rabbit. Better to stay where I was, keep them in view. Here I had the advantage: they didn't know where I was, yet the two of them were in my plain sight.

Eventually they set about making themselves comfortable for the night. In the morning I'd be able to see which direction they took, and if need be, to alter my plan accordingly. I could outsmart them; yes, I could. I didn't believe that in terrain like this they would be able to track one small person moving more carefully than ever.

Darkness settled. The men sat in front of their fire and drank. The tracker sharpened his knives so that the distinct swish of steel on rock was sharp on the breeze. They talked in voices I couldn't hear, but they didn't seem to be taking pains to hide their presence. The aromas from their open-fire cooking maddened my stomach. I felt in my pocket for the wrapped-up pieces of chicken I'd been forcing myself not to eat.

Something about the cold, dry taste made me want to gag. I choked the chicken pieces down and dug a small hole for the few bones, burying them carefully. I needed more; I wanted lumps of that roasting deer meat. Maybe this was Salvatore's message to me, wherever I was. He was still the master; I was still the slave. He could eat and drink as much as he wanted and I could cower hungry and cold as a dog. Maybe he expected me to come trembling out of the wood and drop to my knees before their feast, giving up, turning myself in, half-crazed with hunger and exhaustion.

After they filled their bellies Salvatore arranged more wood onto the fire, then he and his companion settled down and all was quiet. I concentrated on the flickering flames as long as I could but darkness seemed to press down, and as the fire's glow went down so did my eyelids. Every hour or so I'd snap awake. The camp was always the same, the men always there. I marked every shift in position they made. Salvatore liked to sleep on one side, the tracker preferred to be on his back. The night passed tense and quiet and still, and mist rose above the ground and stayed there.

After dawn the mist was still there and the two men were packed and ready to leave. I was damp through and through, shivering with cold. I couldn't remember an hour out of my entire journey when I hadn't been shivering, except maybe when I'd slept in the chicken hut while holding that hen. Later as the sun came out, I'd drape my overcoat and clothes over some branches to have them dry.

The tracker was clapping his hands together for warmth. Salvatore was blowing smoke, not mist. Out of the corner of his ugly mouth a stubby cigar protruded. The two men broke camp without fanfare. Salvatore kicked soil over the fire's embers but I noticed that a good side of deer was still arranged over the smouldering coals. The skin would be crisp and smoky, the meat thoroughly cooked but dripping with natural juice. The rest of the carcass they'd hauled into the trees, but there over the remains of the fire was enough meat to make me mad with hunger.

It was all I could do to restrain myself. I watched the two men ride away, and forced myself not to move until they were a long way distant and had disappeared like motes of dust into the undulating countryside. Today they'd kept away from forestland and hills, going straight into the plains; it didn't seem as if they were heading toward Etna. My brow was creased as I tried to think this through. What sort of trail did they believe they were following? There would be villages and towns in that direction. There could be nothing at all for them to read in the land. Something had led them to believe I'd headed straight to civilisation?

Hunger clouded my thoughts. I could figure it all out later. The succulent deer was waiting.

Birds of every type drifted out of the sky, drawn by the aromas of the spiralling smoke. Nothing would be able to resist such bounty. I cursed the birds already pecking at the slab. That meat would sustain me for days. I'd eat well and carry chunks wrapped in leaves in my pockets.

My heart lifted. Maybe from here things would work out.

By the time I was prepared to risk revealing myself and climbed and tumbled down the dew-covered slopes – crossing a creek bed with a splash of water glittering in it, and keeping to the edge of the trees behind the place where the men had camped, then darting out to feed myself from those remains – the feast was being attacked from all sides, by infighting sparrowhawks and innumerable squawking birdlife I couldn't name.

The carrion fluttered and scattered as I stomped forward. They shrieked at me and I threw rocks and sticks. Wings flapped hard in the desperation and excitement of beaks filled with morsels and tendrils of meat. I saw strips of dangling gristle and muscle being torn away, then I was down on my knees pulling at hot meaty bones and well-cooked flesh. It was warm and tender, and fell away from the carcass like water. My eyes wanted to close with ecstasy as I chewed and savoured a mouthful of this prize. I had more meat ready, but as it touched my lips and teeth I noticed two sparrowhawks fluttering on the ground by the burned wood and branches, and then I knew the trap I'd so willingly entered.

I dropped what was in my hand, spat out all the globs of masticated portions in my mouth, reached in with my fingers and nails and dug around for any tiny pieces of meat between my teeth. Spat out the animal juices. Birds died around me and I was on my knees retching up anything and everything that was in my belly.

Coughing, eyes watering, I wiped my mouth with the backs of my hands then wiped my hands on my wet overcoat. Salvatore and his tracker must have tired of the hunt; maybe they'd realised how close I was, even that I'd been watching them. They knew one running boy would be hungry and scared, and the one would conquer the other, and so all they had to do was leave food for me and soon enough their long and frustrating hunt would be over.

In a fluttering sea of death I watched the birds' heads whipping from side to side, wings shuddering, crooked, out of their natural shape forever. Their screams seemed human. As I dragged myself away from the smoking remains of the fire more birds came out of the air and continued to attack this unexpected gift.

I stumbled forward in a daze, ready to give up, not knowing if I was already poisoned and would simply die here with these creatures, wishing I would be found and shot quickly so that this endless fear and anxiety could stop. But when I saw the horsemen in the near distance, riding hard, having doubled back to the site, and to me, I turned and ran into the trees, wings on my feet. I passed the severed head of the deer and a collection of its raw, bloody hindquarters and legs. My bad leg gave me no pain at this moment and I had no hunger either, and my eyes barely saw where I was going. I simply ran without thought. There was nothing left to do.

The cat and mouse lasted another three days. By that time I'd made a way through the cultivated regions at the base of the volcano, and had started climbing higher into the thickening mountainous woods. What had saved me from being overtaken almost immediately was the almost impassable nature of the forests in the flatlands surrounding Etna. The men had horses that had to navigate thick trees and steep inclines and declines; I could scramble along unfettered by belongings, always losing myself far ahead of them. But they kept coming. Sometimes from some wooded plateau I'd see one man holding both horses, so I knew the other had taken off after me on foot, but I barely stopped to gather my wits, barely paused to catch my breath, and didn't sleep at all. They did, I imagined, snatching hours here and there and finding time to eat. Then something would let me know they were still pursuing their quarry – a burst of birds through the treetops, a shrilly whistle between them – and I'd run, climb, fall, trudge even further, now always heading upward but barely knowing where I might emerge.

Though it had stopped snowing I could see the volcano's peaks painted white. Black smoke poured into the sky. A single tall, sputtering fire jet exploded against the snow. No more came. I'd seen for myself that in the lands surrounding Etna farms grew corn, maize, asparagus and fruit. Then there were the mountain's encircling forests, through which I'd tried to lose myself. Now, higher up the slopes, there began these dry and arid regions burned by fires and lava and sulphur – I imagined this zone would be no different to the ruined valley and the stinking mines I'd left behind.

Exhausted and starving, stumbling forward, the vague plan renewed in my mind was to climb as high as I could and find the deepest cave. Surely amongst such a vast terrain of caverns, terraces, ridges and towers of rock, Salvatore and his man would never find me. They might try waiting me out till thirst or starvation drove me into the open, but the truth was that I would rather perish in some hole than give in to their rifles.

But I wouldn't *let* myself perish – and when this time they really did give up, and I was sure of it, I'd stay hidden in the mountain even longer, making infrequent journeys into the forests and farmlands to raid whatever I needed to survive. I'd bring up food and water and live alone for months on end. I wouldn't leave until I was certain the world had completely forgotten about one insignificant boy.

And Salvatore and his hunter *would* give up, for how could it profit them to keep hunting a worthless chattel? The seams of Salvatore's mine were so profitable yet he wasn't working them while he was trying to find me. He was earning no money, only making expenses for himself. His tracker had to be paid; why wasn't Salvatore thinking about the funds he could have directed to his life with his handsome wife? Why was he bothering with me, what issue of useless pride was the point?

There were times when a blind hatred rose up in me and I would curse myself for not having taken the opportunity to sink that serrated blade into my master's eye until it punctured his brain. My fate would be no different than Angelino's, than Natale's. Than the deer's. Maybe they'd nail my skin to a tree as a warning to other escapees.

I might hear the shot before the slug hit me. I might have a moment to realise. One moment to reflect on my life. Or no moment at all.

My hands constantly shook. Fear, hunger and now the urge to kill.

The last thing I'd feasted on? Raw corncobs and tomatoes, perhaps two days earlier. I'd taken them from a field that abutted the first line of Etna's thick trees. I'd even been able to drink from a pail of goat's milk. A solitary farmer had been working with his flock and for some reason had gone away. I'd made the most of my luck – just as I'd made the most of my luck the night before, by sleeping in the high slats under a short wooden bridge. Apart from the bright eyes of several rats, I'd been completely undisturbed there, comfortable in the enclosure like some kind of rat myself.

Now my stomach was in knots of hunger and I trudged along a surprisingly well-worn path through very crowded trees leading into the crags above. This had to be a route used by hikers and workers, and it only increased my anxiety, as it indicated that this region might be more populated than I imagined.

There was no other way to go – the slopes were now too precarious to try to find another route. And so Salvatore and his tracker would soon come this way too.

I passed a pair of scops owls in a branch. Their heads didn't move but their eyes followed me. There would be snakes here, and those cats I kept thinking about, but what bothered me were the seas of colourful birds. Though it seemed as if the tracker used magic or sorcery to keep on my trail I knew he was reading nature's signs – and birds startled by my passage revealed where I was better than a flag.

Inside Salvatore's boots my feet felt as raw as meat but I told myself not to worry: at most there was another day's hiking then I'd be in the wasteland of the volcano's higher reaches. Among arid rocks and canyons, I couldn't possibly leave signs for men to follow. There I'd find myself a cave, take the load off my feet and live with infinite patience.

As I was considering all this I came to a natural clearing. The dense canopy cover had separated and there was an uninterrupted vista of the great mountain's highest slopes, the perfect blue day around it. I kept to the clearing's edges then slipped through several lines of towering pine trees, stopping, pressing myself behind the trunk of the largest. I listened and listened, as had become my habit. I'd already discovered how well sound could travel in this place, almost in direct contradiction of all the crowding vegetation.

There was nothing. Small insects chirruping and birdsong far away: not the slightest indication that nature was being disturbed by men or horses. Now more confident, I moved back to the clearing and squinted up into the daylight. This was the closest I'd been to the volcano's canyons. As I stood there I saw something I could barely understand. An immense ring of smoke floated in the sky. It was perfectly formed and looked as if it had been suspended there by design. Whose design I couldn't say.

It didn't fade, and gave the illusion of being strong enough to support a rope you could throw up and climb. Then, in a way that suggested the volcano meant to put on a show for any sad creature that needed uplifting, a second smoke ring soared away from the volcano and hovered in the blue. I couldn't see which particular crater or breach produced these miraculous effects but a third soon joined the first two, then a fourth.

There were no more. I stood in that clearing with my mouth agape and my eyes drinking the miracle in. Then a bullet pierced me and the shot rang out through the trees and into the canyons of stone.

I was flung, face first, into the ground cover but I immediately picked myself up and ran without even looking back. I was too close to the start of the arid region of this mountain for the forest to be any more help – the pine trees here were scattered wide and the foliage had thinned, giving no cover. Yet up in the rocks I thought I could see myriad plateaus to hide behind, and plentiful terraces and walls to throw off my hunters.

The upper right of my chest and back were burning, as if a fire had been pushed through me. Another shot rang out, and another. I was hit one more time, but I couldn't tell where. I scrambled over a low wall of rocks and landed heavily on my side. At least I had a moment's protection. I slipped my hand under Salvatore's heavy coat and shirt and pressed my palms to the bloody wound in my chest. It was the size of a fist and blood was pouring out. Pain radiated from the hole so that all the muscles in my body clenched and unclenched, as if to the dying pulse of my heartbeat.

I was already lightheaded, more lightheaded than injured and suffering, and I knew I ought to already be dead. Why I wasn't, I had no idea. But I could see what little hope I might have was to keep heading upwards into rockier and more treacherous terrain. Salvatore and his tracker would have to abandon their horses, and maybe I could outrun them or find a place to hide where they wouldn't be able to find me.

There would be a blood trail, the easiest thing to follow. They needn't even hurry; perhaps by the time they came to my body it would be absent of life.

Gasping, I picked myself up and forced myself to crouch, traversing the length of this natural wall until I saw a vast plateau of rock ahead. A rifle shot scattered stone, but not very close. Another shot echoed far and wide.

Turning a corner, slumping against a nest of boulders, I realised that while I'd been travelling through the upper regions of the forest belt I'd actually climbed much, much higher than I'd realised. A dizzying view of patchworked land and tiny, dotted villages spread out before me. It was a panorama offered by the top of the world, a gift to climbers determined enough to come up this way. I'd never travelled so far or so high. This was the place I was going to die, but I didn't feel any pain nor the slightest amount of fear. It was all right. Everything was fine. I'd travelled further from the sulphur mines than I could have hoped, maybe more than any escaping boy before me. I'd seen the sort of beauty in our Sicily's natural world that none of the *carusi* had experienced with their own eyes – and it was still in front of me, real enough to touch.

Above that panorama were the ghostly smoke rings. If I had the chance I would run and jump from the highest cliff, rather than let myself be shot again. My body would tumble to the rocks below but my spirit would rise up into the rings, maybe make a game of it.

Before he raised the black muzzle of his rifle again I would have liked to tell Salvatore that I'd hoped to stay out here a little longer, and been able to drink from more cold streams, and to sleep on more forest beds.

I stole a glance: the riders had dismounted and now each was forcing his horse up a small hill of stepped rocks. Both Salvatore and his companion had their reins in one hand and their rifles in the other. They couldn't aim properly and couldn't risk letting go their reins in case the horses panicked.

For a brief moment I met my master's eyes. I remembered how he'd waved to Angelino as the boy had tried to scurry away, so I raised my hand in greeting. In that moment, in the way he looked at me, was the reason he'd chosen to hunt me down. In his life he'd dominated the earth, he'd dominated his mine and probably everything and everyone he'd ever known. He'd buggered small boys, and to his great bulk the world had always shifted aside, making way. I was the only one who'd come close to beating him; I'd shamed him; I'd made him as helpless as he'd made those who had to succumb to him. Then he'd been found, and other men had seen him trussed and gagged, and they'd known that a thin nothing of a boy with a limp had made the terrible Salvatore into a fool. All of that was in his eyes. I knew that even my execution, my total eradication, wouldn't wipe those memories from him.

But it would be a very good start.

Salvatore kept his eye on me as he slipped his rifle into its scabbard and reached into his coat. His hand emerged with the very same serrated blade that I'd held to his eye and that had fallen from the hessian sack I'd carried over my shoulder. He dangled the blade between forefinger and thumb, and smiled.

I knew what he planned to do.

My former master slipped the blade back into his coat and with clicks and whistles encouraged his horse to traverse the precarious rocks. The tracker, who was close enough now that I could see exactly what sort of light-skinned, fleshy jowelled, pointy-nosed piece of inhumanity he was, did the same.

While the rocks slowed these men down, and guiding the horses made shooting problematic, I used the last of my strength to make a dash across the plateau.

If I could get across it, turn the corner, there might still be hope, but when I was no more than halfway, the might of the world smashed into me from behind and I was joined to the rock. A booming explosion echoed out from the hills, amplified a hundredfold. I struggled to my hands and knees and made a faltering crawl. To one side I saw a drop into the nearest fissure, and though it was very cold on the mountain I felt the immense heat that radiated upwards, warming my cheek. There was another gunshot and the rock by my right hand exploded, then my shoulder slammed forward as I was hit again.

I tried to crawl, but I was finished. Looking ahead, I saw a stranger stride out from the spot I'd been trying to reach. He quickly pulled a long-barrelled bolt-action rifle up to his eye and sighted.

How could it be that there was a third man, and that he was ahead of me? I hadn't imagined that possibility, couldn't begin to understand how a previously unknown member of Salvatore's party had managed not only to track me invisibly, but even to get in front of me.

I wanted to face him. I didn't want to crawl on my knees in my last moment. I struggled up to my feet and then I was swaying, but standing too. In a way I felt as if this was as great an achievement as any chattel had ever made. There was a gunshot from behind; the slug whizzed off the rock wall nearest to the stranger's face. He flinched slightly but strode straight past me, his long rifle up and steady. I turned and as I did the world also turned and I fell to my knees.

The man shouted something, someone fired, then he shot once, reloaded and shot again.

Salvatore and his tracker lay on the rocks, their horses standing quietly. Neither mare had panicked during the gunfire. I reached out a hand. I think I meant to pat the horse's heads the way I'd used to do with Pino's mule, Luisa. Of course, they were too far away. Everything was too far away. The sky whirled, and now I was on my back and I admired those four immense halos floating in the blue. I could have touched them. There was no sound anywhere, my ears had become like stones. I knew that this was my end and I liked where I lay and the last things I saw. In a moment, a darkness would descend and I could have the peaceful sleep I'd always longed for.

The stranger came and kneeled beside me. He had a satan's face, ugly as sin. He followed my gaze and he watched the halos too, then his eyes brimmed and he did the oddest thing, which was to weep, also without sound.

Green Book

BEHIND THE STRANGER, THE AZURE sky framed immense canyons. I could see the two horses standing idly. This man must have moved me into the shade because the sun wasn't in my eyes. Still, I wasn't very far from the spot where I'd fallen.

'You can hear me, can't you?'

He spoke without any trace of a peasant's accent or a localised dialect. I wanted to answer, but couldn't. If I could I'd have asked why I was still alive. This was simply not possible. How many times had I been shot, and in places that should be fatal? It was also extremely unfair, to have the end dragged out like this.

He nodded encouragement. 'You're aware, that's a good thing.'

Now he had saddlebags and a goatskin water sack over his shoulder. Putting the saddlebags down, he helped me drink a little water.

'For now that's all I can give you. You've been shot three, maybe four times. From what I can tell a couple of the slugs passed through you but they mightn't have been intact. You could have metal fragments . . . maybe other whole bullets. And bone fragments of course. All of that will make you very sick, if you manage to live through the next few hours.'

He looked down at me, maybe trying to work out how much I understood or how much he should say about my condition.

'I can't risk moving you but I've staunched your wounds as best as I can. If I put you on my horse you'll be dead before we're through the forest. So you're going to have to stay here while

I find help. I know a very good doctor. He'll come.' The man squinted up at the position of the sun. 'You're shaded now but you won't be in the morning. It'll take me longer than that to get back. You'll have to cover your own face when it gets bad, do you understand me?'

I neither nodded nor shook my head, simply lay there looking at him. He had odd features, odd because they were so much at variance to the kindness he displayed. His lips were thin and his eyes narrow, his face seemed arched into a mask meant to resemble Satan's cruel countenance. Yet every word he spoke was full of kindness.

'I'll leave water but no food, it wouldn't do to try and eat and I doubt you'll be hungry anyway. You might not have the strength to drink but the problem is that I can't stay. You're wrapped in blankets, do you understand? Lie still. When you need to urinate or defecate, do so. Don't wait on niceties. We'll clean you up before the dance,' he smiled.

I struggled to say a word. Just one word. He heard it.

'*How?* You mean how am I here or how are you alive?' He took a sigh and made himself more comfortable. 'Those two bastards found me last night. We joined camps for a while. My whisky was better than theirs. Let's say the night was more to their benefit than mine. I came here to observe the phenomena of the halos. Wondrous. I don't believe Etna has produced an entire series like that in fifty years. And I saw the women flying through. Did you?'

He gazed down at me. I couldn't make the slightest response.

'Of course,' he went on, 'all those two wanted to know about was if I'd observed a boy. They said I'd know him by his limp. They explained that he'd escaped from a mine and they were coming to collect him. They didn't like me asking why a boy should have to escape. I didn't like the way they drank all my whisky and cleaned their guns.'

He pressed his palm to my forehead and cheek, feeling for fever.

'They said this boy they were looking for was fourteen or fifteen years. In the war I saw too many boys that age given guns and expected to fight. The men in charge of them sent them out of trenches too soon, sent them to unfortified front-lines, simply expected them to die at their word. Which they did. I saw the same expectation in those two. Salvatore the miner and Gino the tracker. So when we parted we went our separate ways, except that I came back and kept them in sight, at a distance. But I never really believed it would come to this. Their bloodlust was up.'

He bit down on those words and now I understood why he'd wept. Then he steeled himself.

'We have the added complication of two dead bodies. I can assure you that no matter how cheerless I feel about what's happened, I've got no desire to be tried for murder. That's what it would come to.'

He sipped from a different flask. I guessed it wasn't water. I would miss him when he went away, his voice was so quiet and soothing, despite the subject matter.

'Those horses are a problem too. I can't take them with me, or take anything at all that might connect me to those two corpses.' He looked into my face again, as if I could provide an answer. 'What in the devil do we do?'

I tried to edge up a bit so that I could view the problem. Salvatore and the tracker, the man he'd told me was named Gino, were still exactly where they had fallen. The stranger got to his feet and went to the horses and soothed them, then he went through the equipment packed onto their backs and found the feed bags. In a moment both horses were munching quietly.

The stranger looked around this bare plain. He walked here and there picking up the broken pieces of his rifle, which he'd smashed to bits in his fury. He threw them over the side into the chasm. Then he looked at the corpses and knew what to do; he'd probably known it all along but hadn't wanted to contemplate actually completing the task.

He took some care in picking up the bodies. He didn't want their blood on him. As he loaded each corpse over the saddle of each horse he rubbed their strong flanks. Then an idea struck him. Removing the feed bags and emptying them over the side of the cliff, he spoke softly and reassuringly, and inverted the bags and placed them carefully over each horse's head so that their eyes were covered.

The horses snorted and shook, tails swishing with annoyance, but he kept them calm and led them in a circle one way and in a circle the other way, making sure they were disoriented.

I closed my eyes because I didn't want to see any more, and with only the slightest sound of screaming the two horses with their burden of dead men and dead men's belongings tumbled into the molten fire of that crease in the volcano's skin.

Why wasn't I dead with such holes in me? The pain had subsided and now the sun was bright and hot. I squeezed my eyes shut then in my dream I remembered what the stranger had said and so I lifted a veil of night up over my eyes. A red haze persisted but it didn't burn so badly, and I wasn't conscious of anything until that veil was drawn down from my face and the stranger said, 'Still with us?'

He turned to his companion, a much older man with a grey-and-white beard, and round, thick glasses.

'See what I mean, doctor? Holes in him and still alive. Thinner than Jesus Christ, but excellent facial bone structure.'

The older man nodded, but not happily, and said, 'Before it gets dark, all right?'

The stranger brushed hair away from my forehead. 'You might make it yet. Doctor Vliegan is going to do his best.'

The doctor made me take a few drops of something bitter and harsh onto my tongue, but when he put an injection in my arm all pain and trouble drifted away. He and the stranger rolled me onto my side and as the older man worked on my wounds I was startlingly conscious of the conversation – even if its meaning wasn't at all clear.

'You're so certain about this boy? I'm not convinced.'

'Oh yes, and he was under the rings. If that isn't a sign . . .'

'The world doesn't give us signs, Domenico, you keep mixing up reality and fantasy.'

'Kristof, please don't start with your nihilistic views again.'

This older man, Doctor Kristof Vliegan, said without rancour, 'It's only when you start with your religious fantasies.'

Don Domenico laughed softly and it was a lovely sound. 'You know religion's got nothing to do with it. Men have made themselves into the only gods they or we need, correct?'

'It would appear so.'

I must have cried out.

'He's feeling too much . . . do you have to be so parsimonious with the anaesthetic?'

The doctor prepared another injection and the pain only lasted a moment longer. But by the time night fell I was aching and burning, as if the doctor had decided to put lumps of red coal into my bullet holes.

'Kristof, he's in agony.'

'And he's not dead. Awake and looking around, incredible.' The doctor was sitting up from the bed he'd made for himself, reaching for his spectacles. He examined me quietly. 'Feverish. But I can't give him any more, it'd do him in.'

'Just a little? Maybe he can take it.'

'Whatever we do,' the doctor shook his old grey-haired head, 'he'll be dead before morning.'

'Then what's a little more going to matter?'

The doctor slid another shot into me. Serenity eased through my veins like a warm liquid. I felt good. Happy even. My eyelids were heavy, but despite so much anaesthetic I was still awake. It was as if I'd been put into a waking sort of null state. The stranger pushed himself to his feet and dusted off his trousers. By the light of an oil lamp he looked ten feet tall. They had a fire going and had eaten well. I was swaddled like a baby. My face was freezing but inside all those blankets I felt I was melting. The doctor's words floated on the stagnant ocean of my mind. *He'll be dead before morning.*

The stranger found what he was looking for and crouched beside me. Carefully, he used the wet cloth to soothe my face. Then he settled comfortably, his back against the rock wall.

'Let me tell you something,' he said to me. 'I have a spirit guide who looks after me. He's not much to look at but he can be very powerful. You saw the men Salvatore and Gino firing at me. Did you see that I wasn't hit? My spirit friend protected me, then I had him shield you from the last bullets. They would have struck you in the back of the head and that would've been that. My protector became your protector and he liked doing it, so I'm going to ask him to look after you a while. You've come this far, boy, with no animal or human spirit to defend you, so I think now you deserve a little help.'

The doctor was trying to settle in for the night. 'Come on, Domenico. Do these inanities have to be the last words your slave boy has to hear?'

This strange man named Domenico held up a hand to quieten his friend.

'Don't pay him any attention. He's a good doctor but he lacks imagination. The only animus that cares for him is an owl that died a hundred years ago, and the good doctor's still angry at the universe. My spirit might be featureless and somewhat pallid, but it certainly gets the job done.'

'*Featureless and pallid,*' the doctor muttered. 'God above . . .'

'But you've had nothing, and that seems miraculous, to survive so far. The best I can do is lend you mine so that if death comes stalking, my guardian will hold him back. You can help by being strong. Believe that you will live and don't submit. If you hear sweet words about how easy and nice it will be to let yourself slip away, don't believe them. Not unless you want to go . . . and I don't think a young boy like you should be ready for that just yet.'

Out of the medicinal comfort there was a spasm of pain that seared through my chest. Don Domenico's hand was close by. I grabbed it and squeezed hard. It was the first time in my life that I sought solace from another person. And received it. When the spasm passed I let go. He took my hand again and I was panting like a sick dog.

'Get your mind off physical matters. Relax. I'll tell you something amusing. I've discovered that a group of naked women use their wings to fly around the smoke rings above this place. Close your eyes, try and see them, take yourself away from these rocks. Are you old enough to like women?'

I heard the doctor grunting his displeasure again, then the world wavered and I no longer heard background sounds. Instead of being wrapped in blankets I was sitting on a monstrously high ledge observing a universe of stars. A white and featureless warrior guarded me. Except that this creature looked as if it was the one needing protection. It was slim and naked and bland as milk. There was no face to see. Nothing at all.

That was all right. It, or he, could be whatever it was.

A hand that wasn't quite a hand touched mine. I felt no pain, and for the first time in days I knew I wasn't going to die.

★

Later Don Domenico Amati would tell me that we stayed on the plateau three nights, until they decided to risk letting me ride one of the horses down off the mountain. Mostly, I remember, I was lying forward hugging my horse's neck while the don guided us along. Doctor Vliegan rode the second horse and saw me to the Amati estate and *palazzu*, but the first real sense I had of the place wasn't until many weeks later.

Most of the time I was in an insensate haze, drifting in and out, faces talking to me, caring for me, trying to feed me, meaning as little as the dreams you forget the moment you awaken – and even the awakenings themselves were no more substantial than dreams, until a day arrived when I had a clear head with clear thoughts in it. I was in the softest bed I could have imagined, the room so beautiful it had to be a chamber of paradise.

Under the sheets and light blanket I was bandaged well, my body clean and washed. Vials of medicine were arranged on a small table, and when I tried to move I couldn't quite do it. Despite the comfort I was determined to get some clothes and find a way to continue my journey. This house wasn't my destination. To me it didn't matter that I'd been saved and that by some incomprehensible miracle I'd survived. The man Domenico might want anything from me. I still intended to escape the island. It didn't cross my mind to wonder exactly who it was I had to run from any more.

A woman quietly entered. She was much older than any others I had vague recollections of. They used to visit me in this bedroom: maids, nurses perhaps, washing me, turning me. This older woman – yes, she'd also been here many times, looking over me, caring for me. I couldn't imagine why.

'Well, you're with us. How do you feel?' She touched my hands and face and wiped my forehead with a damp cloth. 'What do you remember?'

I didn't want to speak about the shootings. I'd never reveal what the stranger had done, though that didn't seem to be what she was asking about.

'Tell me something. What's the earliest thing you can see in your mind, as far back as you can go?'

It was a strange question but somehow, here, it made sense to ask. I thought it over, as I'd done many, many times in my life. The earliest thing? But it was like looking into a fog.

A man giving me to another man. Disappointment.

I shook my head.

'Can you let me know what you need the most right now?'

With words that didn't want to be produced from my dry and sore throat, I told her. She left me with something she called a bedpan. When I realised what it was for and how it should be used, I decided I had to recuperate as quickly as possible.

The doctor visited soon after. There was a twinkle in his eye as he examined my wounds and had a nurse in a white uniform re-bandage me. He assured me I was firmly in the land of the living and that from here my recovery would be fast. Despite his confidence, for this day at least, I could feel myself fading once again. His face shimmered as if in a pool of water disturbed by a stone and I don't remember another thing.

That's how those early days would pass, and for me they were always extremely short. I'd lie or sit awake for an hour or two feeling perfectly lucid, then without expecting it all my strength would go and I'd drop into unconsciousness.

The older woman returned several times a day. Her name was Rosa Bortolotti, and when the doctor wasn't in attendance she gave a small group of nurses their directions. They helped me eat and drink, wash and use that awful bedpan. One day Signora Rosa came in with a tray of food, the plates decorated and the cutlery shining. She helped me sit up, firm pillows behind my back. She put the tray onto my lap then folded her arms.

'Come on,' she said. 'Let's see how you help yourself.'

I was little more than an animal. I managed to hack a portion of meat and get it into my mouth.

Rosa said, 'You don't have a single social grace, do you? Could you please keep your mouth shut while you chew, you're not a dog.'

I did as she asked, and it was as awkward and strange as trying to speak without using your lips.

'That's beef, roasted with rosemary and peppers, served rare to help you build your strength.' She watched me hacking at another piece. 'Do you remember my name? And the doctor's?'

'Signora Rosa.' My voice was a whisper I didn't like, no air behind it. 'Doctor Vliegan.'

'Good. I don't live here and neither does the doctor. I've known Don Domenico since he was a boy. Three sons of my own, so he thought I'd be the best person to look after you. But you've taken your time to come back, and I have to be with my family again. I'm sorry to leave you but maybe one day you'll want to come visit me in Catania.'

There were so many questions I wanted to ask her, but the pressing matter was the food in front of me and the effort it took to feed myself, much less speak. The elegant knife dropped from my hand to the plate. I had the strength of a kitten and the finesse of a boar. Signora Rosa couldn't help herself: she cut the beef into small portions and fed me. I chewed obediently, mouth shut. Then eating cost too much strength and I had her stop.

'Why – did you ask me – about what I remember?'

'You worked in a mine but you weren't born there. Before that a man called Gozzi had you, didn't he?'

I stared at her, trying to work out how she could have known this.

'I want to understand if you know anything about what was before that.'

I didn't, not in the slightest. She must have read the truth of it in my eyes because she didn't pursue the matter. I had no memories of someone who would have been like her, for instance, what normal boys would call a mother. And that image of the man delivering me to another man certainly didn't include a father, I was certain of it. In reality I believed I had no parents at all, as if I'd been born out of the air itself.

I tried to speak.

'What? Please try again.'

'Have – I – got clothes?'

'Leaving so soon?' she smiled, revealing the deep lines in her face. 'You'll have to ask Domenico. I burned everything you came here with myself.'

As Rosa cleared the tray and straightened my bed for me, helping me make myself comfortable, I wondered if I was some sort of prisoner – everything about my life had taught me mistrust; it was the only way to survive.

Signora Rosa put some of the medicine from one of the brown vials onto a spoon. The liquid was milky white and I took it. She told me she wouldn't be seeing me again for some time, looking down into my eyes in a way that said she didn't necessarily want to leave.

As soon as she was out of the room, I spat the medicine into a washcloth and lay restlessly asleep–awake for hours, waiting for nightfall. When things seemed safer I nearly fainted with the effort of climbing out of that bed, then I managed to do it, staggering naked, bandaged and shivering around the room.

There were many closets to investigate: women's clothes with ruffles and velvet, small-soled boots with buttoned-up sides.

There were men's vestments too, and very fine ones at that. I tried a few pieces of the more sedate items but they looked and felt ridiculous, as big as Salvatore's things had been, though of infinitely better quality. Still, I needed to select clothing that would give me protection.

I was angry at how hard I was breathing. I dressed, no shoes, and went to the windows. During my recovery they'd been mostly open, the curtains drawn or undrawn depending on sleep or wakefulness. This was the very first time I looked through them. There was a moonlit night of spreading fields, undulating valleys and the outlines of hulking mountains. Small fires were scattered in the fields and tiny homes glowed from the inside.

I opened the window, checked the sides and found a way, and then carefully climbed down the side of the mansion. My arms felt thin, legs spindly, not wanting to carry me. I had to stop every now and then, catch my breath, wait for nausea and some small amount of pain from my wounds to pass.

There were four levels to get down. I was certain that if I could escape the hellhole of the sulphur mines and travel all the way to the volcano, I could get away from this infinitely more congenial place. I thought of how kindly everyone had treated me, starting with Don Domenico on the mountain, letting me clutch his hand when pain shot through me, but I also remembered his odd stories and visions, the unimaginable goings-on in his head. Naked women floating through the volcano's smoke rings; a spirit guardian: there was no choice, this was hardly the place for me.

My destination would be, as always, the Straits of Messina and the mainland, but now I had an added objective. During some one-sided conversation the don had mentioned his participation in the war. What better and easier way to escape Sicily and Italy entirely, to disappear? Sign up with a new name, allow myself to be shipped off to some mysterious new country, and vanish. A new life on foreign soil. Perfection itself.

Once I had climbed down the brick and latticework of the side of the great mansion no one was around and there were no dogs to bark and snap at my heels. I kept to the shadows and found shelter in a grove of olive trees. My soles were as hard as they'd ever been, sores all healed, but something to protect them would have been useful. I'd worry about that later. What I really needed was better orientation so that I'd know which direction to take. My head was swimming but I pushed myself to move on until the half-moon revealed a trail and then a field of corn.

Away from the overhanging branches I looked around and saw the great dominating glow in the sky. I was closer to the volcano than I'd realised.

The mountain filled me with confidence; a breeze rose up and it was sweet with flowering scents. I took a deep breath and filled my lungs, and that was my mistake.

Don Domenico stood at a nurse's shoulder as she fed me a clear soup. 'That's chicken broth,' he said, 'don't let it go to waste.' I'd resisted at first, but the taste was too good and my body was crying out for sustenance. Watching me he went on, 'If you weren't so used to being a slave I'd put an iron collar around your neck myself. Where did you think you were going and how far did you expect to get?'

His voice was reasonable, even quite playful, totally devoid of anger. He took the bowl and spoon from the nurse and gave them to me.

'You do know how to feed yourself?'

'Yes.' My voice was still hoarse, the effort to speak even greater than to walk.

He sent the nurse away. After she closed the bedroom door behind her he went on. 'Then it's time we stopped mollycoddling you. This is a civilised house so don't slurp like a pig. You're going to need an education.'

I went at it even more noisily, ignoring him, then belched as I insolently pushed the empty bowl away. He threw a napkin toward me.

'You're not a captive,' he said, 'but you're too young and ignorant to know that if you escape from here you'll simply be caught and sent to some new version of the place you ran away from. So try to understand something. If you trust me, I think things can be all right. There hasn't been any word about missing men or a boy on the run. No one's going to look for the likes of Salvatore and Gino very long. There'll be searches, that's certain, but the police will know that anything could have befallen those two. People disappear around here, it's just the way it is. Now that means that if I can live with what I did, life can go on. Same for you. If you can refrain from being stupid you can have a new life, the sort a boy should always have.'

I shifted in the bed, feeling better and with a little more strength in my voice.

'You – own me now?'

'Look around you,' he said, clicking his tongue in exasperation. 'You're in a comfortable warm bed and I'm bringing you food and medicine. Who owns who?'

I didn't see the humour in it. 'Once I'm better – you'll make me work for you.'

'What do you want to do, fly kites and play chess?'

'What's chess?'

He frowned then. A thought seemed to cross his mind. He went to a set of drawers and rummaged around personal apparel that didn't seem to be his, then found what he wanted. He handed me a large book.

'That's the Holy Bible of the Amati grandparents.'

He said the words 'Holy Bible' as if they were amusing in

themselves, but what was curious was the way he'd said 'the' Amati grandparents, not 'my'.

'Find a nice page. Read a paragraph for me.'

As he suspected I would, I stumbled over a single sentence and gave up. At Gozzi's tiling plant I'd managed to learn to read a few words, but not many.

'So we have a first objective. Your education starts today. We'll also consider mathematics, the sciences, the humanities in general. You've got a lot of catching up to do and a lot of lessons to learn.'

'I don't – need to learn – anything.'

'The first lesson is this one, so listen,' he said, choosing to disregard my impudence. 'No one owns anyone. The Amati family thought they owned all those people out there. That was a mirage. But this island of ours continues to believe the church and the rich are entitled to their dominion over the poor. Well, those sorts of days are coming to an end. Whatever happens, I don't want to be involved. By the end of the year a sale will be complete and I'll be leaving this situation I inherited. Let me tell you, that will be my happiest day.'

He reached his hand out to smooth my hair but I twisted my head away.

'I'm lucky enough to be the last legal branch in the Amati family tree. That means I'm free to get rid of this infernal estate. When I do I'll have the sort of freedom very few men experience.'

'And what – what will you do with that freedom?'

'Nothing. Just a place in the country away from prying eyes and other people's interests. It's a nice plan, isn't it?'

'Sounds boring.'

'That will be its best attribute.'

'You're going – to sell all those people outside?'

'They can stay or go, that'll be a matter of contracts and choice.'

'And I'll be sold too?'

'You'll also have a choice.'

'Between what?'

'Staying here with good honest work, or hitting the road. Though there could be a third option.'

I kept my eyes on that odd-looking face.

'Learn to be better than a brute and come with me.' He knocked my woolly skull with his knuckles and I flinched away. 'In here is chaos. So far you don't know up from down.'

'I know enough. I know you want . . . unnatural things.'

'Do I?' he smiled. 'I wouldn't think so. Listen. I'm not ignorant of what must go on in those mines. You can put any of those sorts of worries out of your head. There are better things to deal with. Now, I can guarantee that the acquisition of knowledge can be quite painful, but I'll never hurt *you*. That's my promise.'

'Then what – do you want from me?'

He didn't have to think about it. 'You're already giving it to me.'

From there on Domenico read to me almost every day that he was at the property, introducing me to books taken from his voluminous library, titles such as the *The Adventures of Tom Saw-yer, The Count of Monte Cristo* and *Robinson Crusoe*. As he read, the enjoyment and pleasure in his face changed his satan's mask into something softer. It was as if a light came into him. For the hour that a story possessed his soul, his ugliness fell away, an extraordinary thing to observe. I came to hate those long stretches when he was away, interrupting our immersion in his books, but then he'd return and the tale would be taken up once more, each of us as eager as the other to answer the glorious question: *What happens next?*

Within twelve months I was reading these books myself, either on the veranda, in the shade of some trees, or in my bed late at night and early into the morning. And we were all still here; the great sale hadn't eventuated.

My days with Domenico were the happiest but I was also pleased whenever Signora Rosa returned. She'd stay for a week at a time and give me the benefit of her own teaching. For reasons I couldn't yet understand she didn't like to be away from this mansion too long, but I could also see how torn she was: in Catania she had her own family to attend to.

Rosa's gifts were for more concrete matters than storybooks. Though it was a struggle at the start soon I could recite the multiplication, division, addition and subtraction tables she gave me, and in all directions.

The difference between her type of learning and the don's was that I found the former confusing and virtually impenetrable, and one day when Rosa was trying to drill the rigours and the pleasures of pi into me I stood up from the table with my head throbbing and left the room, and because it felt so good I ran down the staircase, and then the true pleasures of life hit me so I ran out of the house whooping, and took a trail past the homes of the workers into the green fields. First some dogs came yapping and barking at my heels, and some of the younger children followed – little boys in cut-off trousers and no shirts, and tiny girls wearing dirty peasant dresses but with pretty ribbons among their curls – then came all the boys, the ones my age and older, and they whooped and screeched even more loudly than me, running as if on a hunt and leaving their fathers or their masters to watch with dumbfounded eyes, and everyone was so much faster than me, what with my cursed limp, that they all overtook me and ran off like banshees.

I collapsed and two puppies were with me and wanted to be my friends. As I let them tumble over my belly and legs, Don Domenico rode across the plain on one of his mares.

'So this is what my young foundling, Sette, makes of his education?'

I peered up at him, saying nothing. He rarely used that name with me, usually calling me, in his ironic way, 'boy' or 'young man' or 'learned student'. One of the puppies licked the corner of my mouth and I held it away, small legs kicking. The other whined.

'Pi, I'd run too,' Domenico laughed, dismounting. 'I haven't got a head for figures either. Arithmetic, math, scientific equations . . . let's be thankful there are people in the world who can worry about these things for us.' He sat next to me in the grass and took the second puppy in his hands, cradling it and giving it his finger to suck. 'I was watching the way you run. Does it hurt very much?'

'No, it's just . . . slow.'

His mare snorted and chafed at the bit, wanting to take to the plain again. Don Domenico looked into the distance and thought a while.

'You shouldn't have limits. At least not the kind that can be avoided.' He put the puppy down and it joined its brother, the two tumbling like little clowns. The don found his feet, then expertly whipped himself up into the saddle. He jerked the reins, keeping his horse in control. 'Want to learn how to ride, boy?'

'Can I?'

'Why not? I'll talk to Leo. Now let's get you back to Rosa before she thinks she's a bad teacher.'

Don Domenico put out his hand and pulled me up. We rode to the house and he whistled a quiet melody. I recognised it as something he'd been playing on the piano in the downstairs parlour, late at night. If this man was mad, then it was the type of madness the world could use a little more of.

So I thought then, friend, and still do.

When I was stronger I spent my days outdoors, playing with Leo the foreman's children, mostly because it was expected of me – even though I couldn't find the purpose, much less the joy, in kicking and chasing a ball from one side of the green expanse of grass behind the great house to the other.

My limp had managed to get me across country in my unlikely escape, but I was at a disadvantage at this game they called *palluni*. Some days the boys Maurizio and Pietro took pity on me and moved slow and other days they ran rings around me just for the fun of it. Whenever we were tired from the game we would fall into some patch of shaded green grass, and the boys would like to tell me tales about how mad our master was, comically grim histories of the way he had used to light fires as a child and some-times go running naked and screaming into the fields, pursued by maids and servants, but never, they would laugh, his mother or father. Piercing screams would puncture the night and all the workers in their homes would wonder what sort of devil lived inside the masculine Amati offspring. According to Maurizio and Pietro, the boy Domenico Amati only changed for the better after he started to become a young man, and most especially so upon his return from the war after the death of his parents – at which time, they said, his demeanour became almost totally dis-similar to the person he used to be.

He withdrew into the mansion at that time, and refashioned himself into a benevolent but distant overseer of this vast prop-erty he'd inherited. Don Domenico became a steady hand to write the necessary cheques. And little else. He had no wife or children, and the place almost ran itself; whatever authority was needed was now invested in managers and foremen. Even the house was captained by someone else, a great-aunt with a man-nish voice who didn't like her great-nephew one bit, and who never stopped telling the house staff what to do or how to do it better. Despite Domenico's altered temperament and disposition, no one quite trusted him, and certainly no one thought he'd been cured of the ills in his head.

I learned to ride, and for the majority of the next year I worked in the fields, mixing in studies and reading, sometimes being a labourer, sometimes a fruit picker, sometimes even taking a gelding out to ride beside the horses of the overseers and learning the ebb and flow of farming life. These were good days, and they went fast, but when the turning point finally came, the one Don Domenico said he'd dreamed of for years, all our lives changed completely.

Our master finally managed to sell the great estate and with it the last remaining tendrils of the Amati family's business dealings on the mainland. These, he told me, had had to do with munitions, in the application of that earthbound horror once called brimstone, now called sulphur, the integral part of almost every armament manufactured in this world.

I couldn't believe it; this family and this place, now my home, had in fact all been built on the suffering of boys like me.

'So is that why you took me in, out of guilt, because of everyone and everything you've profited from?'

'The Amatis, true, they had no reservations about how they earned their money . . .'

'You keep talking as if you're not even one of them!'

'I —' he started. 'I —'

Don Domenico stammered some more and didn't finish the sentence. There was something important about the Amatis that he wasn't telling me. Still, he managed to calm me down and eventually found the words to tell me a story.

Deep down I knew it wasn't the full story but I took in every word, relieved to finally hear the tale of this peculiar world I'd fallen into.

★

From as far back as he could remember, the young Domenico despised everything his family did and stood for. This rebellion was solidified by his participation in the war. His father, Vincenzo Amati, a giant of the Italian industrial and agrarian sectors, had purchased his boy's immunity from the draft, but Domenico had gone anyway – as much to spite his family as to protect the homeland which, despite its vicissitudes and inconsistencies, he cared for.

The war had proven a bonanza for his family, as it did for any family with interests in the sulphur fields of Sicily. There was a world need, a hunger, a desperation for sulphur, and the subsequent increase in demand upon the world's centre of sulphur extraction, the tiny island of Sicily, led to unimaginable profits – and of course, to unimaginable practices in the urgency of its mining and supply.

Traditional supplies of sulphur around the world, though, were dwindling, and this was as true for the island of Sicily as anywhere else. No resource is infinite. The old fields were being mined out of existence and favourable seams and sites were becoming harder and harder to find.

And then further disaster. No one knew how it happened exactly, but there was a fire that led to an explosion, which created other explosions, which led to blasts destroying entire warehouses and plants in an almost unthinkable chain reaction.

In all, the blaze was to last two full months. The small city that was the Amati manufacturing and distribution plant outside the mainland town of Milan ceased to exist but for ashes, twisted metal and melted rock. Vincenzo Amati, his wife and small daughter Stella, eight years of age, gone, along with countless workers and their families. Domenico, the last Amati – saved, ironically enough, by being busy fighting in the war – was found somewhere on the Western Front and rushed back to Rome, where he was hauled in front of a hostile senate inquiry that seemed to hold him partially responsible for the debacle, for this great loss to the nation.

He was informed that, as a precious and dwindling a commodity, Sicilian sulphur could no longer be left in the hands of one family, much less one sole-surviving family member. The Italian government was seizing control and proprietorship of the Amati mines plus whatever remaining distribution and production channels still existed. The sum offered in recompense was a fraction of the true value. Domenico told the senators, scientists, military strategists and economists they could take everything *gratis*. Not for a second had he ever thought there was anything worthwhile about his family's business.

On his less than triumphal return to Sicily he spent months behind locked doors, communing only with himself and whatever ghosts floated from room to room in the Amati mansion. He said there were many, but only one that meant anything to him: little Stella. When her soul or spirit finally chose to leave the house forever, Domenico opened its doors and windows and all the servants and field hands, the day workers, foremen, managers and staff, breathed a sigh of relief. Domenico signed cheques and honoured labour contracts. The banks honoured those cheques, and the Amati estate didn't collapse the way it had been expected to.

The new don surveyed this empire he didn't care for, and immediately tried to find the best means to divest himself of it. The task would take some doing; many other major families were also shrinking their landholdings or losing them altogether. The last Amati understood that an entire way of life was ending.

Finally a deal was sealed. Domenico's lawyer advised him that an Austrian buyer had signed the necessary contracts. His affairs were so simple that all he was required to do was leave.

The final duty was to let everyone know.

★

In the pavilion where all the workers gathered twice a week for communal meals, the facts were going to be laid out for all to hear, though of course the word had already gone around and this was little more than a formality. There were nearly forty families comprising at least two hundred souls, all present, all of different hierarchies in this working world of adults and children. I was at the back, listening to the rising muttering and grumbling. The mood was surly; any fool could see that it would take very little for things to take a bad turn.

Flanked by his best foremen, including the most loyal and competent of them, Leo, our master spoke in a voice that neither commanded attention nor particularly sought it.

'So let me tell you how things stand . . .'

'Quiet!' Leo's voice boomed out at the assembly.

These people who'd never known what to make of Domenico as their *signor padrone*, were still suspicious about whatever clouds floated in his head. No one was likely to forget the strange things he'd done through his youth and no one liked the way he'd locked himself inside his mansion until the 'sweet spirit of Stella' had decided to leave. Added to all this, easy as his so-called rule was, no one could respect a man so fundamentally disinterested in his own business affairs. They expected that this sale he'd engineered could only turn out well for him and badly for them. I could understand how his workers felt, because whatever Don Domenico did affected me too. I'd been sold and onsold all my life, and here my most benevolent master of all was doing exactly the same thing.

Leo had to pound a tabletop to silence the voices of dissent.

'Let him speak! Listen and you might learn something!'

'This is the news,' Don Domenico went on without fanfare. To hear him properly everyone had to quieten down, which they now did. 'Each family will receive an endowment of two cows, three goats and a dozen chickens. Three acres of land will be placed in the name of each man over the age of twenty-one who is married. Each single man over the age of twenty-one will receive one acre. Every individual whether a man or woman, adult or infant, will receive a cash payment of one thousand lire to their name. Use it for education, your own crops, more animals or whatever interests you. Learn to be self-sufficient. The new owner has promised to honour our estate's current work contracts and I believe he will. However my accountants inform me that even the contract with the longest term left will expire within eighteen months. Everyone here knows what evictions have been happening all over the island, so you can't count on a new *padrone* taking care of you forever. I've given you as much as I can. Please use it,' he said, then finished with the words: '*Siate chi siete*'. 'Be who you are.'

Everyone knew just how serious the economic problems of the island were, and everyone understood how unprecedented this man's generosity was. Don Domenico's father and his father before him had been like other landowners – gentle when times were good and brutal in everything else. Domenico was their opposite. Still, all around there remained nothing but unhappy faces. Some men stood holding their pitchforks and scythes; I had an awful image of them taking to the don and cutting him to shreds. None of these folk saw Domenico as symbolic of some gentler, kinder, more egalitarian new age. Instead he was a living emblem for both the weakness of the young and the corruption of the upper classes. They were terrified for their futures and the futures of their offspring. Despite what he'd just granted them, most found cause to complain even more loudly.

'If you care about us so much open your house! We can live there!'

'If you want us to live well then let's profit equally!'

'Why two cows each? Why not twenty? Why three acres? Why not three hundred? A thousand lire is an insult – squeeze yourself to a hundred thousand!'

The socialist spirit had well and truly seeped into the Sicilian way of thinking and nothing the wealthy classes did was ever going to be allayed by throwing scraps. No man of the people, Don Domenico simply listened to the shouted admonishments with his hands clasped in front of him and an expression of almost complete disinterest in his face.

And the truth is, I was shocked by what I saw, this indifference. He didn't care. He didn't care about any of us.

People even started laughing and castigating him for the odd entreaty, *Be who you are*.

'Who else would we be, American movie stars?'

'Maybe we could be princes and kings!'

'No! We'll be like you Domenico! Rich – but maybe not so mad!'

'So let's take what we want before this new family of bastards comes in and takes everything from us!'

This was the moment the trouble flared. A field hand I knew only as Giacomo overturned his table, pushed forward, and made – I think – to tear the shirt off Domenico's back. Leo smashed him in the face with an elbow. A roar went up, now turned against Leo and the other foremen along with Domenico.

Despite my anger and hurt at the way he'd simply divested himself of all of us, the way a *patruni* might divest himself of a herd of unwanted cattle, I was now terrified at what a mob might do to Domenico. I pushed forward through the throng, avoiding the raised fists. Food was being thrown, bottles of wine were being smashed. I saw naked flames and a torch. Leo and his men were fighting off their own friends and workmates, protecting Domenico – who, I saw, found a way to withdraw.

It took an effort to squeeze through the sudden, fierce rabble. More tables were upturned, chairs smashed; men and women were shouting to be heard and children screamed and cried. It was as if a madness had entered the pavilion and was now raging to be set free. Next, the manor itself would have to be invaded, stripped bare, set alight.

And if they got their hands on the don . . .

When I was finally able to stumble outside, I caught sight of Domenico on a Spanish-bred gelding he'd named Esperanto. The don was no longer indifferent. Perhaps he never had been. His features were strained and his face was white. The horse galloped past me and toward the hills. I asked the mistress of all our house-keepers, Donna Francesca, who had also managed to find her way out of the wooden pavilion and into the open air, where he was going. Her hairy chin quivered, tears of rage running down her face.

'To hell I hope, where his whole family's burning! He sold me with the house! He thinks I can stay on to serve the new master!' She shook a fist at the night. 'No heart! No heart!'

I didn't know if I'd be able to catch up with Don Domenico, or even if I should, but I went to the stables and saddled the most powerful mare we had, Estella, a half-Arabian beauty named for the deceased young sister. I didn't even know if this mare belonged to Don Domenico anymore.

It was a long ride into the hills above these plains of misery, but I found my master's horse where I thought it would be, at one of Domenico's favourite places of solitude. I tethered Estella's reins to Esperanto's, and then I heard a mumbling, a blathering, a long outpouring of words that had no meaning.

The night hummed to his tuneless song. I sat on a rock and watched my master, who was spread out on the flat rocks as if prostrate to some divinity. The endless plains spread before us but he was facing the sky, arms and legs outstretched, his feet kick-ing and his palms slapping. His fingers scrabbled for nothing but stones. His satan's face was a rictus. He grumbled, he cried, he moaned – and he spoke in a hoarse tongue that wasn't Italian, or of any Latin derivative I could imagine.

Nor, I thought, was it anything of this earth.

Watching, I was sick to my stomach. Here was my saviour and master; this was the man who'd determined the fate of almost two hundred lives, including my own.

Then he stopped, the wordless syllables dying on his lips. His body relaxed. Slowly he came to himself. There was quiet. I didn't see why I should hide my presence, and I approached cautiously. The rocky ground and my halting walk probably accentuated the nature of my limp, which, even in the darkness, Don Domenico immediately recognised. He sat up and turned, half-glazed eyes taking in my approach. I didn't know what I expected him to say, but it certainly wasn't this:

'Sette, your leg remains a problem we can do something about. Before you come to the country house you'll have to visit Doctor Vliegan. He lives in Bologna. I'll have Signora Rosa take you.'

Then his eyes showed their whites and he slumped sideways, dead to this world, but perhaps not to all others.

White Book

FROM TIME TO TIME I'd travelled with Don Domenico on the Sicilian *ferrovia*, which took passengers to small villages close to the volcano, and completed a panoramic circuit of Mount Etna, but small-gauge rails were nothing compared to the miracle of real trains. The smoke, the cabins with their open windows and plush seats, the dream-inducing steady rocking of the journey, and Signora Rosa beside me in her best clothes, her hair up and protected with lace, and her gloves and boots – all this combined to make my first trip to Bologna quite unforgettable.

I envied Rosa's sons for their mother. She was a woman of nothing but benevolence and her manner told you that everything was going to be all right, even if there was so much proof to the contrary.

She had bread, cheese and meat wrapped in wax paper, but more than anything she had that smile, as if my every action, whether voluntary or involuntary, gave her pleasure. I daydreamed she was my own mother. Some terrible calamity had forced me to be taken away from her, and something prevented her from revealing the truth, a mysterious secret, good enough to occupy the novels in Don Domenico's library.

When we stopped at major stations she gave me the coins necessary to buy cold drinks from the concession stands. We overnighted in a good hotel, and in its dining room full of civilised people she ordered seafood and pasta coloured with squid ink, and my first glass of champagne. She liked the fact that I'd learned to eat properly and could carry myself like a young gentleman.

'How old do you think you are?' she asked. I had to admit that I didn't really know. 'Sixteen? Seventeen? What about your birthday?' I told her that was a mystery too. 'You'll have to agree a date with Domenico. You need your own day.'

There was a time in the recent past when I had nothing at all of my own, and no prospects for the situation ever changing, yet delicious food was now in front of me and I was drinking champagne with a woman I wished was my mother. Rosa caught the look in my face. I'm sure her sons were able to get away with nothing at all.

'Your new life is a little confusing, isn't it?'

I wanted to tell her about the boys left behind at Gozzi's plant, and all the *carusi* in the Amati sulphur mines. Most of those boys would be dead now, or close enough. New underage workers would arrive to replace them then more again to replace those. Yet I was here.

'Believe it or not, Italy and even the rest of the world is against this type of slavery. In America they changed the way they were allowed to treat the black race and abolished slavery completely, but here we're too smart. The children aren't called slaves. They're supposedly doing work that will benefit their families.'

'But that's all lies,' I said. 'And obvious ones.'

'Of course. Therefore many people work against it.'

'Including you?'

'Women can be very effective in this regard,' she smiled. 'Forty years ago a Catholic priest named Father Luigi Sturzo started the movement to stop child labour. Some great successes, yes, but real and absolute change always comes slowly. The sulphur pits are the hardest to conquer – though nature has been kindly lending a hand. People estimate the mines will be almost completely useless within a decade. But that's a decade too long.' She put her hand over mine. 'All *you* need to worry about is our life ahead. Leave the inequities of the world to we do-gooders. I promise you this evil will end within our lifetime.'

We travelled on to Bologna, and while I enjoyed this cross-country journey I also found myself wanting to be back with Don Domenico. Since that night of his announcement to his workers, after I'd found him suffering in the hills, I felt more protective of him than ever. He hadn't sold me. He'd never even thought to abandon me.

Domenico Amati wasn't a god-like figure, nor was he even what I believed a strong upright father might be. He was simply a person I might be able to help as much as he'd helped me. So when the moment came when we started across the Straits of Messina on the ferry, I felt no inclination to slip from Rosa's eye and disappear into Italy and beyond. For better or worse my place was in Sicily with Don Domenico, a master who wasn't a master, a father who was anything but.

We arrived in Bologna, and spent an initial night in the sort of hotel I was getting used to. Signora Rosa said she would stay with me for the duration of my procedures with Doctor Vliegan. I had very little idea what these procedures would be or why she would choose to be my companion while her family were again left to cope without her. I had no *hope* of understanding – Don Domenico hadn't told me the truth of what he knew about me, and hadn't explained the full reality of this world I'd been rescued into.

Signora Rosa and I had one day to spend as tourists in a wonderful city. Of all the churches and ornate porticos we wandered through, plus boat rides along the river and coach rides through the old quarters, my favourite visit was to the university. Doctor Vliegan greeted us and told me this was the oldest such institution in the world. He showed us around the medical school and I stood inside a wood-panelled sixteenth century anatomical theatre as if in another type of church. Here various sciences came together and were researched, taught, studied and practised – the culmination of which would do something special to make my leg a little less the burden it was.

After I was brought into the hospital and I made the transition from being a normal person with an affliction to being a surgical patient, I learned why Signora Rosa's family should have to be without her, and I had to be in her care. The knives of Doctor Vliegan and his associates cut me, their saws rendered bone, muscle and flesh, their science sent me into wracking screams that no anaesthetics could quell. I had to be strapped to beds and gurneys. I was never left alone. My fingers scrabbled at locked windows and I broke my nails on iron bars. Every day I cursed Doctor Vliegan and his surgeons and assistants. I spat at the nurses then pleaded with them. I begged Rosa to get me out of there.

No one listened. The procedures continued.

Long months later, my master waited for me at Catania's central station. Signora Rosa had needed to leave me at the hospital during the last stages of my recovery and rehabilitation, and now I disembarked alone. Domenico turned my face this way and that, pleased to see me again. I was pleased to see him too, even if I remained a little resentful. The truth that I had to admit, however, was that my leg was healing very well. Though the long lines of scarring still caused pain, I was already walking more freely.

Don Domenico tipped my hat off my head and mussed my carefully brilliantined hair.

'Look at you. That stride brings out your natural nobility. Don't you think the boy "Sette" has finally gone?'

We were moving away from the main platform, each of us

carrying a suitcase. They were stuffed full of good and fashionable clothes purchased for me by Rosa on his account. To my surprise, the don had got himself a motor vehicle. It was a dark green Fiat 501 Torpedo, top-down, more beautiful than a work of art in a museum. We put my bags into the back seats.

'So what will we call you?' Don Domenico cranked the 1460cc engine. 'You're reborn, so let's make the process complete. Your profile's always so Roman to me, like an emperor. No less than Caesar maybe. "*Cesare*". Do you like it?'

He could give me any name. I didn't care – I simply wanted to be someone new. Before I'd met this man I was nothing, now I wanted the new start he offered and I wanted the transition to be complete. Domenico opened the side door for me and as I climbed up he watched.

'Hurts?'

'I've been off the crutches for a month and the bandages have been off almost as long, but Doctor Vliegan gave me exercises —'

'Don't worry.' My master nodded with rare impatience. 'I know exactly what will help.'

What he had in mind was simple: long treks through quiet, undulating countryside. I saw these rolled in abundance from the small, private manor he now called home.

We arrived and there was no one around for tens of kilometres. The fields that surrounded this place were full of meadows and flowers. Nothing had been tamed by women or men. At his new house Domenico had no staff, no cook or gardener, no handyman or field hands. He had so completely given up his previous life that he might as well have given *himself* a new name. Instead of the past trappings of a padrone he now had a car, a truck with a smoking, rattling engine and a wooden tray, two horses, one of which was the half-Arabian mare, the other the Spanish hothead, a small number of pigs and goats, and several good cultivations of vegetables. There were also shaded groves of orange, lemon and olive trees, plus the manor itself – small by the standards of the previous Amati home, but, I thought, much more beautiful with its stucco rendering and red-tiled roof.

It contained a single fireplace and chimney, and rooms with pleasing dimensions: none was monstrously large, none was too small. Two cool bedrooms and a nice-sized kitchen. The heart of the place was a study that had been fashioned by removing walls from a previous dining room and library. This was the don's sanctuary, a large and comfortable room lined with shelves of books and furnished with deep armchairs and an overstuffed couch. Its rugs and sideboard, the upright piano moved in from the Amati mansion, and most especially the overcrowded writing desk and comfortable chair gave my master an obvious satisfaction. It was the sort of sensual pleasure that I imagined other men took in lovemaking and drink – but Don Domenico experienced it most strongly when he was in here, alone. Something told me that if I ever had the chance, this aspect of his life might be one I'd like to emulate.

Of his books, these days he most pored over the many volumes of memoirs by the writer he referred to as 'The Venetian', Casanova de Seingalt. One day he showed me a quote and asked me to copy it out:

Man is a free agent; but he is not free if he does not believe it,
for the more power he attributes to Destiny, the more he deprives
himself of the power which God granted him when he gave him reason.

I thought I understood Domenico's message and intent; they were good ones for a boy with my background in slavery and sulphur. But it wasn't until much later that I learned the true import of these words, and how vital they were for both of us to keep in mind.

*

It didn't take long before we settled into a companionable routine, like father and son – or perhaps simply like brothers. The relationship was in no way one of master and serf. At first Domenico would rise with the sun, make coffee, dress into whatever was appropriate for the weather, then go tend his small community of livestock. Swill for the pigs, grain and leftovers for the chickens and goats. His chores would go on until midmorning, when he would finish by watering and grooming the horses. Soon I let him know that these were tasks I preferred to do. I didn't need Don Domenico's supervision and neither did I need his constant company. I liked the quiet of this place as much as he did, and though it might seem we had completely withdrawn from the world, neither he nor I felt a moment's loneliness or a moment's longing for anything else. At the time I had no explanation for why this was so.

Domenico acquiesced and I enjoyed the work, finding it neither onerous nor dull. After I finished those morning duties, on the kitchen table I would find various books and academic texts set out and waiting. Don Domenico had recorded exactly where my old studies had reached and here always was the way forward.

While I occupied myself and felt what it was like to live unshackled, unsupervised, unpunished for infractions real or imagined, he would work in the study with his papers and notes and books. Some days he emerged excited and eager to continue with whatever it was that he was doing; other times he was drained, as if he'd worked outside in a long day of blistering heat. But whichever his demeanour, he was always ready to sit down at the table and review what I'd read and learned, and try to explain the things I hadn't quite grasped.

He was a good teacher because he made up for those areas in which he wasn't knowledgeable by calmly retracing his steps through my books until he made sense of things. Above all, he was interested in my progress.

'What will you study at university?'

I remembered those gorgeous grounds, the thrillingly dark cloisters and lecture halls at Bologna, and was horrified he might think I'd want to become a part of that world.

'Nothing at all. I don't want to study. This is enough here.'

'But you're young,' he would explain. 'You can't stay out here in the wilderness forever. A young man has to make his own life. Reading about characters in books and all the exciting things they do isn't enough.'

'Enough for what?'

'Young men have needs that go beyond the present. If you don't fulfil them, Cesare, you won't live.'

'But I'm happy. I only want what we've got.'

'Then what will you be?'

I couldn't mix with students, with teaching masters and intellectuals. I was a slave from the sulphur mines. A new name and a better leg didn't change that.

'I want to be just like you.'

'Like me?' he asked, feigning incredulity.

'Yes, just like you.'

'And what exactly do you think I am?'

It was a better question than I could have imagined, and for the present it went unanswered.

That evening we took the horses and rode until it was too dark to see ahead. This was something Don Domenico liked to do whenever he'd completed some substantial portion of his work. I wasn't completely certain what his work was supposed to be, but it involved papers, pens and endless pages floating around the floors of his study. Often it was punctuated by melodies from his piano, his thinking time.

We camped by a stream, built a fire and grilled fish I'd caught on my line that afternoon.

'You can't do anything from here,' he said, and we'd become

so close that I knew he was continuing our earlier conversation. 'Life doesn't stop in our home and this island should be too small to hold a young man's dreams.'

'What about you?' I asked. 'You're not so old, and I don't see you going any further. So why can't that be enough for me too?'

He took a drink.

'Maybe think of it this way: all Doctor Vliegan had to do was fix your leg. He's got no solutions for fixing what's wrong with my head.'

Domenico glanced at my expression and smiled, even though I tried not to give anything away.

'I know you're aware I'm not quite right, but in this place I'm fine. The reason's simple enough. Peace. Peace and beauty. When I'm not around people and when I don't have to deal with troubles, the fire in my head stays away. The countryside and our home are perfect for me. It won't be like this forever. There've been wars in Sicily and over Sicily for thousands of years, nothing will change that. And the more I know about world events the more I realise we're in the eye of a storm. There'll be another war. This is simply an *intermezzo*.' He took more sizzling fish out of the pan and savoured it. 'Well, let's not worry until there's something to worry about.'

I struggled with the feelings I needed to express. He was happiest away from people and the truth was that I felt the same way. Why did I have to pretend differently?

By the flickering fire he now gazed at me, his eyes steady.

'When you've become more worldly and when you understand more about the substance of the human soul, then you can come back. You have to become who you are, Cesare, and that's not me.' He thought a moment longer, becoming pensive. 'You, I think, are something a little better than what I am . . . and maybe you shouldn't be as alone as I've been.'

'What if I won't go?'

'You'll go. You're too smart not to.' He studied the dark shape of Etna. 'You'll need proper papers, a family name,' he said.

'Amati?' I suggested.

'We wouldn't want to connect you to those fools.'

The flickering firelight made his satanic features seem even less of this world. Above us was the black mountain where I'd been both killed and saved.

It was as if he'd read my thoughts.

'"Montenero",' Domenico said, and so I was made.

My master used his influence and money to get me papers, documentation, a birth certificate and a passport. All of this was no easy task and would take him away for long journeys into the city of Catania, and once further afield to Palermo. That's where he told me he had to grease the greediest but the most useful palms. I didn't accompany him on any of these trips, remaining where I was to work the gardens and tend our livestock. Always he would return exhausted and harried, white-faced in fact – and I would wonder if on his own in hotels, or in public, on trains or in government offices, for example, his 'head on fire' returned, and how he'd dealt with it.

As if to provide himself with a salve for all the public effort he'd had to undertake, for weeks Domenico joined me in my outside duties and together we planted new trees and new vegetable and herb patches. I was enrolled and had to wait for the university year to begin; it would have pleased me if war had broken out in the meantime and all institutes of education were closed down. For now we constructed rock walls held together by mortar we learned to mix by perusing Domenico's encyclopaedias, and we even found instructions for building ponds. Ours became a large and deep tract of water fed by the clear stream running near the house. When we were satisfied with our accomplishments we hiked or rode as far and as wide as we liked. In those excursions we only altered course whenever we saw groups of people along the way.

In a similar manner we also continued to give one another our privacy. Domenico returned to his habit of spending long hours in his study, and I worked my way through the library from Alighieri to Zola, with plenty of stops for more volumes of Casanova's fictions and further memoirs, and writers such as Chekhov, Tolstoy, and foundlings such as Lawrence and American writers in new Italian translations. I was also just as happy to care and play for our new dogs: three puppies, white, black and brown. Three seemed to be the perfect number for the villa, and I learned to train these young dogs in good behaviour and obedience. Soon I could trust them to sleep in my room with me, which they did without creating the slightest nocturnal disturbance.

One day Domenico came to help me as I slaughtered two chickens for the pot. The birds lay twitching, then with absolutely no foreshadowing at all my master and I hesitated in going any further. Plucking, cleaning, the dogs salivating as they waited to be fed the entrails they knew would be coming – all at once this seemed a barbarous task. We sat down in the cool of the shaded courtyard. Something like this had never interrupted us before; Domenico and I had feasted on almost every form of livestock, all of it fresh from the knives we wielded ourselves.

'Why don't we stop killing?' he asked. It wasn't really a question. Somehow the thought, the feeling, the *change* had already occurred between us.

And we smiled our agreement.

In his study, sometimes Domenico worked at his desk, but the majority of the time he stretched out on the plush sofa, feet up and with a large embroidered pillow in his lap, where his pages were supported on a flat ledger. His ink wells would be close at hand and he was so comfortable in this position that he could sit for hours composing whatever story or stories, whatever scenarios involving whatever people, that came into his head.

I did my best not to intrude and had never been tempted to sift through that ever-increasing stack of handwritten pages, but one day he offered a clue about what he was doing by telling me the title.

'*Sulphur.*'

'And?'

'The active ingredient of gunpowder, and the source of the Amati fortune. Source of misery and slavery, but because of it we'll never want for anything.'

'Called "brimstone" in hell.'

'Yes.'

I thought it had to be a history of his family's armament dealings, but when he finally presented the entire manuscript of seven hundred and ninety-three pages to me, the first paragraphs introduced the travails of a five-year-old boy sold by his peasant family into labour.

'If you could give me some thoughts I'm sure they will benefit the manuscript. I've written others but the only person I've been able to ask is Signora Rosa. She's no help; simply not a reader.'

'You mean you've written other books?'

'Manuscripts,' he corrected me. 'Garbage not fit to be printed. I've been doing it all my life.'

That night I started reading, and over the next three days I learned that Domenico had fashioned a tale out of my own story.

In the end the boy escapes his master and the sulphur mines and survives an epic journey across land and mountains to hide in a cave in the barren regions of Etna. The boy, however, is tracked mercilessly and eventually found. There is no rescue by an unexpected saviour. He retreats deeper into his cave, travelling so far into an increasingly hot and monstrous pit that the rock around him literally steams and the stench of hot sulphur permeates the air. When all seems lost, the boy feels a gust of cool breeze from a tiny passage in front of him. He scurries through, then uses rock to wedge the opening completely shut behind him. As he emerges into a vista of blue sky, the hunters suffocate in the underground, having lost their way.

Domenico stopped me before I could say anything. 'It's too long and it isn't truthful.'

'In parts . . .' I replied, with some hesitation.

'I was never there.'

'So you can't know it exactly.'

He gave a nod of agreement and passed me a blue ink well.

I didn't like to use his study, or any room indoors, so I started to revise and rewrite his manuscript at a shaded table near the vegetable gardens with the dogs at my feet. Sometimes I shivered in the cold winds rushing down from the mountain, and sometimes perspiration fell from my face right onto the pages, staining the blue ink. There would be the sound of the piano from the house. On one of our trips into a larger town for extra produce and grain Domenico had found a deceased estate's entire holding of music books, and so the strains of Tchaikovsky, Chopin and eighteenth-century Italian composers such as Alessandro Scarlatti, Domenico Scarlatti and Luigi Boccherini poured out of the house.

I could never have created this work from a raw beginning, but for whatever reasons of my real experience with slavery and sulphur, or of a better sense of written composition itself, I was able to follow his blueprint and recreate it into something stronger than it had been. I also meticulously excised all the varied allusions to floating winged women, and characters who travelled the Sicilian plains with spirit guides at their side.

To my surprise Domenico agreed with these changes. Our

disagreements had to do with more mundane matters: the best way to express an emotion or the simplest way to describe a face or a hand.

Every day that Domenico read my work he either nodded in agreement or patted my shoulder and said, 'Keep going,' which I did, until an official date intruded and I had to drop the project. I found myself on a train again heading north, leaving my master to his solitude and the things he did or didn't see around him.

Bologna was as beautiful as ever and the university was full of lovely young faces from all strata of society, but I travelled through those few years like a ghost. Sicilians were in short supply and the ongoing joke among northerners seemed to be that the island was inhabited by monkeys from Africa who'd barely learned to talk. They regarded my language as a bastardised dialect of their rarefied Italian, some abomination that wasn't worthy of a great nation – but Don Domenico Amati had long since taught me the truth, that the Sicilian we spoke was its own language, a combination of all the civilizations that had ruled over us as our masters, diluting our blood and turning us into what we ourselves called '*i bastardi puri*' – 'the pure bastards'.

My master had taught me to speak the mainland's language without any signs of southern inflections, but I wouldn't hide my heritage, only the catastrophe of my early years. There were times when I sat in lectures or in a café or at a train station, or merely when walking down the street, that I wanted to shake my fellow students out of their airs and affectations, out of their easy contempt for everything that wasn't *of them*.

Don Domenico had sent me to learn these lessons myself, but to me the privileged student class was like a kindergarten of little children. In their high education they were totally uneducated, and in the politesse with which they carried themselves there appeared to exist a complete lack of understanding of what men could do to others.

To my fellows I was Cesare Montenero from the dreary Sicilian isle, a thoroughly 'B' student no matter how I worried over my papers or how diligently I consumed the pages of musty books for my exams. People were told I was the ward of a fallen nobleman from the great agrarian and industrialist Amati family, and it took some time before I understood the true connotations of the word. What everyone assumed was that I was some decadent ex-nobleman's kept boy. Now I'd been sent to receive an education so that I wouldn't be too embarrassing in Society. Once started, the whisper never stopped, and it hardly helped that I avoided contact with fellow female students, with waitresses, with the few local bawdy houses. Sex had simply never entered the equation of existence for me: I had none of the urges I read about in Lawrence, cheap books, or heard other boys and young men speak of with such longing and hunger.

And as it was true for me, I suspected it was just as true for my master.

To combat the milquetoast tag attached to me, I joined a university boxing team and for the first year hammered at bags and my opponents like the brute Domenico didn't want me to be. The coach fumed at how regularly I was beaten by young fools I ought to have dominated, at least until I learned the dance of the quick step, the blur of the lightning jab, the endless combinations that could be put together in order to lay flat a man otherwise made of oak. Then I started to win, leaving bloodied noses and cracked cheeks and split lips in my wake, and the word went out that the Sicilian ought not be toyed with. My chest should have puffed with pride, but I found that this was just another barrier I'd placed between myself and others. None of it brought me any joy, of course, so I dropped out of the team just as I was climbing their rankings.

Other students had shared living arrangements in apartments and dorms but I was able to stay on my own in two very clean rooms. Doctor Vliegan had kindly found me employment at his hospital, and I worked part-time picking up after him and his surgeons, wheeling patients in distress and those who'd just died, and I fed the fires in the great basement furnace with bloodied bandages, clothes that had been cut off accident victims, not to mention limbs and other body parts recently removed. When these activities became too much I had an outlet, the field track below my window. Boxing had been for show, studies were for Don Domenico, but running was for myself.

My gait had become powerful and smooth. Scouts would come to watch and I was often asked to join various athletic teams. Though I liked the fact that they wanted me I always made excuses. Organised sports weren't for me; I preferred to run to the rhythm in my own head and no one else's.

Be yourselves, Don Domenico had admonished the people on the Amati estate he'd been leaving behind. Well, I *was* being myself, for better or worse, in this long fallow period when no one loved me and when I allowed myself to feel no love in return.

Looking back, I find it hard to believe that the thin façade of my life and everything that I was involved in hadn't been more transparent to me, but Don Domenico had established his world with care and my background as a boy-slave had left me prone to be unquestioning about matters that I should have looked into more deeply. Added to which, of course, I was so much like my master that I skated over the surface of life in Bologna and was like a ghost when it came to the everyday ebb and flow of human intercourse.

The change came simply enough, and the façade, when it fell, vanished as if by the flick of a magician's wrist.

The lectures this day were particularly dull, commencing with a consideration of Kant's *Critique of Practical Reason* and ending with a long-winded analysis of Italian philosophers from the Eliatic school.

I made beautiful notes in artistic script: Southern Italy, 400 to 500 BC, Parmenides, Zeno and Melissus. Being exists, non-being does not exist; what is rational is real and what is real is rational; truth exists but is clouded by illusion, prejudice and preconceived ideas, therefore to uncover truth thinkers must free themselves from common sense and its convictions.

For reasons I couldn't yet define, this refined discourse on the nature of being and non-being soured my mood. After the class ended, I returned to my rooms exhausted and enervated. I had no mother and father and no early memories to fall back on; there was nothing except a man delivering me to another man, whom I now believed was Gozzi. I had no parents but I still existed; I had no childhood experiences but I was still real. I hadn't fallen out of the air, I hadn't been made out of nothing – I was here and I was flesh and blood. Yet I lived like a ghost; I spoke to people only when necessary; my dreams were of living like Domenico, totally alone. What was I then? A being or a non-being?

The books we'd discussed said that to uncover the truth, thinkers had to liberate themselves from common sense. Common sense said I was a boy who'd been sold by his parents at an extremely young age into slavery. That explained the lack of memories, that was the sensible answer, but a voice of pure *unreason*, of nonsense, told me that none of this was so.

Then what? Then what?

I had no answer.

It was time for my evening shift at the hospital and I welcomed the fact that I could put these thoughts aside and go immerse myself in that place of other people's miseries.

I ate in the kitchen quickly and without enjoyment, then

caught my usual trolley car for the start of the eleven p.m. to six a.m. shift. These were the best hours to work, I found, being neither very populated with hospital staff and patients *in extremis*, nor being particularly demanding. For the most part this shift involved cleaning and burning, and would lead into lazy Saturdays when I could sleep and read the day away or do whatever it was I wanted until my classes recommenced the following Monday morning.

Tonight however I was surprised to find that Doctor Vliegan was in attendance, conducting a surgical procedure in an operating theatre that was very seldom used, at least in my experience, as it was on one of the older and dismally unrenovated floors of the great hospital. This section of a smaller building contained facilities that were by no means as modern as those taken for granted in the more widely used theatres. My suspicions were aroused, but at least to this point, not unduly so. At this time of the evening it couldn't be that there were no other surgical theatres available, so something of either some significance or of some secrecy had to be taking place.

As I watched through the glass of the adjoining room, and saw Doctor Vliegan at work with only one nurse rather than his usual retinue of assistants and fellow doctors, I assumed that in several minutes I'd be transporting a dead foetus or half-formed baby into the fires of the basement furnace. This occurred with some regularity, and even though the activities of abortionists were strictly forbidden, there were enough incidences that couldn't be avoided: of diseases, accidents, threats to the physical well-being of mothers, or of the simple pity by doctors who believed in their modern ways that women had the right to control whether they should or should not become mothers. That Doctor Vliegan had chosen to conduct this particular procedure in this particular place gave me added suspicion; though he was quiet and unassuming, I reasoned that in all likelihood he was aborting a baby that he himself had helped conceive. Well, I had no judgements to make, and so I simply waited where I was to be called when needed.

Soon there was the tinkling of a bell. I wheeled my disposal trolley inside. Doctor Vliegan, in a lather of sweat and with an expression of distress, turned toward me. I saw the alarm come into his face.

'*Cesare,*' he said, using the new name, which he'd adopted readily enough. He'd either not realised or had forgotten my roster; why he should have cared whether it was me who was there or some other hospital worker mystified me.

I glanced at the individual on the surgical table. I'd been mistaken. Though this person was completely covered in sheets – even to the extent of hiding the head and face, as well as the feet, which was extremely odd – this was definitely not a woman's form.

'Who else is there?' the doctor asked.

'Only me. What's to be done?'

Doctor Vliegan was exasperated and tired. I hadn't seen him for a number of months and thought he even looked a little unwell. Whatever was going on in this theatre, it was clear he'd run out of time.

'It was an amputation. Just the disposal please.'

He moved to wrap a severed arm with rags and a bloodied sheet. No doctor ever bothered to do this; it was usually the task of underlings such as myself, who of course usually failed to bother with such niceties. Human parts simply went into the trolley and into the fires without ceremony or decorum.

I noticed that the nurse had not turned or lifted her head, and was in fact doing her best to keep her face hidden. Curious, I slowly stepped toward her and she edged away. Like a dance I half-circled her. She couldn't hide. Signora Rosa stared back at me.

'Cesare,' she said to my dumb gaze, 'it's a little hard to explain.'

Though I'd always known she'd been well trained in nursing,

I'd had no idea she ever worked here in Bologna, and certainly not for Doctor Vliegan. Something in my head wanted to swoon. The earlier nausea and throbbing of the temples had returned. A voice told me I ought to understand what was being played out: take away preconceived notions, take away illusion and ignore what you know is common sense, and the truth is in front of you.

'Please,' Doctor Vliegan said, 'we're wasting time.' He placed the amputated arm into my trolley. 'Cancer.'

Now I saw that his face was grey. Sweat beaded his forehead and had gathered at his upper lip. Not only that, but the man definitely was in pain. His hand involuntarily moved to his side, low down.

'Will I return for the patient? Which ward should he go to?'

The doctor shook his head. 'No, we're finished here. After you've made the disposal please go on to your normal duties.'

I tried not to make anything of this, or at least not to let them see that I already did. The person under the sheet was certainly not dead; the cloth rose and fell over the chest area and there was an irregular fluttering where the nose would be. Then why should this patient's face be covered?

'Thank you, doctor,' I nodded, glancing at Signora Rosa as I wheeled the trolley away.

Doctor Vliegan's voice stopped me at the operating theatre doorway. But for the three of us, and the poor one-armed soul on the table, there was no one else around. This basement area was silent as a tomb.

'Rosa is going home to Catania tomorrow. I apologise, Cesare, but please don't feel slighted. There simply wasn't time to arrange a social gathering.'

I dipped my head. How much they believed in my nonchalance was reflected in the unhappy expressions in both their faces.

'Good night, signora,' I said. 'Thank you, doctor.'

★

There was something about the furnace room that could remind me of the mines: heat, putrid air a torture to breathe, the way the walls themselves seemed to sweat. A pungency emerged from your own body in competition with the ghastly odours that seeped through that place. My years of mining experience meant I could sustain myself here far more easily than my fellows – in comparison to those pits this place was dreadful but hardly enough to complain about. When a great pile of human detritus accumulated – hands, feet, legs, arms, organs, meat – and had to be gotten rid of, my fellow attendants would pool their trolleys and beg me to do it while they smoked cigarettes in the cool outside.

So now I entered, shut the door behind me and opened the grate into the furnace. The all-consuming flames leapt up. I lifted the wrapped and dismembered arm. Throw it in and go, I told myself. Don't pause even a moment. Raw heat seared my face but I held back. I left the grate open and sat down away from the fire, in a wooden chair by a far wall, contemplating the bloodied sheets of the wrapping.

Doctor Vliegan had done it carefully. Doctor Vliegan and the woman who'd been like a mother to me, at least the only mother I'd ever know. Why was she here? Why had they been working together in that neglected old theatre? And why was a patient who was still breathing hidden under a sheet? To hide the individual, of course, but not specifically from me. Doctor Vliegan clearly hadn't expected me to be there. So the person worth hiding probably wasn't someone I knew, such as Don Domenico, for instance. What then? A person of importance – a politician, a leader of the church, even a famous musician, singer or actor?

Common sense told me that it was certainly one of these things, but the irrational part of my thinking screamed, *No, No, No. It's something else.*

I knew I oughtn't do it but I did. I lifted the dismemberment out of my trolley and laid it on a table. Gingerly I picked away at the corners of the bloody sheet and tightly wrapped rags until I started to reveal what was there.

Yes, it was an arm, a perfectly ordinary arm. Its only features were that it was not attached to a body and seemed almost bloodless. Had it been drained?

The arm was the colour of milk, and not only that, it was completely smooth, utterly hairless. Otherwise it was unremarkable: an arm.

What ridiculous conspiracies had I already conceived? Yet I couldn't resist studying this thing more closely. I found that the bone that had been sawn through was soft, almost gelatinous. Horrible. I hadn't studied anatomy or human diseases; was this what cancer could do to the human body? I was about to feed the fire in disgust when I noticed something else. The hand, which was curled in on itself, had perfectly formed fingernails, but the palm was completely unlined, like that of a doll. I touched it, ran my fingertips over it. A man's hand totally devoid of character. I fitted my own hand into that palm in the attitude of a gruesome handshake. I could feel this was a true hand, that it was correct in bone structure and form, muscles, ligaments, tendons, what have you. It was even a little warm from the life that had been in it. Strange.

Suddenly overcome with revulsion for this dead thing, I threw it hard into the furnace. Its wrappings followed. I slammed the grate and slid the main bolts until they locked. In seconds there would be nothing left.

I didn't feel well. My stomach was churning and my head hurt, and something that was human without quite being so was already smoke and vapour, no ashes.

During the night shift, as I was finding excuses to visit various wards in case a one-armed patient might have been settled there,

I received word that I was wanted in the main building immediately, in the duty registrar's office.

He was tapping his fingers, a tiny man with a narrow moustache, soulful eyes and a prematurely receding hairline.

'I'm sorry, Cesare, we can't use your services in the hospital anymore. Here's your pay packet. You'll see it's up-to-date and includes a small amount for severance.'

He pushed the envelope across to me.

'What have I done wrong?'

He made a face.

'It's not my decision, my job's to pass on the news. You know the hospital lurches from financial disaster to accounting fiascos on a weekly basis. There's probably been some decision to cut more corners than usual, so don't take it personally. Part-time staff will always be the first to go.'

The first to go from any place, I thought, were sure to be those who'd seen things they shouldn't have. Doctor Vliegan had to have made the decision on the hospital's behalf.

'When should I finish?'

'Well, it's quiet. I was told there was no need to make you see out your shift. You're free to go immediately.'

I took the envelope of cash and slipped it into the pocket of my trousers beneath the light blue apron and smock that constituted my workwear. Then I extended my hand. With a little surprise the registrar reached up and extended his.

As I firmly shook his hand I said, 'I'd like to thank the hospital for the employment here. If financial circumstances allow it, I'd enjoy the opportunity of returning.'

The little man's face broadened into a smile. He hadn't expected a lay-off to display such charm; Don Domenico had taught me well in the art of good manners and sincerity.

'May I drop off my workwear and say goodbye to one or two co-workers?'

'Certainly, and the best of luck with your studies, young man.'

I left him and walked with every semblance of nonchalance down the corridor, even forcing myself to stop and have a friendly word with two nurses I barely knew. One, who also happened to be the prettiest, actually blushed deeply and found it hard to meet my eyes. I wondered why I'd never bothered to try to engage any of the young females working in this place in conversation but, as always, the thought had simply never occurred to me.

Pleasantries completed, and out of their sight as well as the registrar's, I hurried towards the wards housing accident victims and patients recovering from recent surgery. My curiosity was now at a fever pitch. So was a vague sense of dread, plus the churning sickness in my belly. I wouldn't be put off. That severed arm with its soft bone and the inhumanly unlined palm meant something that was as clear and precise as a mathematical equation, but I couldn't seem to focus my mind on its solution.

As I took a staircase at a trot I knew I ought to be safe enough to make this investigation. Word couldn't have spread that my employment had been prematurely terminated. I imagined Doctor Vliegan wouldn't have wanted to tell anyone except those who needed to know. And within the vast labyrinth of this major hospital, with its five separate buildings, each a labyrinth in itself, very few staff knew me personally anyway. My outfit and the fact that I knew what I was doing were the only access pass I needed. Outside a maternity ward, where a new mother was wailing more loudly than the now disturbed group of babies, an elderly doctor even stopped me and asked for surgical gauze and strip bandages to be found as quickly as possible. I served him in minutes. He hurried back to his patient but had no further task for me.

It took the better part of four hours before I was convinced that the one-armed patient hadn't been moved into any of the wards or even into private rooms meant for wealthier patients. Had the individual in question been taken away from the hospital? It was a possibility, even a probability now that I'd failed to unearth him in this place. What with the awful concern in Doctor Vliegan's grey face, not to mention Signora Rosa's inexplicable presence and my own termination, anything could be happening and this patient could have been sent anywhere.

I took a winding staircase in the smallest hospital building, the one that housed the old theatre where Doctor Vliegan's operation had taken place, and returned to ground level. Before I was prepared to remove my hospital clothes and give up I decided there was one more possibility: the ambulance bays.

Drivers were asleep on gurneys as they waited to be summoned to emergencies. In the small staff office the two who'd been assigned the watch were smoking, eating cheese and listening to American music on the radio. They both knew who I was – a large proportion of my work had involved wheeling people from the backs of ambulances into waiting rooms, theatres or the morgue.

'All quiet?' I asked, helping myself to a small slice of cheese. I felt in the trouser pocket that held the envelope and took out my severance pay, which was a generous wad of notes. I counted several bills and placed them on the table. 'For the kitty. Thank you for all the coffee and snacks you've always had available. I've been given my marching orders.'

Though they didn't care about my employment one way or the other, their mood immediately brightened. If there was any kitty at all it was probably for alcohol and the illicit medications that allowed these men to remain alert through the unforgiving hours to daylight.

'Quiet all right,' the first said. I remembered his name was Andreas. 'One pick up all night.'

'Accident?' I asked.

'Maybe.' The man rubbed his jaw. 'Arm. But not from the street.'

'Where from?'

'We had to collect him at a doctor's own home. Ugliest individual I ever saw.'

'The doctor?' I laughed, feigning ignorance.

'No, the patient.'

'You mean something happened to his face?'

The second man shook his head.

'There wasn't a face for anything to happen to,' he said, and I felt something slither through the pit of my belly. 'The doctor had him on a stretcher. The poor beggar was already anesthetised and couldn't move. Whatever's wrong with him, it's serious. Could've been an accident, I suppose. While we were moving the patient into the back of the ambulance truck the sheet covering his face slipped off. The doctor put it back fast. But we saw.'

The two men glanced at one another.

'Yes,' Andreas spoke, 'we saw.'

'And what did you see?'

'I'll only say this once. Then I want to forget it forever. There was nothing. Nothing. Isn't that right, Stefano?'

The second driver, Stefano, nodded and offered his opinion: 'These things happen from cursed births. Babies born with two heads, or an extra hand, or a third eye here.' He indicated the centre of his own forehead.

'That's what you saw?'

'No, no. Nothing. We saw nothing. Just a white head and no hair. Like a wax doll. No features at all. And that means no eyes either.' He shuddered. 'Skin pale as milk.' They both shuddered. 'It was just a glance before the doctor put the sheet back. He told us that people with such disfiguring defects usually die very quickly after birth, but this one had miraculously survived into adulthood.'

I took a deep breath. Stefano's words had hit me hard. They made me recall what Domenico had said when I'd laid wrapped up and bleeding on the mountain: *My spirit might be featureless and somewhat pallid, but it certainly gets the job done.*

Could this be it then – or be something *like* Domenico's vision brought to life? There wasn't much information to go on, but my suspicions were aroused. Doctor Vliegan's involvement, what did that mean? And Rosa's? The hair on the back of my neck literally bristled. And in my mind were the words, *Run. Run away.*

'So you brought him in. Has this patient gone out again?'

They looked at one another.

'There's only one way that poor beggar's leaving here.'

To hide my astonishment at everything these men had said, I ate a cookie from the plate on the table but immediately wanted to retch it up. The illusion of not being all that interested was now almost impossible to maintain. I forced myself to say nothing. My thoughts were electric with images and possibilities, but the most dominant sensation inside me was fear itself.

Andreas and Stefano started to discuss a recent football match in the main stadium outside town that had attracted thousands of spectators and had ended in a dubious draw, then one of them stood to brew more coffee. Neither man was interested in bringing up the case of the patient without a face again.

'You know,' I started, interrupting them, 'I've got an interest in things like this. In the mysteries of what can go wrong in the physical development of the body. It's part of what I study at university.'

Stefano looked up. He'd started cutting cards for a game.

'That's what you study?' he asked.

'Yes.'

'What a waste of time.'

'No, the human anatomy,' I improvised, 'how else can we help people?'

Stefano looked at Andreas. 'Another saw-bones in the making.'

Andreas shrugged. 'The world always needs more doctors.'

'I'd like to see this man you're talking about.'

'He'll be somewhere around,' Andrea replied, waiting by the small stove for his water to boil. I knew by the look that now passed between these two men that they'd been sworn to secrecy. They'd probably have their termination papers handed to them by morning.

'If the doctor you mentioned was going to operate on this individual,' I told them, watching for their reactions, 'I suppose he'd want to do it quietly. And if the patient came to grief he might even want to dispose of the cadaver privately.'

'They all think alike, these medicos,' Andrea said with some resentment, studying me as he would a ghoul.

'But I'd love to see the patient before he leaves this earth completely.'

I took out the pay packet again. My wage and severance. I stacked it by the cookie plate. The men made up their minds with the barest eye contact. Ambulance officers were always of a mind to make a little cash on the side, though the people who greased their palms were usually journalists or private investigators, not lowly university students like me.

Stefano had a key ring in his belt. He unclipped it and carefully flicked through until he found the key he wanted.

'You're right about using the quietest theatre in the hospital,' he said, and described the old room I'd attended. 'You know this wing was the asylum, until our more enlightened days? My money is on one of the cells in the basement. Haven't been used since before the turn of the century.'

'Which basement?'

'Here, in this building.' Stefano took a sheet of paper and the nub of a pencil. He wet the end with his tongue and drew a rough sketch of corridors, steps and rooms that existed, supposedly, behind that section housing the main furnace.

Observing my scepticism, he said, 'It's there all right, we've seen it for ourselves.'

Andreas poured steaming water over his coffee grounds. 'If someone finds you down there, tell them you got lost looking for the boiler.'

'You won't be able to explain having this skeleton key,' Stefano added, flipping a key across the table with the practiced air of a card sharp flipping up the Joker. 'If you're found, we'll be saying you stole it from our belongings.'

I thanked them both. Stefano divided the lire equally and handed Andreas his share. When I was gone I knew they would discuss me as one would discuss members of the lower and uneducated classes who giggle and shiver at circus showings of two-headed goats and bearded ladies.

Maybe that really was me.

I passed several staff members, but none of them were people I'd worked with. Through open windows I saw the dawn had started to rise. Better placed patients were already out and taking their constitutional in the grounds. Family, friends and well-intentioned visitors would be arriving in order to assist loved ones with breakfasts, bed-baths, the changing of bandages, and so on. In the general Italian way few trusted the staff to do their jobs properly and, in truth, to the running of these public hospitals such assistance was crucial.

The daily general theatre schedule would soon commence and there would be an influx of disposal activity making use of the furnace. If I wanted to take a look at this strange one-armed man then I had to hurry.

Heading into the bowels of the building, I examined the rough pencil sketch Stefano had made for me. It was clear enough and soon, in the huge unused laundry next to the furnace room, a place good only for breeding rats and other vermin, which I could see was more than living up to its unintended purpose, there was a thick metal door.

The skeleton key turned in the lock, then there was a corridor exactly as sketched and rough-hewn steps descending into more corridors that ran underground. What the map didn't show was that the walls and ceiling were cut from dark rock, as if they formed the battlements of a great castle. The hospital was old but I would never have guessed that there was this infinitely more ancient sector. If Andreas and Stefano were to be believed then this was where lunatics and the depraved had once been incarcerated.

I shuddered, but it wasn't the physical place that unnerved me. Only the possibility of what it might still hold.

Stefano hadn't told me the corridors would be well-lighted with electric globes, all of them burning. Electric light could have been added only within the last ten years, which was curious, given that the area was supposed to have been long closed-off and unused. And why were they illuminated now? Either Doctor Vliegan and Rosa, perhaps others, were still down here, or they'd left the lights on as a matter of course. Why – for their return? Or because they were still needed?

If someone was here to catch me spying, let them. I wouldn't resort to more subterfuge. I wasn't the one conducting activities that demanded secrecy. I looked at the paper in my hand – this left corridor that I'd turned into was the limit of Stefano's sketch. I went down its narrow path and took another equally ancient corner. Here the ground was so cold that it chilled my feet through my shoes. My breath hung like mist.

Then I came to the cells.

Every old battered metal door was open and every room inside was hewn from rock. Each cell was perfectly bare and windowless, offering not the slightest human amenity. I walked on more carefully, imagining the echoing howls that once must have filled this place. Here now was a closed door, the only one that had been shut. I went to it and pressed my hands against the metal.

Freezing. There was a handle and an eye for a key and nothing else. I stood back. No, there was one more thing. At the base of the door was a hinged metal flap which bygone nurses and warders must have used for sliding daily trays of food. I went down on my knees and carefully lifted the flap. There was nothing to see; there was no movement. Just a bare stone floor.

I rose to my feet and slid Stefano's key into the eye. The lock was heavy but the tumblers moved decisively. When I turned the handle there was no ghastly creaking and as I pushed the door open there was no monster-house screech of rusted metal against metal.

The one-armed man stood in a corner and he was turned towards me. Though he had no features other than two holes for his nostrils and a very small crooked line that was his mouth, without lips, he was attuned to the movement of the door and to my presence. There were bandages over the stump of his arm and he was dressed in rough hospital clothing. His head wasn't shaped like a human head, but was instead elongated and quite narrow. There were slight ridges where his forehead and cheeks and chin should have been. His blankness didn't have the effect of a man wearing a featureless mask. Features simply *weren't there*. They weren't a part of the picture and never would be.

Now I was certain that this was Domenico's dream creature come to life. My temples pounded. I could have doubled over for the pain in my belly.

What accident of nature had caused this creature to be? I stared in amazement, then it struck me that nature hadn't had much to do with what was before me. I stepped into the cell and he – it *was* a he – followed my movements with sharp jerks of the head. I didn't go closer; I leaned back against a cold wall and simply took him in.

Though I felt ill, I wasn't frightened by this man-thing. Instead, a strange affinity rose inside me. It was the sort of empathic reaction that often escaped me in daily life. The people of the outside world, my fellow university students, the great swell of life itself, all of it left me cold.

But this.

Then there was a welling in my eyes and how useless that was, to let tears run freely when I was whole and this being was not.

How did he eat and drink? That gash must have been enough for sustenance to pass through. He didn't see and he didn't speak: two blank nubs where eyes should have formed and two small snot-caked holes for breathing. It seemed impossible that this creature had survived to become fully grown. How had it looked as a baby, as a boy, an adolescent? And by what sense did it understand that someone was here?

I wiped the tears off my cheeks. I had to stop thinking of 'it'. This creature was a man, maybe young or old, but human. 'He'. *He*.

Stepping away from the wall I went to the metal door and pulled it shut. In the cell there were two chairs facing one another. I guessed one place was for Doctor Vliegan, where he'd sat to address this patient and care for it.

Care for *him*.

This man, or this half-man, had been allowed one further amenity: a steel bucket in the corner already stank of workmen's latrines. There was no hand basin or running water by which to wash. I sat in one of the chairs. Presently this man, this thing – this *individual* – edged forward with his one white hand extended. He found the back of the second chair and felt his way around so that he could sit facing me.

We sat. He reached out carefully until he found my face. He touched it, then touched his own, and I was certain he knew I wasn't the doctor or Signora Rosa.

Looking at this individual's waxen head was like looking into some unfathomable purity. The sight moved me so much that

I felt more tears. I forced them back. By some transference I couldn't understand, the individual seemed to understand my reaction. Those two tiny holes of his flared and moved. Soon a clear, watery substance emerged from one.

A droplet, then another.

The individual sniffed and drew heavy breaths. His shoulders shuddered, then for a moment his entire pale body was wracked with spasms. That gash of a mouth twisted, revealing no teeth, only the bright redness inside. The individual was weeping. My head was light, as if I was living some unimaginable dream. This creature was crying – and why shouldn't he?

Suddenly the individual stood up fast, and his chair toppled backward. His head twisted on that slender neck, twisted this way and that way, turned upward to the ceiling. His milky fist was clenching and unclenching.

The individual shuffled backwards to the same corner where I'd first found him and he stood there trembling. He wanted me to come forward; that single hand made a small beckoning gesture. Slowly I did as he wanted. I moved forward until I was standing right in front of him. The mouth worked as if trying to form words. None came.

The individual was wearing a light-blue hospital smock beneath a more conventional masculine dressing robe. Doctor Vliegan's, I imagined. The belt holding the robe together had come undone and the smock was now twisted aside, revealing a patch of his white, smooth, waxen chest without a nipple, and the wrapping of bandages that went around the right shoulder. The smock's twisting also revealed ample masculine genitalia, but without any hint of pubic hair. I wanted to help him, and straightened his clothing for him.

What else could I offer this man–thing?

Not food or water or wine or conversation. Not comfort – I wouldn't know how. But now he let me know what he wanted, and he wanted it more than anything in this world or the next.

The individual's hand felt blindly around until he found my right wrist. He pulled it up to his throat. I pulled my hand away. With strength, the individual struggled to regain my hand and he pressed it into his throat once more. He tried to spread my fingers around his delicate windpipe. Again I snatched my hand back from him. The third time he fought my hand up to his throat, a high mewling sound emanated from his tiny mouth. A cry, a scream, an appeal. With a shock I realised that I was now the one weeping, drawing gasps and sobbing. My hand stayed where it was, and the individual reached for my left hand and closed it around his throat also, and pushed hard against my hands, willing them to squeeze.

How many times had he begged Doctor Vliegan? How many times had he begged Signora Rosa? Would this have started when he was a boy or had the desire for death only come later, when all hope in its spirit had finally disappeared?

In *his* spirit.

He pressed harder and harder into my grip and he tried to hold it there as if in a panic that I'd let go. The mewling sound was soft and high, not even that of a newborn kitten. I wanted to run but I didn't. I shouldn't have accepted the responsibility, but I did. Good sense told me not to acquiesce, but I did it.

I did.

The strength and determination in my hands were things I would never have believed myself capable of turning against a creature that lived, against a creature that I was certain possessed a mind and a soul. As I squeezed I felt his gratitude and longing for release, for this eternal nightmare to end. I was sure I wasn't imagining it.

To this day, friend, I'm certain it was there.

So I didn't allow myself to relent, even when the strength went out of the individual's body and he dropped to his white knees. Still, his one hand held onto mine as they squeezed. The head fell forward and spit crawled from a corner of his mouth. I followed him onto the cold floor and kept on until the body finally lay to the side and no rasping or whispering breath emerged from the holes of his nostrils. Only then did I pull my hands away. They were cramped with effort. I collapsed beside the individual. His hand was limp and still milky, but the head had darkened to the colour of hay.

I held him.

I held him and in a corner of my mind wondered if I'd also destroyed the spirit guide and protector who lived between Domenico and me.

Then I wept for so long I thought I would simply stay where I was until someone found us. Time passed, and when I was able to get myself together I stood and hefted that sad corpse into a fireman's lift. I opened the metal door and laid the body outside, then re-entered the cell. I don't know why I straightened the chairs, but I do know why I hurled the foul contents of the steel bucket around the walls and floor – so that in their scrawl Doctor Vliegan could read my message to him.

The furnace room wasn't being used. I unlocked and opened the grate and fed the corpse into the licking flames. He weighed perhaps half what a man his size ought to weigh, but still I had to push hard and use the poker to get him in completely. My eyebrows were singed as I struggled to shift the body even more deeply inside. I hurled the grate shut with a heavy clang, then slammed the locks and stood back from the pervasive heat, my eyes closed and my lungs burning.

I don't know how long I stood like that before I was disturbed by the familiar rattle of trolley wheels. Two of my fellows were coming, now here they were in the furnace room with great mounds of soiled and bloodied bandages.

'Don't tell me the heat's finally got to you, Cesare,' the first said. 'I suppose it gets everyone sooner or later.'

The second moved his trolley closer to the grate and pulled on the heavy gloves everyone other than me had to use for accessing the fire. If he opened that metal door now, the burning, liquefying body would be revealed. I knew just how long flesh and bone needed before they would become ash, even with such immense temperature. Even then troublesome bits such as skulls, femurs, hips and spines needed to be smashed up with an iron poker if you really needed rid of them.

I was beyond worrying, I decided. Maybe that poor abomination should have been brought to light after all.

As he opened the grate the boy said, 'We heard you've resigned?'

He started to throw bandages in. They caught alight, and there was nothing in the flames, nothing at all, to impede their destruction. The individual had completely disappeared. I took off my blue hospital coverings and threw them in as well.

'Yes,' I told them. 'My last job's done.'

Don Domenico came to the door in the gloom of the evening as he heard me arrive. I'd caught the mainline train, then a regional connection, then the local *ferrovia*, then hitched a ride with a farmer in his cart down into the valleys. The last kilometres I'd walked with my bags on my back. My master greeted me with warmth and without surprise, though he did seem unusually downcast. He helped me in and there was a vegetable stew in a pot over the fire, and then he told me straight out what I'd accomplished.

'Kristof discovered what you did and went home and gave himself a terminal injection of morphine. His wife found him in his study the next morning. The man was being eaten alive with bowel and kidney cancer and he knew what he had ahead of him.

Even though that creature was imperfect Kristof was still holding out hope.'

I collapsed into a chair as if the blood had run out of me. I suddenly understood, it made a sort of sense: the creature was being kept alive for some purpose, some research. Something that would help Doctor Vliegan, and I'd taken that away.

'The truth is that there wasn't a shred of hope in either direction,' Domenico went on, trying to push his own sadness aside.

Then there was such kindness in his voice that it made me want to break.

'Tell me something. The creature wanted release?'

It was hard to meet his eyes. I gave a small nod.

'It was human, Cesare, which means freedom of choice, and you helped it the way Kristof never would.'

'Him,' I said. 'I helped *him*.'

'Yes,' Domenico replied.

The creature dead by my hand, and the doctor dead by his own hand – because of me. I thought I would never be able to meet anyone's eyes again, including my own, and went outside and sat in the cold, my face and my heart growing numb as one.

My master left me alone for as long as I wanted to be alone. The evening was darker and the wind bit and howled. I stared out at nothing, and time was nothing too. So was I, of course, a piece of worthless flotsam blown back to Don Domenico's house after committing a horror that had led to something equally appalling.

Kristof Vliegan, with his round spectacles and concerned face, how many times had he helped me?

The frozen night made it impossible to stay outdoors any longer. Full of shame, I had to return inside. I had no idea what the time might be. Domenico was waiting. In the lamplight he'd been reading and now he put his book down and went to the fire.

'But what was the creature?' I asked him. 'Did Doctor Vliegan expect to use – I don't know – parts of it, to try and cure himself?'

I could see the effort this was going to take. Domenico moved closer and we sat at the kitchen table.

'This may be a little difficult for you to understand, but that creature – let's call him "a man" – that man was supposed to have grown into Kristof's image a long time ago. Something went wrong right at the start, however, and Kristof didn't have the heart to destroy it. He held out hope, but it was so obviously in vain.'

I shook my head. This made no sense.

Domenico said, 'Let it sink into you.'

Let it sink into you. As if this was something I ought to already understand?

'All those years,' I said, 'Doctor Vliegan kept this man in his home?'

'Yes, from the moment of his inception he cared for him. Until it became too sick. It – excuse me – *he* was likely to have died very soon. Though of course a creature like that couldn't have any way of knowing what was happening.'

'He knew,' I spoke. 'He knew what was happening. He knew a great deal.'

I saw the way that sad individual's long plain head had twisted and turned in anguish and despair, heard again the mewling cry from his throat.

Domenico simply nodded, remaining downcast.

'But are you saying —' I started, but found it hard to construct the right question. Domenico had been more than correct – what we were speaking of wasn't only difficult to understand, it hurt too. In my belly and in my heart. And it *was* sinking into me.

'Are you really saying he was meant to become Doctor Vliegan, exactly him?'

'Well, no one's ever certain of the precise outcome,' Don Domenico replied. 'The procedures have never been perfect. It seems the good scientists of old were never able to predict whether the creatures would become true doubles of the people they were seeded from, or if they'd become something else entirely. In Kristof's case, if things had worked out properly, then yes. The creature would have been him. But without his memories and experiences and so on. There's no transmigration, nothing at all esoteric like that.'

'Transmigration?'

'Of souls or of memories. Not the psyche. The heart, if you like. The creatures are simply human beings reproduced from the person in question.'

'Their children.'

'Almost their perfect children, because the creatures' make-up comes from only one person. The individual being seeded. It's an extraordinary achievement of science, even if it's never turned out quite right.'

This was the door I'd been standing in front of all my life and finally it was being pushed open.

'You are referring to us, aren't you, Domenico? You and me.'

'And people like us, yes.'

I swallowed hard and looked at my hands. They were a young man's hands. Not a thing's. Not a sad creature's, nor some milky individual's.

'There are more?'

'Yes, there are.'

I was shivering now, and not from the cold. Domenico looked at me with kindness, a satan's face of kindness.

'So that's all we are then? Remnants of other people?'

'We're hardly remnants. If anything we're more like the product of humankind's dreams. Of course, you could say that's what normal children are too.'

He was watching me to see how I received this news. In fact, a little of the shock was passing, some of the pain too. The shivering subsided. I reached for the bottle of wine on the table and poured myself a glass and one for Domenico. Now my hands were steadier. I drank. He didn't. It was as if I'd known these things all my life but had never possessed courage enough to face them.

'It's not so bad for us,' Domenico spoke more gently. 'Despite their intentions to the contrary we've managed to become ourselves, haven't we?'

Yes, of course: *Be who you are.*

And those lines from The Venetian that Domenico loved so much: *Man is a free agent; but he is not free if he does not believe it* ...

Don Domenico wanted me to believe it.

He stood up and took the saucepan from the stove, then ladled stew into the bowl that was always mine. Despite everything, despite what I'd done and what I now knew about myself, and him, it was good to be here. It was good to be home.

I was famished and tired, and couldn't think of a single reason why I'd want to leave this place again.

In the wintry morning I went outside with Domenico and helped him with all the simple tasks that I wanted to take over once more. The pigs were fat and the goats were annoying. Domenico saw my smile.

'You're really so happy to be back?'

I made room for the largest pig to take its food from the trough, then we stepped back and watched.

'Tell me something, Domenico, why did you send me away?'

We sat down out of the freezing wind and watched the animals in their simple activities. Domenico idly scattered grain, and the chickens came and pecked near our feet.

'I never intended to keep secrets from you, but I did want you to experience life and your own potential before putting you face-to-face with the truth.'

'Maybe you thought Doctor Vliegan would tell me what we are?'

'Possibly. He should have, really, because he understood the science involved. I wanted you to work with Kristof and maybe even join one of the teams, but he was a man who had problems with trust. Learned over too many years of keeping secrets. And your grades – unfortunately they didn't quite reach the right levels.'

He gently bounced his shoulder against mine when he saw me start to hang my head with shame.

'But there was something that was equally important to Kristof. He worried over philosophical questions. He wondered whether it was right to let you know at all, or if it mightn't be *more right* to simply let you live like normal people.'

'I'm not normal.'

'You have to be. You have to make every effort to be.'

'Why should I?'

'Here . . . in this place here we can live in silence and solitude. That suits me and I know why it's so. My affliction is that I can't bear the presence of others. Simple human demands. Even if it's in friendship. People's ideas and their dreams and their needs confuse me, and that makes me lose my equilibrium. But you still have the chance to go forward, you can still learn how to be a man in this world. One country house in one small island of the Mediterranean can't be enough for you.'

'You tell me to be myself then you expect me to be something I'm not,' I replied. 'I didn't ask to be made this way, but if it's how I am then let me be. I never want to live anywhere but here with you. Is that so wrong?'

'When you were a slave you dreamed of other countries, didn't you? Freedom and wild imaginings . . .'

'That's because I had to escape.'

'Don't you think the need to escape is what drives all people?'

The friendly ease of the morning was beginning to slip away. The further this conversation went, the more my temples started to ache. I didn't want to speak but I knew I had to.

'The world —' I started, but could barely bring myself to say what I felt. It was such a coward's thing to utter. 'Domenico, the world is full of horror.'

'And always will be.' He shrugged, but not unkindly. 'You can change, Cesare. You're young and you can become anything. Our antecedents don't necessarily curtail our futures.'

We watched the animals in their unhurried and unworried grace. I thought this was a pivotal moment. My heart cried out for Domenico not to send me away, not this time or ever again.

He said, 'While you were among your fellow students, other young people, did you feel any sense of connection, a feeling that you wanted to become close to them?'

I shook my head.

'What about females? Did you sleep with many?'

I shook my head again.

'Not one?'

'Not one.'

'Do you have urges?'

'No. Or not often. I look. Sometimes I think I want to act, or I know I ought to, but I can't. I don't know why that is.'

He accepted this without surprise, but didn't seem happy about it.

'Why are you asking?'

'It strikes me there can be more to your life than solitude. Look at our books, the stories they contain. Most have to do with people together, the things they share and the things they can't. The things they want and the things they need. There's love and pain in equal measure, and people, they seem to be at their finest when they seek these things out. When they let one another into each other's lives.'

'Maybe you and I have that already.'

He shook his head. 'I like you being here, Cesare, but if you go, *when* you go, I'll like that too. I'm talking about something

172

infinitely deeper. Aren't you curious about the love between a man and a woman?'

'Not really.'

'I'm hoping you'll find it, Cesare.'

'Maybe I can't. Maybe I just don't have the means.'

He nodded, thinking it through. 'There are a number of characteristics that define us, and from there we do or we don't individuate. A number of things we inherited from the originals and some other things were encouraged by design. A major characteristic appears to be what you're referring to, the lack of sexual urge. More important is the lack of emotional interaction as well. It was considered important to take these away. The need to procreate was never going to be sympathetic to the tasks we'd be set.'

'The tasks?'

'You're aware the Amati family were leaders in munitions development and manufacture, but historically they were also researchers into other means of winning wars. Going back many generations. At a certain point the family's work became government sponsored, and very obviously by more nations than simply our own.'

'Then it's been replicated in other countries.'

'That's a reasonable conclusion. Italy's not exactly an industrial powerhouse.'

'So that was the intention? To make a type of soldier?'

He nodded slightly, and he was watching me now, his gaze attempting to penetrate my heart.

'How did you feel when you killed Kristof's creature?'

'It seemed —' I struggled for the word. It was the most vile word I'd ever spoken. 'It seemed easy.'

Don Domenico kept his eyes on me, and the picture of him on that ridge striding toward Salvatore and Gino with his long rifle drawn, and the two perfect shots, finally made sense.

'Who am I?' I asked this man, the only person capable of telling me.

He thought it over before replying.

'In the wider world, that's a question the young always have to find their own answer to, but of course we're different. Before I try to tell you, remember that beyond anything else, you are yourself. No research into science and no intrusion of the hand of man changes that. They never succeeded in making us servants.'

'Tell me.'

'You and I share a sort of parentage. I'm led to believe there were many, many surrogates for the seeds. Women who carried and delivered us. Women who've long since been paid and forgotten. My seed was the essence of a boy named Domenico Amati. The sad creature that went wrong, that was taken from Kristof Vliegan in an attempt to give his life some kind of a renewal once the cancer overtook him. And you – well, I believe you were from one of the minds most involved in all of this.'

'Who?'

'The patriarch, Giovanni Amati. He didn't start the family's interest in creating new men, that predated him by generations, but he certainly took up the reins.'

'Giovanni Amati,' I repeated. 'The father.'

'And me, of the son.'

We gazed at one another, Domenico with a wry smile. The world was upside down and the two of us with it.

'What about females?' I asked, clearing my throat, trying to make sense of this news, wondering if it would change the relationship between us. 'What about women?'

Don Domenico spread his palms. He honestly didn't know.

'All I'm clear about is who we were seeded from, and despite all the hopes that went into us, the project failed. New people such as ourselves have too much potential for illness and disease.'

'All of us?'

'That's unclear. But enough to ruin all the plans. One example is the way Kristof's illness was multiplied in his creature. There has been a predisposition towards cancers, though there have been other unexpected problems too. Of the mind. Discovering all this, I believe the project was abandoned and funding was reallocated into the production of more traditional armaments.'

'Was I one of the last?'

'Possibly.'

'And you were involved?'

'No,' he said, shaking his head. 'I was nowhere near the Amati family. In my fifth year I was sent to live with Rosa and her husband and her sons, obviously an experiment to see how a new child would fare within a normal family. I fared badly. Much later, when I became friends with Kristof, he told me that the difference between me and the majority of other new children was that, physically at least, I grew into the mirror image of my seed. I looked like the original Domenico, and that's rarely the case. But of course I didn't know any of this until after the Amati factory was destroyed and I was withdrawn from the battlefields. Before then I'd never heard of the Amatis, much less been to their mansion and property.'

'That's why you seemed so strange there? And wanted to get rid of it?'

'That's correct.'

'What about the destruction of the family's plant in the north, was it really an accident?'

'Everything points to an eradication. I was sent to take the place of the only son, the original Domenico, who'd had the good grace to die quietly and without fanfare in an asylum. Hence several of the more obvious issues I've had to deal with,' he said, gently rubbing an index finger along his right temple.

The howling in the great Amati manor that the workers had never forgotten, the setting of fires, that had been the work of the true Domenico Amati – but the man who'd sold the property and who I'd found babbling in the mountains, scratching and kicking at the earth, that was my master.

'But we are ourselves,' I said with what I hoped was a new conviction. I was the image of no one. I was Cesare Montenero, exactly who I wanted to be.

'Yes. And so they failed,' Domenico agreed. 'The important thing for people like you and me is that living prototypes had been sent out into the world before the project collapsed. I was one and there must have been more.'

'I wasn't sent. I know I was discarded.'

'That's also correct. We can be grateful that the men who were so disappointed with the way we turned out didn't decide to end the lives they'd given us. They simply let the older ones continue and they set the children free.'

'I wasn't free.'

'They put you, and boys like you, where you could do no harm. None of us was of any use but they knew that we'd never overburden society.'

'What does that mean?'

'It's another of our shared similarities. We don't desire sexual activity but more important is the fact that we have no ability to procreate. It's impossible. So when we die we die, and with the last of us the enterprise becomes a part of history.'

We fell silent. Despite everything my master had told me the world seemed clearer and somehow less frightening.

He might have read my thoughts, for Domenico added, 'We have a future. There are things we can hope for. We all get to live, that's the gift we've been given, despite the dubious intentions of our creators. And like everyone else in the world we carry our own burdens but also our own joys. The *potential* for our own joys.' He smiled, his satan's features softening completely. These were matters he'd considered all his life. 'If we allow ourselves to go find them, Cesare.'

The wind had picked up. It found us where we sheltered and whipped at our faces. The chickens pecked and the goats drank and the pigs kept eating. Our three dogs shivered. Back at the house we could hear the shutters rattling. There wasn't anything else to say and it seemed too cold for more chores, so we returned inside and poked the coals in the grate, then as the dogs drowsily slept we sat together in the yellow shimmer of the fire's warm glow.

Red Book

THERE WAS NO MORE TALK of the need for me to go away. Domenico must have decided that I now knew enough to make my own choices. On the one hand he wanted me to go find my fortune and life, but on the other hand my presence was pleasing to him. We had no need for others, for new companionships or broader horizons, and so the ensuing months were spent living and working in the sort of tranquillity I still believe few in the outside world can ever achieve.

Then we returned one afternoon from three days' riding, hiking and camping, and found a collection of tired and quite emaciated horses tethered at the troughs. The manor's front door was ajar. Domenico's features became tight but he rode on as if this was an everyday occurrence.

'Keep going,' he said quietly, betraying no outward concern. 'When we get to the courtyard ride around to the back of the house. Get yourself the handgun and fresh ammunition for the both of us. Have everything ready.'

There were six horses. I wondered if six men were inside and how we'd protect ourselves if these individuals were after more than water and a camp site. Visitors were acceptable, but the open front door was the problem. We did our best to continue displaying no reaction. Eyes were probably already on us. Where were the dogs? Now I wished that we'd brought them with us, but we'd been riding into rough terrain to see the new waterfalls and rock pools formed after a full ten days of storms.

Now here were these dusty horses, and the dogs didn't greet us, and the grounds of the villa were silent.

As we approached Domenico drew his rifle out of its leather scabbard. It wasn't the bulky army rifle that had killed Salvatore and Gino, but his usual .22. Something about that resonated in the back of my mind, and if the situation had been different perhaps an important truth would have struck me right there and then – but of course there were more pressing matters at hand.

The only weapon I had with me was a small axe used for chopping fire wood. Domenico leaned toward me. 'Go now,' he said, but two gunshots rang out and clods of earth jumped up in front of our horses. They reared back and we fought the reins to keep them straight.

Then a booming voice: 'Throw down the rifle and dismount.'

Domenico whispered, 'Let's be smart,' and dropped the rifle. I noticed he made sure it didn't fall too far away from himself.

The owner of the voice was no fool: 'Ride ahead twenty-five metres.'

We had no choice but to do what he said, then we slowly climbed out of our saddles. Our horses were parched from riding, so I led them by their reins to the trough where they could drink with the others. As I did this I waited for the explosion of white light that would repay such foolishness. It didn't come. I returned to Don Domenico standing unprotected in the courtyard. Four men decided it was safe to emerge from our home, then two more walked over from the direction of the barns. All of them were armed.

The leader was the thinnest and the tallest, and I had a vague memory of him working on the Amati property. Some field hand. Then I remembered; this was Giacomo, one of the first to lose his temper the night Domenico had told everyone on the Amati property that the place had been sold.

'We're sorry for the dogs,' he said. 'They wouldn't let us alone.'

I spat at him, mostly hitting the side of his dirty and unshaved face.

Giacomo didn't retaliate at me directly but flicked his fingers at his men, and they shot our horses where they stood. Estella's head whipped once and she was still, and Esperanto twitched and kicked through another three slugs in the head. By then I was screaming and being held down in the dust on my knees, and Domenico, far from transforming into the decisive hero he'd been on the mountain when he rescued me, started to froth at the mouth, to shake, his eyes bulging.

'Amati lunatic,' Giacomo said. He stepped forward and shot Domenico point-blank twice in the chest, his body blowing backwards. Then he turned the smoking muzzle to my fore-head. 'Lucky I remember what a good worker you were. But you shouldn't let yourself be a servant to scum like this. Leave this bastard die and come with us.'

The men holding me let go and I scurried across the dirt to cradle Domenico in my arms. Flies had already found the bloody rents in his shirt and coat. Blood bubbled from the wounds.

These thin, sunburned, half-starved criminals took everything they could from the house and split the booty. There was plenty of cash and silver and pearl. They wheeled out Domenico's automobile from the barn and destroyed the engine and tyres, then smashed the wheels of the truck and buggy. They'd already filled their bellies with all the food and wine and milk they could, and their packs were replenished with foodstuffs they'd stolen, not to mention the salted meat of our pigs and goats, which they'd slaughtered and prepared in our absence.

As they were leaving, Giacomo circled me on his horse. 'His family took everything from us then this bastard sold us like chickens and whores. And look at you holding him, faithful little puppy dog.'

For a second time he chose not to shoot me.

By nightfall my hands and the instruments I'd used were covered in blood, but the slugs were intact and drying on a small porcelain plate. Domenico was unconscious and breathing. I used a lot of clean gauze to pad down the wound and wrapped his chest in bandages. Help was a good two days' walk away. I didn't know if this impromptu operation would save my master, kill him or make no difference at all. At least, following the books and encyclopaedias I'd tried to absorb like air, I hadn't cut a major artery. He hadn't died in my hands. In the bedroom where I'd laid him down I kept listening to the slow rhythm of his breath.

My master's hair was awry and his colour was milky white, and to my surprise he came awake. It was the most unnatural awakening I could imagine. His eyes were abnormally wide and his pupils large and round. He barely blinked. When he focussed on me he pulled down my face and kissed me on both cheeks. His breath had an odour like sulphur.

'How do you feel?' I managed to ask.

'I don't feel anything,' he whispered and made himself sit upright. It was like watching a corpse rise. Then he fell back and slept.

Hours later, with the glimmering of dawn, my head jerked up.

Domenico was propped on both elbows gazing out the window. His eyes still had that strange quality to them. His face was no longer pale-white; it had darkened considerably.

'What is it?' I asked.

'Those women are beautiful,' he whispered. The staleness of his breath carried – I can't quite explain – a sort of absence of life, as if he was already quite dead.

I followed the line of his sight, which took in the grey-blue above the ridges of the distant mountains.

'Are they?'

'I wish I'd been able to have more women,' he said. I felt his hand. It was neither hot nor cold. The pulse at his wrist was slow. 'Like the ones up there.'

'What can you tell me about them?' I asked, loosening the main bandage around his chest. The gauze underneath was bloody but seemed clean enough. There was no odour that equated to poison.

'They must live by *cratere centrale*. But don't tell anyone. If any of these peasants around here found out about a marvel like that they'd go spoil everything.'

'You've seen them often?'

'Not really . . . only when the smoke rings are in the sky . . .'

He slept and dreamed again. Somehow he wasn't in pain.

There were no narcotics or anaesthetic in the villa, but Domenico seemed to be experiencing some kind of bodily numbness. Or maybe the lack of hurting had something to do with what we were. Domenico slept peacefully for several hours and whenever I closed my eyes I felt as if I was falling from a high place.

In the evening he was looking at me with those abnormally bright eyes. Their expression was beginning to unnerve me. In a voice no stronger than it had been in the morning he said, 'He protected you.'

'The spirit.'

'He did very well,' Domenico nodded. 'He'll stay with you now.'

I forced myself not to look over my shoulder.

Domenico said without breath, 'Can you help me into the study?'

I didn't want to move him, but it was what he wanted and so I helped him walk carefully through the rooms. I settled him into his big couch. He lay sideways, propped up with pillows, his legs stretched in front of him. The way he lay like that made it look as if he was ready to take up his blank pages and start writing again. He was happier in this room, but his face had turned almost black and his torso and arms were livid, as if all the dark blood had pushed its way to the surface and had stopped moving. Only his ankles and feet still remained white as plates.

Then he spoke, again without any wind to drive his words.

'Before I was conscripted I used prostitutes . . . a few times . . . maybe six or seven in total. Then one more time in a northern town . . . before we were sent to Isonzo. There was a queue of fifty men . . . all of us ready to use one of the three women. I waited . . . mine turned out to be sixteen, seventeen. She was nearly worn out but managed to be pleasant and sympathetic. I tried not to take very long . . . as I was leaving I told her, "This will be my last time." She thought I meant that I expected to be killed in the battlefields . . . and so she gave me a long and very sincere kiss. The kiss meant more than the coitus. I don't forget it . . . what I'd meant to tell her was that our transaction had given me less pleasure than it did her . . . it was something I didn't have any more need for. That's the way it's been . . .'

I wondered why he was telling me this now.

'It was a mistake . . . I should have found a way. Don't be as cold as me, Cesare . . . the coldness turns in on itself.'

'If that's what you think is best.'

He nodded. While he'd been talking his dark face had developed a sheen of moisture. I'd read accounts of men killed in battlefields, beyond the trenches where their friends couldn't reach for the sniper fire. Over the days that passed those helpless soldiers reported seeing their fellows' dead faces turning white, then yellow, then purplish-black, then becoming wet as if sweating. Domenico's flesh was proceeding in exactly the same way, except that he wasn't dead.

It was hard to keep looking at him; he had the manner of an

animated corpse, and deep inside I couldn't help shuddering at the horror of what I witnessed. This wasn't a human occurrence; it was part of what we were.

'I'll sleep in a minute,' he breathed, 'but if you could help me . . .'

'Tell me.'

'The title page of our manuscript. And something to write with.'

The pile of pages was arranged on his desk. We'd had so many other things to do that I'd neglected to finish my work with it. I took the first page and placed it on his lap with a firm ledger beneath it, then dipped his *stylo* into the blue ink well.

He scratched out *Sulphur* and very carefully wrote a new title: *God is a Young Man*, then added the author. It wasn't his name or our two names together but mine on its own.

'The man who shot me . . . Giacomo. He was right. The Amatis were — what they were. Their name should fade. Disappear from memories and this world forever . . .'

'But this is your book, not mine..'

'Not anymore,' he said with as decisive a shake of his head as he could muster. 'One hand passes on to the next, Cesare. Isn't that the way we renew ourselves?'

'And the title?'

'They bred us for hatred. For the worst of what's inside human-kind. But whenever I look at you, Cesare, I see what God meant everyone to be, in the first days . . .'

He closed his eyes and his fingers tried to push the page toward me. I took it from him and eased the pen out of his fingers.

'There's a lot of money,' he started to say, eyes still closed, 'just waiting . . .'

I thought he'd sleep, but as I arranged his pillows he was look-ing at me again. And smiling. Finally there was some life in his eyes and a little more breath to drive his words.

'In that cabinet, a long thin bottle. If I could have a glass, and something alive on the phonogram.'

I chose the *Rites of Spring* then found the bottle in question. Vodka. I poured his drink. Domenico seemed quite his old self and finished it in two deep draughts. As he savoured the taste he looked around and said, 'We're far from alone.' I poured him some more, and he laid his head back and closed his eyes and died so peacefully that the glass was still loosely clutched in his hand, a few drops still in it.

I stumbled outside and tried to make myself busy, burying my dogs and the pathetic remains of the pigs and goats. I couldn't imagine what to do with the fly-strewn horses.

Domenico left no will and the state seized his property. I had no official role or place in the Amati world so the authorities gave me five days to vacate the premises. I filled a pack with all his wads of handwritten pages, my new ones, and left with nothing else other than a few bundles of clothes. At first I was lost, but then a single sentence sprang to mind and impelled me toward the long road again: *I'm sorry to leave you, but maybe one day you'll want to come visit me in Catania.*

Signora Rosa Bortolotti welcomed me more warmly than I could have expected. Of course I should have come to her; of course I had to stay. She'd heard about Domenico's death and had been pestering every government agency she could reach for the whereabouts of the boy who'd lived with him.

She gave me a room. Her sons were grown now, and in this city house she lived alone. Her husband had passed away after an accident that involved too much alcohol – his worst failing, she said.

Signora Rosa wasn't a lonely widow. Her sons might have been overseas, but in Catania everyone was her friend and people were always dropping in for coffee or long sojourns at her dinner table. Soon visitors came to understand that Rosa's lodger didn't like company. I would remain upstairs doing the only thing that gave me satisfaction: finishing the work on the manuscript, my way to keep Domenico in my mind. When it was done I asked Rosa about other manuscripts, the ones Domenico had told me he'd given her to read. Shamefaced, she took four thick-bound piles of paper out of a bureau and told me she hadn't been able to read them.

'But why, if he wanted you to?'

'Domenico was as much a son to me as my three boys, and to read the secret thoughts in his head . . .'

'I understand.' I hesitated. 'I've finished working on one we were making together.'

'Can I see it?'

In the bedroom she sat at my desk, carefully turning pages. Then she took in the title page and my name inscribed in Domenico's hand.

'That's the problem,' I said.

She shook her head. 'Your name belongs there and to do anything else goes against Domenico's wishes. Do you know what a typing machine is?'

'Yes,' I replied, 'but I've never used one.'

'You won't have to.'

She took the manuscript of *God is a Young Man* and over the next three weeks carefully typed it up on her machine for me. She politely refused her usual visitors. Pages on which she made mistakes she simply tore up and typed again.

In the meantime I read Domenico's older manuscripts, and though they were wonderful artefacts of his mind, each in its own way was strange and confused and . . . oddly meaningless. It struck me they were academic exercises, not the products of living. All of them except for one, which was connected to his last halting conversation with me about women and sex.

It was a mistake . . . I should have found a way. Don't be as cold as me, Cesare . . . the coldness turns in on itself . . .

Domenico must have reflected on this coldness his entire adult life. It was in these pages. So I started work on *A Life of Disappearances,* the tale of a young man who has no great love for himself and even less for others, and those to suffer most from his emptiness are of course the women he beds. His complete rejection of social conventions is reflected in a lack of concern for anything but his own pleasure, which is by no means great.

What I thought elevated the book was a less realised political theme: the efficient brutality of the Italian state and the increasing disregard of the needs of individuals and communities in exchange for easy economic deals and catchphrases. Newspapers Rosa accumulated daily were full of simplifications and expediencies in political thought and action. In a way the perfect foil for this trend was my late master's young nihilist, 'Donato Alberti'.

When Rosa finished her typing on the first book, she told me she would only send the manuscript to the most reputable publishers in Italy. After some time, polite letters of refusal started to return: 'Dear Signora Bortolotti, would you please inform your Signor Montenero that unfortunately . . .'

We settled into a comfortable rhythm of life in her house, and I noticed that Rosa gradually relaxed with me, though it came with some effort. She was warm-hearted but had lived with secrets for so long that being cautious, being silent about certain topics, was now simply a part of the way she was.

One night with glasses of port and special *dolce* set out for a group of her friends who hadn't arrived because of an unseasonal thunderstorm, she drank more than she normally did and became positively talkative. She told me that in the weeks following the destruction of the Amati facility, officials had twice come to this house and had combed through it carefully, taking anything and everything that might be a link to the project. They helped themselves to all her husband's papers and records; he'd been a colleague of Kristof Vliegan's and had once been his direct supervisor at the university in Bologna, where ancillary research for the Amati project was carried out quietly.

So Doctor Bortolotti had been yet another element in the Amati's endeavour. His specialty area: genetics and the mutations of species. His published work had achieved such distinction that in 1919 he was invited to Russia to work with a scientist named Vavilov in helping to set up the Laboratory of Applied Botany in the then Petrograd, later renamed Leningrad. This facility proved to foster a vast growth of research into plant breeding. Later he was invited to present at the International Congress of Genetics in Berlin, but it was his extended sojourns in Russia that reflected the Soviet interest, instigated by Lenin and Trotsky, to marry science and socialism.

'Those two things go together?'

'When a country's wracked by famine, yes, I think so.'

'But how did this have anything to do with the Amatis?'

'All new ideas are like a jigsaw puzzle, aren't they? Findings here, research there, beliefs overlaid with opinions and scientific data ... I remember my husband was most excited by two events in Russia. A man he helped to train, Karpetchenko, crossed two plant species. It was the first time it had been successful. Then an old friend of his named Koltsov developed a theory about inheritance within species that has to do with chemicals and templates.'

'Chemicals and templates.' I tried to make sense of this information, but in reality I was more interested in the reaches of this research, which countries had contributed. 'So the Soviets were involved with the Amati family?'

'In the early part of the century. The revolutionary government sent scientists all over the world to learn and to collaborate with others in their field ... but the Amati plan goes back well before any of that. The Soviets were latecomers.'

'But important.'

'Very.'

I thought it over. The most apparent truth was that none of this information helped me in the least; I was no better or worse off for knowing these small, disparate facts. But I did put the small pieces together to form a larger truth.

'Then if so many others were involved in the project, it's not right to think that the destruction of one facility would stop something so —'

I tried to find the correct word.

'Important, Cesare?'

It came to me: 'World-changing.'

'Yes,' she agreed. 'World-changing.'

A big word and a bigger concept – so how could I be the sad result?

The officials scouring her house had been at pains to ensure that Rosa had no personal diaries or letters that gave accounts of her involvement. They even took a vast majority of her family photographs – all the ones that incorporated Domenico as a member of the Bortolottis. She now had no pictures of him as a young boy, and all his school books, writings, drawings, toys and clothes had been gathered up and destroyed as well. Rosa signed papers that forbade her from speaking about her husband's research and either of their involvement. In return she received an ex gratia payment large enough to buy a lifetime's silence. Several lifetimes' silence. Her three natural sons profited with access to the best education money could buy. When it came time to set up their own lives and homes, there were ample funds.

I looked into Rosa's eyes. They held the tears an old woman was practised at holding back. For all these benefits there was also a life of lies, and I was certain that in her soul, as must have been the case with many, many other innocents such as herself, she wished she'd never heard of the Amatis.

Halfway through my work on Domenico's *A Life of Disappearances,* an unexpected event occurred, something that stepped straight out of the pages in my hands.

I was out in the afternoon looking at well-stocked storefront windows and had stopped at a bar, first for coffee then for a glass of Cynar, the aperitif made from artichoke essence and other herbs and plants. This was an ordinary outing for me – I couldn't stay indoors twenty-four hours a day – and despite my reticence, sometimes I did try to be in places where there were women. To look at their faces and clothes, to be close enough to smell perfumes and soaps, to try and understand the attractions between men and women. If a female ever looked in my direction I dropped my eyes immediately. I knew that I blushed all over too.

When the writing was difficult and I couldn't find my way through a certain problem, some days I'd take the train from the east side of the island to the west, and watch the young girls and women of the chaotic former capital and adjacent wealthy resort towns. The power and beauty of different countries were written in all the faces and accents: Germany, Sweden, France, even the Americas. Still, I walked among these women, but never *with* them.

This particular afternoon I sipped my Cynar and read the last pages of Italo Svevo's fine novel, *As a Man Grows Older.* I closed the book, finishing the aperitif. There was Rosa's dinner to go home to, but I'd also developed an affection for the movie theatre in town and thought I might go see what was playing. Exactly as I put down my empty glass, though, the waiter stopped at my table and gave me another shot glass of Cynar. He moved away before I could tell him he'd made a mistake. A couple then passed my table and the female partner dropped a folded note almost into my hands. The man left the establishment first, and the woman stopped in the doorway to glance back at me. She had the lightest eyes I'd ever seen – they reminded me of a cat's. The wisps of hair that showed under her hat were the colour of honey. Then she was gone.

Curious, I opened the note.

It was a street address with an apartment number and a single word that wasn't part of the Italian language: *Now*. What did this note mean? Maybe this strange '*Now*' was an acronym for something. Or a foreign name. I drank the Cynar and put the note into my book, thinking I would forget it immediately. I didn't. What would Donato, the no-good protagonist of *Disappearances* have done?

Paying my bill, I asked the bar owner if he understood the meaning of this three-letter foreign word. He didn't, but called over a waiter, who also didn't have a clue. As I was putting on my coat and hat the waiter came to find me, having worked it out with the assistance of one of the more worldly cooks.

'It means "*Ora*". "*Il presente*". "Now". "The present moment". You understand?'

It wasn't a difficult equation: a word, an address, a glance.

Domenico's book was meant to be full of this spirit: sexual liaisons out of nowhere, passions quenched with absolute strangers. He must have imagined, or perhaps had even wanted, these things, even though he hadn't possessed the will to gratify himself. My hands, inexplicably, had gone cold with nerves. What an adventurer I was. Rosa's dinner, the movie theatre, or this address? I knew the hotel and I knew how to get there; it was a few street corners away. But what would I actually *do* when I was there?

And what about the man with her? It could be the case that I was comically misinterpreting the note's intention and the woman meant to procure a boy for *him*. Or what if they both wanted me? In Domenico's book was the real answer: it told me I had much to learn.

Three street corners. The hotel, a busy porter, carpeted stairs, wandering guests, the door with the correct number. The corridor was so gently lit and silent there might not have been anyone at home in any of the rooms, however the door in question wasn't fully shut. I was about to turn on my heel and run but the man was there, and he tried to smile. I could see he was tense though probably not so much as I was. The woman stood in the room behind him and her hair was down, and she was drinking something. The man spoke. When he saw that I didn't comprehend, he opened the door wider and motioned me in, saying three times, '*Permesso*', which was the wrong polite Italian word to use, but at least this time I understood what he meant.

I left late that evening knowing a little more about myself and the unseen currents running so mercilessly through people's lives. The couple, they'd shown me by way of a world map, were from Great Britain. The woman had been drinking tea that she'd made from English leaves brought with her in a travel case. They'd offered me a freshly brewed cup as we attempted to converse without understanding one another's words, resorting instead to broad, comical sign language. At first I was so nervous I could barely bring my cup to my lips. Then as I gradually understood I wasn't the only one suffering this way, my hands steadied and I began to relax into the situation.

In fact, I felt myself taking command.

His anxiety revealed itself in the jittery way he smoked. She was much more reticent, as if she wasn't even present – but when she lay across the bed and opened herself, and with unexpected tenderness drew my face down over hers, nothing in her manner was reticent any more. I was transfixed by the movements of her eyes, her mouth, by the way she lightly bit her bottom lip.

Her name, they told me, was Veronica. His name, they said, was James. They had both smiled at my own name and repeated it together. They made me understand that his participation in the war had perpetrated something terrible upon James, but it wouldn't be allowed to ruin their devotion to one another. He waited in the main room with cigarettes and port. When I was done, Veronica lay in my arms, satisfied and unsatisfied at the same time. She slowly used her elegant fingers to bring herself to orgasm.

I had no clue about what I'd done. Was this lovemaking? Was this pleasure I experienced the centre of the lives of those around me?

When I stopped kissing her cheeks, her forehead and her mouth I saw a tear run down the side of her face. We emerged from the bedroom. I let the green-eyed Veronica go first, having watched the way she stood naked by the window and slowly pulled up her nylons. I saw how much she longed to be back with her husband. She'd never know that she was the first woman whose body I'd seen and held. If she ever thought about me again it might only be to remember a particularly inept young man in the quaint Sicilian city of Catania.

Veronica and James embraced. There was something both very happy and sad in the way they held one another. James offered me a glass of port but I shook my head and straightened my tie.

'*Buona fortuna*,' I told them, and James's brow creased with incomprehension, just as it had done through all our attempts at conversation.

'Fortune?' he asked in his language. Veronica took up their phrase book and found the expression. She showed it to him on the page. 'Ah, "good luck"! Well, *bor-nah for-tuna* to you too young Caesar,' and that was how we parted, with his faltering smile following me, and his wife's green eyes already turning away.

I stopped on the way home, and sat in a booth with a glass of wine, liking the way Veronica's perfume remained on my hands, on my neck and face, and of course under my clothes. I'd bathe once I was at Rosa's but for now it was if I was alone in a meadow, letting its scents seep into my skin. Jasmine, that was it, jasmine from her hair. I glanced at all the others in this bar without making eye contact. There were couples, groups of friends. I wondered how many of them had made love today or would make love later tonight, enjoying the complicity of tenderness and pleasure.

Domenico's book was wrong. It was too harsh in its summation of the currents inside people. In the people of the world there were cruelties and there were selfish needs but there could be such gentleness too.

One day, I thought, I'd write something of my own – and it would say things the right way.

Rosa was awake and waiting for me, which was not her usual way. There must be bad news, I thought, but it was the opposite. A light shone in her eyes. She didn't want to come straight to the matter and so I played along.

'Come and sit down,' she said, 'it's late and it's time to eat.'

I kissed her hand. 'Tomorrow I cook for you.'

'You do that, but for now enjoy this.'

Rosa always respected my desire not to eat meat and tonight she'd saved me lentil and potato soup with hard cheese cut into it. Simple and delicious. We made small talk while I ate slowly, Rosa sitting across the table from me. I pretended not to notice her mischievous gleam, and thought that if this was going to be the first time she told me she had a great friend with a delightful daughter, then I was ready, I'd gladly meet any angel.

When I was finished she reached into her blouse and withdrew a letter.

'My Dear and Gracious Signora Bortolotti,' it read. 'Would you please advise your Signor Montenero that he has written an Important Book and one which Deserves to be Published and Published Well. I humbly offer my Services, and the Services of my Firm, in the Cause of achieving this Aim. We are a Family Company with a proud History, and among our Esteemed Authors we number . . .'

Not only were the words and what they meant extraordinary, but I recognised the names of three-quarters of the authors mentioned. I could have reeled off their works without thinking. The writer of the letter was a man named Bruno Pasqua and he said he was the son-in-law of the company's founder, a well-known patron of the arts who'd passed away ten years earlier. Signor Pasqua and his company were based in the great textile and manufacturing city of Milano. However, his letter pointed out, Pasqua's parents were from no less than the wonderful province of Catania, which was such an agreeable coincidence, and he would be journeying to their seaside town, Riposto-Giarre, within the month. He would very much like to pass by and meet Signor Cesare Montenero – that is, as long as Signora Bortolotti didn't think a short visit would cause too much intrusion or interfere with the good sir's writing schedule.

With absolute delight, Rosa asked, 'And would it cause too much intrusion to the good sir's busy schedule?'

'This belongs to Domenico,' I told her. 'Success belongs to him. Now that he's gone it won't hurt that the correct name goes on the book. I'll write to this man and let him know the facts.'

Rosa took the letter, looked at it, then looked at me.

'You don't know anything about business, Cesare. First, let me write to our Bruno Pasqua on your behalf. His terms may not be favourable and if you have an intermediary it will be easier to handle negotiations. Second is something more important. Domenico didn't want his name on this book. The Amati name *cannot* be on this book. There should be nothing in this world that provokes public interest in either him or his background.'

I hung my head. I could understand, even though I didn't want to.

'Domenico *did* want your name on it. He wanted you to have this future, and now that he's not with us anymore it's even more certain.'

'But —' I started. It made me sick to profit from the dead, more so because it was Domenico.

'But what? But you know better than Domenico? Listen. He spoke to me about you. He told me that if it ever came to it I was to help you find your way in life. Why else do you think I was trying so hard to track you down after I heard he passed away? There's no last will and testament, men always think they'll live forever. The state's gobbled up just about everything, but you need your own income.'

'That's true, but I've got no right to anything of Domenico's.'

'This book isn't Domenico's. You made it your own. It's what he wanted, and it's always been your story anyway, Cesare. The small boy sold into slavery who makes his escape, was that Domenico's life?'

I looked at my empty bowl and rearranged my cutlery this way, that way.

'What is it?' Rosa asked.

'I can't meet Bruno Pasqua.'

'You're joking?'

'He'll see through me straight away. All I am is a fixer, the way I'm doing with the next manuscript upstairs ...'

'Then don't meet him,' Rosa said. 'Good. Cultivate your air

of genius and mystery. I'll write and say you're far too occupied with your latest work and may we kindly see the details of what he offers, including his financial proposal?'

I sat back in my chair. Rosa was perfectly determined to take this route. The thing is, everything she told me made sense, as if Domenico himself was whispering instructions into her ear.

We talked some more, then we cleaned the kitchen for the night, finally putting out the lights. At the top of the stairs Rosa took off her small glasses and let them hang from the chain around her neck. She held both my hands and squeezed them, and smiled into my face. Without words she was telling me how happy she was that my life had found something of its road.

Well, maybe it had, and I knew who to thank.

Both my exhilaration and my anxiety had passed. As I closed the door to my bedroom all the warmth and good spirits I'd felt that day and night were no longer with me. Instead I felt curiously empty, and wasn't sure why. I lay over the bed covers with a book. After thirteen pages I realised I'd absorbed absolutely nothing by a writer named Poe. I felt unutterably lonely. Not because I had no friends, woman or family – Rosa was as close as I came to all these – but because, as far as I knew, I was the only one of my kind.

But I wasn't quite so different to the rest of the world, I thought. Isn't that what being with Veronica had revealed to me? I did have needs and I did have longings and I could even satisfy them as normal people did. What if, as Domenico had believed, there were others born like us? Hundreds of others? Couldn't I make a life with them just as I'd done with my master? If so, where and how would I find them?

I rubbed my face and my temples.

Domenico's own words: 'We're far from alone.'

I'd assumed he'd been seeing his visions in the room, but he might have meant that other individuals like us were wandering in other circles, also looking for their place. I was lucky to have found him; I was lucky to have found Signora Rosa Bortolotti, who was not one of us but was of our world. The alternative would probably have been to go through life with no clue about what I was and why the great world seemed so far removed from me.

And finally a thought struck me. By its very obvious nature it had managed to never strike before. Or perhaps I'd never allowed it to.

Domenico and I *had* found one another. In fact, he was the very first person I found upon my escape. It was almost miraculous.

No: Domenico had found *me*.

His story was that Salvatore and Gino had come upon him during their search and asked if he'd seen a running boy. Something about them worried him and so he'd followed, being on hand to save me and not a moment too soon. But hadn't he also said that he'd only been travelling into Etna to observe the phenomena of the smoke rings? Then why had Domenico, such a man of peace, been carrying his most powerful weapon, the long-barrelled army rifle? It was bulky and awkward, and would only have been an impediment to his sightseeing. On all our journeys into the mountains or across endless plains he'd only ever wanted to bring the .22, and even that was left behind most of the time.

So he'd been prepared. He'd deliberately set out to rescue me.

And now in a way I'd been rescued again. I was safe with the woman who'd not only brought Domenico up as a son, but who glowed for joy at good news coming my way.

Her husband had worked for the project; Rosa had been one of Doctor Vliegan's nurses; she might even have borne Domenico in her own womb.

I strode from my room and knocked on Rosa's door. Then I rapped harder just to make sure she heard me.

'Rosa, come back to the dining room. I have to talk to you.'

I went down and waited for her, bottle of brandy on the table and my first snifter already drained.

'Am I your son?'

Signora Rosa had let her hair down and she was in her night-gown. In the flickering light she looked older by ten years, as if she'd feared this discussion ever coming. She closed her eyes and spoke with them shut, the lids trembling slightly.

'No, you're not. They put you in me and I carried you to term. The term was less than three months. Then they cut you out. I'm no more your mother than the bed you slept in when you were a baby.' She opened her eyes and they were full of shame. 'You weren't the first.'

'Who were the others?'

'Domenico, and also the creature you killed. The third and last was you.'

'They let Domenico live with your family, but not me?'

'Five years after the delivery they brought Domenico back to see how siblings and a family life would affect one of the special children. He was with us before the sad occurrence of the second. I let myself be talked into a final experimentation and then I was done. I never laid eyes on you, Cesare. Never held you. The understanding was that you'd be for something else not to do with families. I didn't know what. I only discovered the facts later. Your test was an investigation into what could be brought out of the new children by using brutal circumstances as a tool.'

'I remember other children. And disappointment.'

'That's why they decided to force the worst out of their children. None of the plans had proceeded properly. They put you with Gozzi and they kept watch on you. The surprise was how much you wanted to please your master. They'd expected you to turn into an animal.'

'Expected or hoped?'

'Both. Then they decided you were no more use so they let you be. Gozzi divested himself of you immediately.'

'If you knew all of this why didn't you come get me?'

'I kept an eye on you from a distance. I was horrified at what was happening. So was my husband. It was so removed from the original plan. We —' she took a deep breath. 'We did try. At first we were warned away, then when my husband kept pressuring the higher echelon for you to be removed from your circum-stances and handed over to us they saw him as a major problem. In a meeting he made threatening remarks. Things about the press. The prime commandment of the project was Silence. We'd already joined an international campaign to end child slavery, and with the help of hundreds and thousands of people in Italy it was building momentum. Next came his drowning. No one involved with the program was fooled. It was a warning to me and to everyone else in the project who'd allowed themselves to become attached to the special children. If these men would do away with one of their own scientists then what else were they capable of? I had three sons to think of.'

'This happened when I went to the sulphur mines?'

'Yes.'

'How did Domenico become involved?'

'He was the only person I could turn to for help. All I could do was keep track of you. I'd already made sure my sons all worked overseas but even I could see that the tentacles of these men extended around the globe. My boys were vulnerable. Any action I might take would affect each of them.'

Signora Rosa's voice shook. I poured her a little brandy and she took a sip before continuing.

'I asked Domenico to find out about your life in the sulphur fields, about your new master and how you were treated. The plan was that he would eventually buy your so-called contract out from that man Salvatore. You managed to escape. So Domen-ico set out to follow Salvatore and his tracker, hoping they'd lead to you. They did.'

'Then he took me in.'

'Yes.'

'And now you're caring for me and giving me another home.'

She tried to meet my eyes but couldn't do it.

'So I have to thank you, Rosa.'

Signora Rosa finally wept then, quietly and without hope.

'You have to hate me. You're right to. I loathe the Amatis and their legacy. The things they've done under the guise of good works. Under the guise of helping humanity. The things my hus-band let himself do. I don't feel anything but pity for all the other women like me, but most of all I hate myself for what I did and didn't do . . .'

Her tears came from a sickness that had burrowed deep into the soul.

'No,' I said, and I was sure I meant it.

Rosa's hands trembled so much that when she covered her face it was as if she suffered from a kind of palsy.

'Listen,' I told her. 'You gave me life and then you saved me.'

I made her lower her hands and I held them firm.

'Then what's to be angry at, Rosa? What?'

Yellow Book

ROSA SOLICITED AN OFFER FROM Bruno Pasqua, which she refused in my name, and when he doubled it Rosa visited a lawyer versed in these sorts of affairs. She said I should see him with her so that I could understand my own business. I couldn't have cared less. The signora had the measure of things and whatever she thought was good was good enough for me.

Bruno Pasqua sent contracts which I signed, scrawls on the official documents to get them out from under my nose. He'd repeated his request to visit, but I hadn't changed my mind. Instead I was more and more absorbed by the possibilities of this new manuscript. As I wrote about Donato's sexual encounters I even began to see myself as him, seducing women, using their bodies, making pleasure the centre of my life. The idea of some kind of statement about the coldly opportunistic politics of Italy and Europe now seemed ridiculous and irrelevant; what did I care about governments and society? I cared about Donato and his women, whom I undressed in vivid detail.

If the English woman Veronica had still been in that hotel room I would have visited her and begged to watch her in her nylons again. Her red lips on my mouth would have comforted me. I sublimated the desire by writing ten furious pages about longing and fucking, then tore them to shreds. I wrote it all out again, this time putting Veronica herself into the story. Donato was me, holding her naked body in a hotel bedroom while her impotent husband smoked and drank outside. Donato kissed her pale cheeks and covered her warm mouth with his own as she fingered herself into the climax he hadn't been able to give her.

Veronica's hand rested, and Donato kissed her fingers.

Donato kissed her fingers and tasted them in his mouth.

My body trembled and I came into my hands.

Then I heard someone using the brass knocker at the door downstairs, probably one or a few of Rosa's coterie of friends. I definitely wouldn't be joining them in the parlour.

When I took a glance down to the street from my window I saw a well-dressed man waiting, looking around, taking everything in as if he was a jungle cat scanning his terrain. I knew immediately and without doubt that this was Bruno Pasqua. I'd made Rosa reply to him three times, always saying I was too busy to meet, yet here he was not taking no for an answer.

I stormed downstairs and Rosa was politely letting him into the inside landing, where he was taking off his hat, scarf and overcoat, saying ' . . . of course, unannounced like this . . . the height of rudeness, but —'

'But nothing,' I interrupted. 'But you choose to come here anyway and abuse this good woman's politesse by putting her in a position where she can't send you away. Even though we've made it absolutely clear how unwelcome any sort of visit is —'

'But,' Bruno Pasqua went on smoothly, yet with an edge, like a man revealing the handle of his pistol, which was, so far, still in its holster, 'I need to ensure that the extraordinary manuscript I'm about to acquire for quite a bit of money on my company's behalf is indeed written by the personage whose name is on the title page, and that the events depicted, while not at all required to be real and true, are at least real and true to the circumstances they depict, by which I mean, young man, that what's in those pages is a true reflection of life in our island's abominable sulphur mines, and not some fancy dreamed up by a child in pyjamas.'

Two in the afternoon and I was wearing pyjamas. Not only that, his words meant the man wasn't so stupid as to swallow whole whatever was sent to him. And one more thing: even though I'd signed the contract documents, he hadn't.

Rosa invited Bruno Pasqua into the sitting room and I trudged upstairs to dress. By the time I'd done that and had run a brush through the mop of my hair, Rosa had served our unexpected guest with espresso coffee.

I awkwardly stuck out my hand. 'Cesare Montenero, and I apologise for my behaviour.'

He stood and his grip was dry and strong. Pasqua was a short man with a powerful build. He didn't seem in the least bit book-ish. His hair was long and thick, falling to his shoulders. His nose had been broken some time in his youth, and though he was middle-aged and handsome, one of his cheeks was slightly indented. There was the look of sunburn to his face. His lips were chapped. I thought he was more of a retired boxer or wrestler than a man of the arts.

'And I must apologise again at this intrusion,' he said. 'My excuse: book contracts are partnerships and I suffer from anxiety when I don't know my partners. I won't trouble you very long.'

We sat. He took me in, a fool who'd been in his pyjamas in midafternoon, unwashed and unshaved. Neither Rosa nor I had the slightest clue what to say.

'I don't have the chance to come home very much,' he filled the silence, 'but whenever I do I like to make a worthwhile trip of it. My brothers and uncles are fishermen in Riposto. I've been out with them for days now. The taste of the salty wind,' he smiled. 'The next *Mattanza* being planned. Books are good, but the sea – well. Is your family from the coast?'

I gazed at him. So the inquisition begins.

'I never knew my parents.'

'You don't remember them?'

'As in the book, I was too young. And they never came to find me.'

'The boy in the book is in fact you? It's a true story then? Of your slavery?'

We played like this for an hour. I was a slave and uneducated yet I wrote like an angel. How so? I never knew my family but I'd become this 'Montenero' – where did that name come from? I worked in the worst sulphur mines, not those that were open-cut, which were hellish enough, but in vast tunnels underground – yet my health seemed excellent. My lungs weren't destroyed by sulphur or my back destroyed by labour. Why had I survived so well?

Almost everything he brought up led to a new line of inquiry. We drank two pots of coffee and ate cake. If he stayed much longer Rosa would have to feed him dinner.

How is it so? and Why did it become? and Who was that?

I was surprised I could handle his questions, and he liked my answers. I never strayed too far from the truth. I told him things exactly as they were, except for the fact of who wrote the book's originating material and the true manner that the late Don Domenico Amati and I had come together.

'Now,' he said, 'I believe you're immersed in a new book. Are there any pages I might peruse?'

I didn't mind. I thought it would provide proof to the things I'd told him. I went upstairs and gathered up the new manuscript I was making out of what Domenico had left behind. It was three-quarters done. When I returned to the sitting room Pasqua was telling Rosa how much he liked his life in Milan but how greatly he always looked forward to his visits to Sicily – even though it was hellish being away from his wife, and his son and young daughter.

Bruno Pasqua looked up and I placed all two hundred and seventy-six loose-leaf, handwritten pages into his hands. He was delighted.

'May I?'

'May you what?'

'May I peruse it?'

'It's not finished.'

'To get the flavour.'

Tiresome man – but I could see the benefit. He had a new manuscript written in my own hand, what better verification could there be?

'When?'

Bruno Pasqua turned the title page over. 'Now, of course.'

He was perfectly serious. He'd already started.

When Rosa quietly shook me awake I thought it was morning. It wasn't. I was in my clothes and I'd been asleep over the bed covers. The windows were dark and in the streets below the last people of the night were taking their evening *passeggiata*.

'He's asking for you, Cesare.'

I went downstairs yawning, and in a minute Pasqua was pumping my hand. I could see the last page turned up: *Donato kissed her fingers* . . .

'We must redo the contract. I want this, unfinished or not, I want it.' He couldn't hide his enthusiasm, then leaned in and whispered, 'I can taste those fingers myself.' For Rosa's benefit he said in a louder voice, 'And please, let's meet tomorrow night, after you've had a good day's work. There's so much to discuss.'

So I met Bruno Pasqua the next night at a place that was supposed to be the finest restaurant this side of the island. I didn't know if it was true, but the first king of the united Italy, Vittorio Emmanuel II, was said to have dined there in his day. Framed photographs on the wall showed Italian presidents and prime ministers who'd also passed through.

One of the many things I'd liked about living away from society with Domenico was that I'd never had to dress for any particular occasion, or shine my shoes, or attend to such menial tasks as my own grooming. Cold water in the face got me through the mornings and bathing every week or every several weeks had suited me perfectly. Now I was in a much different world, and Rosa had made sure this particular day had been spent not in the gainful writing that Bruno Pasqua had suggested, but in being shepherded around the city like a lamb. She had me fitted out with new trousers, new dress shirts, several pairs of waistcoats, a jacket, silk ties and finally a hat in the new style supposedly all the rage in the best circles of France.

She even had me carrying bags full of new undershorts and undervests, not to mention socks so sheer they looked as if they ought to be worn on a young girl's slender foot. Rosa left me at the barber, who was instructed to turn his unhappy subject into something resembling a gentleman. It was a challenge. The barber said my hair was unhealthy, a symphony of split ends, and it would simply be best to start again. He gave me the shortest style of cut possible that wouldn't make me look like a man just released from prison. He softened my face with hot towels and shaved my beard, and set to work with tweezers and small scissors, excising hair from places I didn't even know hair grew. He scrubbed my ears to a hot pink finish and attended to the tufts in my nostrils the way Domenico and I had attended to sturdy weeds in troublesome corners of our gardens.

By the time I was standing inside the restaurant at the Villa Marconi I was uncomfortable in my new clothes and felt semi-naked on top of my head. I'd handed over that ridiculous hat and intended to neglect to pick it up on the way out. My toes pinched in my new shoes, which made an impertinent squeaking sound whenever I took a step. The maître d' wanted to show me to the table reserved by Signor Bruno – they were on familiar terms with him here – but men were standing drinking, smoking and talking loudly at the bar and I preferred the anonymity of disappearing behind their crowded mass to waiting alone, self-conscious and nervous at a table.

I drank two incredibly smooth whiskies in quick succession, my stomach in turmoil. In the street, on the way in, I thought I'd noticed a woman glance in my direction. Her gaze had held me for just that one moment longer than necessary. I didn't know what to make of it, but I imagined Veronica's face, her scent, her hands, her secret places: my one woman. How would I ever get a second? Did I even need one?

Bruno Pasqua found me in that corner of the bar.

'Two more,' he ordered. 'The corner, good, it's quiet here.' I looked at him and knew he sensed my distress in a place like this. 'Don't worry about it,' Bruno Pasqua told me. 'All these people have got more money and position than brains in their heads. The important thing is that the food and wine are good and my friends here understand what gentlemen like at the end of a very successful week.'

He didn't elaborate.

Bruno Pasqua was shorter than me but seemed bigger; he was older than I was but far younger at heart; he lived the great north-ern Italian life, but now, this second time I was meeting him, he already seemed more of a Sicilian than me. Dark craggy skin, a twisted mouth, deep-set black eyes and hair worn long, as if he lived in distant hills tending flocks and didn't have to worry about what people thought of him. The man immediately dropped all the airs and confabulations of High Italian and started to speak to me in our good Sicilian, Catanese to Catanese, and he had a lot to say.

'I don't know where it comes from, but you've got something strong in the way you put things. Your work's tough and clear, as if you know what you want to say and you haven't got time for bullshit or fools. From what I've seen of your two books we've got something new on our hands. You were schooled in the hardest places I can imagine. With, I'll wager, some of the stupidest and cruellest pigs God ever put on his good earth. But it made your vision clear. I like that. I like that very much. In your first book you can feel the whip crack, the meat tearing out of the body. In the second book you can feel the engorged prick going into a woman's hot flesh.

'My family are all fishermen. They're not the happy-go-lucky sorts you see singing songs or cooking up pots of fish stew for everyone on the docks. My people are tough and they're vicious. If someone tries to take what they've got they smash them down and enjoy it. They like to fight, and when their country calls them to war they go out and kill whoever they're told to. I grew up with them and in the middle of all that I was the only one who loved books and stories. What do you think my life was like? Nine-tenths of my family can hardly sign their names but I've made my course through the two worlds: on one side the sea and blood and on the other side literature. I think in your life you'll also navigate the two.

'Now, you want to eat? I do. Then I want a woman and I don't mean some fat Catanese prostitute with tits like a cow. What did you write, Cesare? "Donato kissed her fingers and tasted them in his mouth".'

Bruno Pasqua laughed so loudly the group of well-dressed older men next to us turned. Pasqua shook his head and swallowed a new shot of whisky.

'The secret is that we know exactly where those lovely fingers have been and what they must taste like . . . you can almost smell them off the page. And a young man who can write something like that knows his women too.' He took me by the shoulder. 'Or he's got a wonderful imagination, right?'

He gave me the chance to answer which of the two possibilities it was, but I couldn't say a word. Pasqua grinned and looked down at my clothes.

'Who dressed you like such a faggot? Don't let me see you like this again. I preferred you in your pyjamas. Come on,' he said, and led me to our table.

I made up my mind to definitely forget to pick up that hat.

Bruno Pasqua ate with gusto, saying that the swordfish on our plates had probably been captured from the Mediterranean Sea by his father and brothers, and, if not, then by Sicilian fisherman just like them.

I understood that at least part of the reason he loved *God is a Young Man* and the coming *Life of Disappearances* was because the island of Sicily was so much a character of the stories. If he could profitably have run his business from Catania or Palermo he would have done so. At one stage during the evening he referred to the 1860 unification of our island with the mainland, except that he called this the 'Italian invasion' and decried the hundreds of years of our rule by everyone but ourselves.

Then when the dinner was done and he'd drunk his fill – which was plenty, even though he didn't seem in the least bit inebriated – Pasqua called the maître d' over and told him to 'Charge the bill as usual' and to 'Tell them we're coming'.

Soon we were leaving the restaurant by a discreet side door that didn't lead into the Villa Marconi's marbled reception area, but to a smaller separate establishment. There we were greeted by a matriarch named Signora Granbassi. A young man immediately brought us a bottle of French champagne and crystal flute glasses. We sat in a semi-lit room full of overstuffed furniture. A record was playing, a woman singing in French, I thought.

'It's been too long, Bruno,' the signora said, not afraid to use his name.

'Too busy, it drives me crazy. When I'm in the north month after month you know how I get.'

She smiled into the plump rolls beneath her chin. 'And a young friend, also a northerner?'

Pasqua looked warmly at me and used a local saying few outside of the island would have made sense of: 'No, *Sicilianu ca scorcia*' – 'Sicilian with a thick crust.'

'What's he after?'

'Ask him.'

'What would you like tonight, young man?'

Bruno Pasqua had to rescue me.

'I think he's the type to go for one of our own, but someone with a bit of finesse. How about Paulina?'

'Not with us anymore.'

'Francesca?'

'Got herself married.'

'Huh,' Pasqua said, 'it really has been too long. Well, bring them all out and let's have a look.'

We drank the champagne as she arranged it. Bruno Pasqua was extremely matter-of-fact about the business at hand.

'First time in a place like this? By Sicilian standards it's about the best you're going to find but once we get on the road I'll introduce you to several venues you'll never forget.'

'The road?'

'We might have to travel if other countries want to translate your books, but that's to discuss another time. Now listen, I can see you're nervous. Just take it easy. The signora and the ladies here only want to please us so there's nothing to be worried about. And if you're concerned about disease ask for a prophylactic and your girl will give you one. Take your time, enjoy yourself, there's no hurry at all.' He brightened. 'Ah.'

Signora Granbassi led in the parade of young women. I was relieved that they were dressed demurely and seemed perfectly normal, though for me there was nothing normal in being so close to nine available females. At first I kept my eyes averted. Bruno Pasqua rose to his feet and greeted each woman with a bow.

'What's your name?' 'Where are you from?' 'Your eyes are almost turquoise, you know that?'

He chose the one with coal-black hair who said she was from Albania, then, as a bonus, a young blonde named Asta who spoke fondly of her village outside Oslo. How coerced were these young women? How much slavery was in this room? I wondered if they were living lives equivalent to the life I'd been forced into – yet they maintained an air of perfect normalcy. There was no unhappiness etched into their faces, no fear, and they seemed as average as the young women I used to see at the Bologna university.

Bruno Pasqua said, 'Come on, who do you want to accompany you?'

Getting any words out was like spitting up stones.

'Whoever wants to,' I spoke in a very small voice.

I was surprised anyone even heard me.

'I will,' replied a bright voice, and I wasn't very much conscious of who'd spoken until we were in a colourful bedroom together.

'If we don't work we don't get paid,' she said, 'and I need the money. So what can I do for you, young man?'

Her name was Klarissa, she said, and she was in her late twenties, though, close-up, she looked much older. She told me she didn't have any children, which for some reason I also didn't believe, and that her husband had been killed in the war. She was born in Trieste and had come to the south for the weather, even though her accent seemed as Sicilian as mine. Obviously she had a picture she wanted to paint, but it didn't quite come together. What interested me more than this brothel or this room or even this pleasant woman was the skill with which lies needed to be spun and threaded together in order to make them work. Hers didn't – but what Domenico and I had done on the page, and that I continued each day, easily demonstrated the skill. For some reason we had it, the ability to make lies seem real.

And now of course Bruno Pasqua had been drawn in by my further patchwork of untruths. He'd be far from amused if he ever learned that I wasn't the sole author of these books; I could picture the black blood that would come into his face, the rage that would tremble in his hands.

After ten minutes of chitchat Klarissa wearied of my timidity and turned in the couch to face me. As she spoke she slowly inched her dress up above her ankles, her knees and finally to the top of her thighs.

'So you've asked me where I come from and now you know. And you've asked me about my family and now you know that too.'

She crept her dress up to her hips and spread her knees wide. She wore nothing underneath.

'And I asked you one tiny question and you didn't answer me. Oughtn't a handsome young gentleman answer a lady? I'll ask you again: What's your pleasure, young prince?'

Klarissa ran my hand between her legs then caressed herself, but only for my benefit, I thought.

'If you want to go slow, I'm in no hurry. Your friend won't mind paying for an extra hour or two, will he? I could make you last all night if you wanted it that way.'

She slid down to her knees and put her hands on my thighs, then ran the tip of her tongue over her bottom lip.

'Would you like me to start you off?'

I caught her hands. 'Can we just say we did it?'

She stopped and looked at me then I helped her up. Klarissa sat facing me again.

'We can. Do you prefer boys?'

'I apologise, it's the situation . . . I don't . . .'

She put her index finger against her own lips. 'Shh, in here whatever you say or don't say is the law. But we act as if we did it, all right?'

I nodded a little more enthusiastically than I'd meant to.

'Well, we've got time,' she went on. 'Your friend paid for some very good champagne. Will I get it?'

'Yes.'

Klarissa slipped out of the room and I studied my palms. I felt as if I could breathe again. Despite everything I'd been imagining while writing Donato's story, right here not a single part of me desired a woman or wanted to be attended to. My hands weren't cold and I wasn't consumed by fear, I simply felt as if I wasn't present.

When Klarissa returned she had a new bottle of champagne and three glasses – the young woman from Norway had come in with her. They shut the bedroom door, laughing together like girls. We toasted one another's health. Asta needed the champagne more than me and certainly more than Klarissa.

'Wore me out in twenty minutes. The man's a bull. He's giving Elena a run for her money, let me tell you. But he's not without pity. When he realised I wasn't keeping up he said I could go, and gave me a tip too. And such a tender kiss. He said that maybe he shouldn't have been so greedy.' She drank some more. 'Cock thick like a leg.'

We spent the hour drinking the champagne and discussing the latest showing at the local movie theatre. When I left the bedroom the signora was waiting in the reception area with some of her women, all of whom were waiting for new clients. She asked if I was happy with the service and I said that indeed I was, and would definitely return. She whispered that Bruno Pasqua probably wouldn't surface until the morning; he'd asked for the pipe to be brought into his room.

Whatever that meant, I didn't mind. The night air was crisp and the cold bit pleasantly at my ears, and by the time I was halfway home I realised I really had forgotten that stupid hat.

Bruno Pasqua had a relative living four blocks from Signora Rosa's house, and three weeks after we packaged up and posted the completed manuscript of *A Life of Disappearances* to his office the relative sent her ten-year-old twins running to collect me so that I could come speak to him on their intriguing mechanism, the telephonic machine.

'My only regret,' he said, his voice echoing on the line as if he was speaking out of some distant dream, 'is that I can't publish this book at the same time as the first. It's everything I hoped for, Cesare.'

Relieved that I'd served Domenico's memory well, I didn't want to make an immediate start on what I thought could be a third and final novel. Working carefully through those remaining manuscripts Rosa had showed me, I saw the strangeness, the confusion, the lack of true experience that could be cut away to make a last book, something tender but true. Domenico had been writing about the old feudal life in Sicily and I liked the idea of bringing something like that to life. It would have to wait, however, because this city living had completely enervated me. I needed to get away into more familiar surrounds.

Pasqua was publishing *Young Man* at the start of the new year, and Christmas was already approaching. Signora Rosa's house was beginning to fill with guests and her sons were due to arrive, new families in tow. The deal with Bruno Pasqua meant I had money, not a lot, but enough to let me do what I wanted.

Instead of renting myself a country cabin or purchasing a ticket for some exotic location, I visited the local stables until I found myself a good horse, saddlery and camping equipment. It only took a few days to put together the supplies. Rosa didn't want to see me leaving, especially not in winter's festive season, but I told her I knew what I was doing.

On the telephone Pasqua asked, 'You're going where?' His voice was half-concern, half-envy.

The horse was a good one, an intact male with plenty of fire. He reminded me of Esperanto. The stable manager smirked when I picked him, knowing what I was getting and already thinking I wouldn't be able to handle him. When we were free of the constraints of the city and its environs I twitched the reins and took Thunder away from wide thoroughfares busy with motor vehicles and bicycles. He snorted and fought me. He didn't want to pick his way down an embankment and then a hillside towards the long, flat green plains ahead. He knew by the time we got to the bottom who was boss. His flanks quivered with the exertion and the stress of the steep descent. I patted his neck and leaned close to his ear, rubbing and scratching, telling him good things and making sure he knew the sound of my voice.

'How about a run now? That's what you really want, don't you?'

It took three attempts to get Thunder to understand what he could do. The stable master had kept his beast in enclosures far too long.

'Come on.' We wheeled in a circle. 'Straight ahead.'

His head shook and his nostrils flared, and finally the message made sense in some primal part of his brain. He shot forward and picked up speed. There was plenty more in him, and we raced across the plains toward the foothills of the volcano.

★

While everyone else observed the ritual of the Christmas season, I observed the snowfalls over the peaks of Etna. While warm kitchens created feasts for gathered family members I cooked lentils, chickpeas and potatoes over open fires. As loved ones slept in their homes in the warmth of their beds and the safety of their rooms I huddled in the sorts of caves I'd been looking for when Salvatore and his tracker hunted me down. I had blankets to wrap myself in against the icy drafts that howled around these peaks and plateaus, and I didn't miss anything or anyone. I did think about Domenico. I could hear his voice sometimes in my sleep. I did think about Veronica. I'd wake up out of some dream and realise I'd been smelling her hands and neck.

Then one particularly cold night, the creature came to me and I saw what Domenico saw all his life. The fire was embers and I'd been sleeping restlessly, and when I opened my eyes it was standing back several steps shaking and quivering. It wasn't facing me, and it drew no comfort from what was left of the fire. At first I lay where I was as if in some waking dream. Maybe this wasn't a creature but a man made eerie by a trick of the light. I rubbed my eyes and sat up. It sensed my movement and turned toward me.

'What do you want?'

Of course it couldn't answer.

Mist seemed to melt out of the rock walls. Thunder skittered and I unwrapped myself from my blankets and went to the thing and draped the warmest covering I had over its shoulders. The individual was as milky white as Doctor Vliegan's sad creature had been and just as blank, just as featureless, but it had two arms, and something else that the other one had lacked.

The creature wasn't cold at all. It shook from the rage that flowed from its body like magnetic waves.

Thunder neighed, unsettled. I had to sit down. Those waves caused a nausea that ran from my belly to my face. My temples throbbed. The good meal I'd made myself before sleep came up in one violent spasm. I coughed and looked at the creature and it was Domenico. A hand seemed to blot out my vision and when I looked again it wasn't the creature or Domenico or even Doctor Vliegan. It was me. My face, my body, and still with such fury. I looked at myself and saw that in the throes of this anger I was capable of destroying men, women, untold lives.

Then I was wrapped in my blankets and Thunder was quiet and the embers created a friendly glow in the cavern. The dream was a warning: I knew now what Domenico had been seeing and what the nature of his so-called spirit guide and protector had been. It was no guardian.

It was himself, the horror of what had been done to us embodied in a terrible vision. It was *rage*. It was what had been bred into him and what he had forced himself to fight every day of his life.

Domenico had *kept it down*. My dream told me I had to do the same.

There was no more sleep that night.

Soon, everything had to go back, including Thunder. I didn't mind – the expedition now seemed tainted. By my reckoning we'd been away sixty-six days; the world was well into another year.

When we rode through the outskirts of Catania a steam train hurtling on its tracks blew its deep throaty whistle. I saw blurred faces at windows. The closer we came to the city the more slowly I proceeded. Thunder sensed my mood and ambled with the gait of an animal that doesn't want to go where it's being directed.

With the increase in the general population and the density of the streets, I thought it better to get out of the saddle and lead Thunder by the reins. He didn't react to the individuals around him or to the children who simply had to touch and caress him. I tried to keep to quieter streets then, as we passed a small tavern and a smaller bookstore beside it, I stopped in my tracks and collected my thoughts, and went back several steps. The shopfront window was full of books, but it was only one title in multiples, and there was a discrete banner attached to the window's glass and it said one word: *Sensation*.

I didn't want to tether Thunder and leave him unattended, so I tapped on the bookshop's glass door until a dapper man opened it to see what I wanted. He had brilliantined hair and a small moustache.

'We *are* open for business if you'd care to come in.'

'This book,' I said.

'Yes?' He surveyed his display. 'It arrived last week and I put it out immediately. As the banner reads, it's something special. Would the gentleman like to examine a copy?'

My book had a grey-black cover with the title and my name and a line from a northern newspaper: '. . . the writer has created nothing less than the sensation of the season.'

It was difficult to leave Thunder behind, but after I'd settled matters with the stable manager I walked to the relative of Bruno Pasqua's house and wondered who'd created this sensation, me or Domenico? Wasn't I a simple leech feeding off a corpse?

'Cesare!' Bruno exclaimed as soon as he heard my voice on his cousin's telephone machine. 'We thought you'd dropped off the edge of the world! Now listen, the advance reviews are good. I can't guarantee the public will catch on but we've made the best possible start. I hope your travels haven't worn you out, because we're going to France, you and me. I've got companies in Paris interested. They'll want to meet you so they can see what they're getting. Your Italian words translated into French, would you like that?'

'Why do I have to go?' I asked.

'*Sicilianu ca scorcia!*' Bruno Pasqua laughed. 'I'll be in touch soon.'

In Paris we had a number of publishing companies to visit. We could have got this business out of the way in a day or two, but Pasqua scheduled only one meeting per day with a weekend in the middle, and more days off for sightseeing.

We met up at Milan central station and Bruno Pasqua's wife and children were on the platform with him. Signora Stella Pasqua was taller than her husband, fine-boned, smooth-skinned, with grey eyes only a little too far the wrong side of tired. In her mid thirties, she was probably fifteen years Bruno's junior. She turned heads and had a soft lilting voice. Her father had set up the publishing firm, and that was how she'd met Bruno, a southerner brimming with passion for books and life in equal measure.

Wife and husband had a manner of standing very close, some part of themselves always needing to touch. In those days of formal, even severe, public decorum this was quite something. They seemed so loving it was hard to believe he could feel the need for physical comfort from anyone but her. Heads were also turned by the Pasqua children, who at eleven and six were so beautiful it almost hurt the eyes to gaze upon them. They ran and played when they were allowed to, and when they were told to wait with us they did so without complaint. Stella's eyes glistened at the final goodbye. Bruno's voice broke a little when he hugged his children and told them to be good for their mother. The youngest, the girl, cried to see her adored father departing on a train without her.

In our private cabin, Bruno Pasqua broke out a fresh bottle of whisky as soon as the train set off and all the fluttering handkerchiefs of our fellow travellers, not to mention his own, were stowed away.

'It's like this whenever I go,' he said, and we drank up. 'Leaving. Even when you have to, even when you want to, it never stops hurting. When you've got your own family you'll know what I mean.'

In the new city a carriage took us to the rue du Roi de Sicile, where Bruno Pasqua kept an apartment. The street name had helped him decide on the purchase, of course. We lugged our bags up six floors, going around and around an ancient spiral staircase.

His caretaker, Madame Seguin, was waiting for us. By now it was midmorning and she'd opened the curtains, so these rooms were bathed in a sort of gold I wouldn't have believed possible unless I'd seen it for myself. The effect made you want to touch the arms of the chairs and the flat surfaces of the tables just to see if some of that gold could come into your own person.

Bruno Pasqua greeted Madame Seguin with kisses on her cheeks and he spoke to her in French. His languages, he told me, included German, Spanish, a little Greek and, of course, English. He'd also dug into the Sicilian language's roots and could converse at a superficial level in Arabic. He had no interest in learning any Asian languages.

Madame Seguin was in her sixties and had lost her husband and her son in the war. She had two daughters in Paris. Later, when I noticed she was packing, Bruno told me he'd asked her to go visit one of the daughters for a few days. This seemed to be something of a code between them, one which only took effect when he travelled without his family.

'We can look after ourselves, can't we? We'll get along fine, true or not?'

'True,' I said.

For this first evening, though, Madame Seguin was staying.

Bruno wanted us to eat and then indulge in the famous Parisian *noctambulisme*, which, he explained, was the pleasant sport of wandering around the streets of the city.

Madame Seguin served dinner. First came crême of asparagus soup, then what she called coq au vin. He'd either neglected to tell the madame I ate no meat or he'd done so on purpose. I hesitated, the steaming casserole dish in the middle of the table and my portion already served. I drank some wine and felt myself succumbing to the seduction of the scent. Since the day Domenico and I had decided to stop eating living creatures I hadn't felt any urge for what I was missing, but when I took a small forkful of the madame's cooking I knew there was no turning back.

I polished my plate two times over. With a grin, Bruno said, '*Bienvenu à la France.*'

Madame Seguin cleared away the table and he smoked a cigarette, absently picking tobacco flecks from the tip of his tongue. His cigarettes were Turkish and very strong. When he was finished he went for his coat.

'Where are we going?'

'In this city you don't need a destination.'

It was past eleven and I thought this was a ruse; in minutes we would be inside some brothel that would welcome him like a king. It turned out Bruno Pasqua was completely sincere. From rue du Roi de Sicile in Le Marais we walked the quiet streets of the quarter, taking in an area I never suspected I would one day come to know as perfectly as I had known the twisting tunnels in Salvatore's sulphur mine. We crossed to a major thoroughfare, the rue de Rivoli, and followed it to the enormous square of L'Hôtel de Ville, then followed the Rivoli for a long time, walking just briskly enough to shake off the cobwebs of a long journey and the effects of the whisky and champagne we'd drunk along the way. Place de la Concorde, les Champs-Élysée, l'Arc de Triomphe – I liked the overall sense of peace in the Parisian night. We strolled under and around the great arch, looked at the inscriptions, then headed home via quieter and smaller avenues. It was hard to believe my book might be sold in little stores in these streets and that Parisians might even read it.

I tried to remember the boy who'd slept on a pallet in rags and who carried sacks of rock on his back through tunnels hot enough to cook human skin. When I had this image I held onto it. There's so much magic and wonder in the world, I thought, more than I could have imagined, but I didn't want to let myself be swept away. My bastion was always going to be that small boy I used to be.

The first publisher we visited was a fool in immaculate clothes, with fat wet lips that seemed to have a life of their own. It was clear that his staff lived in terror of him. Walking through his offices was like walking through a gentrified version of the old mines. Young women worked at typewriters with downcast eyes; they were overseen by a harridan who lacked only a whip. I was uneasy even before we sat down and I fidgeted in my stiff shirt and starched collar.

His name was Maurice Chaumeil and he spoke no Italian. I sat there dreaming while he and Bruno Pasqua took coffee and smoked thin cheroots that smelled like burning cow manure. The two men seemed to be catching up on family and political matters as much as they were discussing business, and I couldn't tell if Bruno liked this man or not. Once they started talking about books and new lists, and my work in particular, Bruno translated for me.

When we were free of his office Bruno said, 'Thank God that oaf doesn't want your book, but it would have been bad for business not to go through with the theatre of offering it. He has, unfortunately, some of the best authors in the world.'

To clear ourselves of an unpleasant encounter we wandered the afternoon away in the Bois du Bologne, among trees and grass and chirruping birdlife. As evening fell, we stopped by a small restaurant and ate a light meal. Something told me we wouldn't be going straight home; soon Bruno Pasqua took me down so many side streets and turns that I thought I wouldn't be able to find my own way back to our district.

We ended up in a busy quarter a long way from my easy central marker, the Seine, and we were in a strip that was as full of people as any city centre at midday. Gaiety was in the air and food sizzled and steamed from vendor's carts and small pavilions. Here, Bruno Pasqua seemed more at home than ever. Carriages, horses and automobiles competed for space in the narrow streets, and my companion took me by the arm so I wouldn't be lost in the melee. We ducked down an alley that stank of wine and garbage. I thought we were headed for some miserable place even more stultifying than the office of Maurice Chaumeil, but at a heavy black door Bruno rapped hard and two well-dressed young men greeted him like a long-lost friend, and from behind them out spilled the sounds of an orchestra, a strong female voice singing, and many people laughing and talking.

We passed on into a place that was ornate, immaculately designed, busy with men and women. The hubbub was astonishing. We left our hats and coats at the check-in and received our receipts. Bruno tipped the three young ladies at the counter. One of them, in what I took to be a negligee, came around from her position and linked her arms with ours. The gossamer material showed the full roundness of her breasts and the red of her nipples, not to mention her bare, stocky legs. I liked the way her hair hung in playful bunches. I thought she was going to spend some time with us but her job was only to pass us on to two slightly older women, who relieved Bruno of a significant wad of cash.

I heard him say the word 'Champagne', and then in a lighter tone 'Celeste.' Was he looking for someone? The two women kissed Bruno's cheeks. We left them and Bruno strode through men milling in good clothes and women in mostly nothing, until we went into a separate grand chamber resembling a ballroom. The chandeliers were bright, and here was where the orchestra played. They made music with real verve, backing a singer who sounded as good as anything I'd heard on Domenico's old phonogram. Twelve angels in silk danced with the expertise of trained ballerinas. A handful of times Signora Rosa had taken me to the theatre and the opera, and in movie theatres I'd learned something of the frivolity and beauty of dance and music, but this was something else again.

At small circular tables, happy groups of men drank and watched the performance. In larger booths at the more darkened corners of the room even more angels were mingling, sitting on laps, caressing fat, thin, smooth, bristly, handsome or repulsive cheeks alike, and receiving kisses. A bottle of champagne in an ice bucket was opened for us. A silver platter of hors d'oeuvres arrived.

'It'll be quieter upstairs, but let's get the lay of the land and see who's around, all right?' Bruno said.

As she poured our drinks I gazed at the barely covered breasts of a lovely girl with a head of cute red curls. Despite the cloying cigarette and cigar smoke hanging like a pall I could smell perfume like strawberries. Bruno tipped her. She looked at me and spoke something in French, and with a flounce of her pretty hips went to assist the next table.

'She said that if you're in the mood, think of her. That means you only have to mention the name "Françoise" and if she hasn't already become busy, she's yours.'

The dancers were coming closer to our table. I felt myself grow tense. 'What's this place supposed to be?'

Bruno Pasqua took out his handkerchief, wiped his brow and straightened his collar. He looked around as he spoke. Thankfully, the group of dancers had decided to veer away.

'People like fancy names, but it's a bordello through and through. Wonderfully legal in this country. There are others – some a little bigger, some a little gaudier, and then of course there are the more exclusive places. Half-a-dozen girls and a single madame. They're my preference but I thought I'd start you with the most dazzling type. How do you find it?'

'I'm dazzled. Who is Celeste?'

'She works here. She also works for me. A very interesting young feline, you'll see.'

Bruno touched his fingertips to his brow, acknowledging a heavy-set man in his seventies or thereabouts who sat with a number of younger men. Three young women exactly like Françoise were feeding him canapes.

'Actor, surrounded by better actresses than he ever was,' Bruno said. 'American films, always played the hero. We looked at his memoir last year but it was extremely dull, hardly a shred of truth in it. God-fearing war hero, etc., etc., when everyone knows he likes young pussy and fat cocks. You'll find bloated egos in here and massive self-deceptions. There for instance is the French minister of defence. A good man, but let's hope there's no war soon. Pacifist at heart, even if he enjoys being beaten.'

'It seems very expensive here.'

'Die with your money in your pocket then, see if it makes you happier.' He snacked and drank, then said, 'But they're very civic-minded here as well. Thursday nights are for war veterans, especially the ones who've suffered the worst injuries. They're entertained and ministered absolutely free of charge. Ninety percent of establishments do the same. It lifts the heart, doesn't it?'

Françoise was back and refilling our glasses. After an inquisitive gaze, which I didn't return, she took our platter away.

'Hurt her feelings, Cesare. Aren't you ever going to take a woman?'

A waiter delivered a new bottle of champagne packed in fresh ice. The orchestra's lively tune slowed, became moodier, and the dozen dancers left to appreciative applause. The lights turned low and four new dancers, naked except for diaphanous ties around their waists, performed with a well-built young man in a golden jockstrap. He was as powerful as a wrestler but moved like a cat. Their performance wasn't in the least bit sexual. With the use of nothing but lighting and their own muscular control they created a number of wonderful human tableaux. Even I could see how exquisite it was.

Bruno Pasqua had grown impatient. He stopped Françoise as she passed. She didn't stoop to hear his voice but actually went submissively onto her knees beside him. She must have hoped he'd decided to choose her. They spoke in French, and Françoise had news he didn't seem to like. He thought a moment then asked her to get him something. I watched the performers create a final scene. This was a funeral procession: the dancers lifted the man high and carried him like a fallen hero or king, their heads bowed.

The audience applauded with genuine enthusiasm. The waitress returned and gave Bruno a sheet of paper, a pencil and an envelope. He scrawled a note then felt in his pocket and detached a key from his chain. He sealed the envelope and gave it back with a nice tip. Françoise leaned in and kissed his neck, the bright red of her lipstick leaving a mark on his skin. His hand caressed her voluptuous backside as he said to me, 'Well, enough art for one night, let's go upstairs.'

'It's a bit —' I couldn't find the right word.

He stopped and looked at me, relaxing back into his chair. 'Overwhelming?' he asked, perhaps understanding me a little better now. 'It's quiet upstairs and the girls don't simply offer themselves for fucking. You'll find they're consorts trained in providing friendship. Without them men would go mad.'

I put my hand on Bruno's thick forearm, stopping him from rising.

His brow creased. 'Is it a matter of religion? Or do you find it coarse to be in a place where women are paid for their skills?'

'Neither. There's nothing wrong with this place. But I'd rather go.'

Bruno's smile was twinged with regret. 'God allows us one life,' he said, 'and whenever you limit yourself you limit the experiences you have before your time's up. Who knows when that will come? Please don't get the wrong impression. I need my outlets, but the centre of my life is my family. Nothing makes me happier or more of a man than the embraces of my children and my wife. They're the gifts heaven's allowed me.' He thought a moment. 'But the idea of God and the eternal is so abstract. Now, are you sure?'

He used the pencil to write our address down, telling me to ask for help by showing it if I couldn't find my way home.

'Avoid beggars and damsels in distress, I don't want to be collecting you from the morgue. Find a gendarme if you need directions.'

Rays filled my room, and the open windows let me hear men and women calling in a market somewhere. If there was any rush to go out and visit the second publishing firm I was sure Bruno would come banging at my door, so I let myself stay in the bed, French voices and drifting scents of cooking giving me the illusion that I was a part of Parisian life. When I finally did rouse myself I found that Bruno must have stoked the fire during the night – it still glowed warmly. I broke eggs over the griddle and added mushrooms, making coffee as they cooked.

I went to Bruno's closed door and asked if he'd join me for breakfast. There was no reply. I thought I could smell a cigarette. Maybe for once Bruno wanted privacy. I went to the bathroom to wash my face, and as I pushed the door a young woman slowly turned and looked at me from the claw-footed tub. A magazine was open across a sort of half-table, which also held a daintily patterned teacup and an ashtray for her cigarette. Her hair was pinned up and her breasts were pert and the colour of snow. She exhaled a plume of smoke.

'Bonjour, monsieur,' was all I heard as I retreated.

The mysterious Celeste.

I checked the main bedroom and saw that the big bed had been slept in. Bruno wasn't there. Delicate clothing and shoes were. He hadn't returned home, even though she'd come and let herself in, using the key he'd sent her.

She emerged from the bathroom wearing a red, clinging dressing robe with blue and purple toucans embroidered into it. I thought she was maybe twenty or twenty-one but her eyes were infinitely more knowing, as if she'd lived a lifetime or two already. As she unpinned her hair she stood at the kitchen's entrance, barefoot. Her toenails were painted a deep red, the colour of fire.

She spoke to me in French, very lightly, but I didn't understand a word she said.

I stumbled over, 'Made-moi-selle . . . Italiano . . .'

Her face slowly lit up. In French-accented but perfect Italian she replied, 'And I'm certain you'll tell me your name is Cesare Montenero.'

Turquoise Book

CELESTE STOOD AT AN OPEN window and used a towel to dry her long hair as I made her two fried eggs with thin pieces of ham. I sliced several ripe tomatoes and served them seasoned with olive oil and oregano. She draped the towel over a chair and poured two cups of coffee. We both took it black. She wanted to know why Bruno had brought me to this city. As I explained she listened and chewed. Though she was slim she ate passionately, which I liked. She wanted more so I made her more.

'But you're here and Bruno isn't. Did you do the rounds with him last night?'

'Just one place.'

'*The Gilded Cage*. I see. And you had better things to do?'

'Only to come home.'

Hazel eyes took me in as if I was some kind of surprising creature, then she surprised me herself by asking, 'Have you met the wife?'

'Only once . . . not for very long.'

'I'm sure she's very beautiful?'

I didn't have an answer. She smiled quietly and for the second time finished everything on her plate. She helped herself to the tomatoes in the side dish and wiped that up with chunks of bread. Finally Celeste dabbed her lips, content with the meal but not with Bruno Pasqua's absence.

'For more than a year now he's employed me to report on the manuscripts he thinks of acquiring. It's an arrangement I like very much. When I'm not doing my other work, I like to read. Nice to be rewarded for it. He sent me yours, but only to satisfy my curiosity. Nothing was going to stop him from publishing you. Are things working out?'

'He seems happy.'

'But you don't have an opinion?' She looked at me with some interest, then found a cigarette. 'I planned to be at the salon last night. Instead a Danish pig I had an appointment with decided nothing I could do was going to please him. The minor aristocracy, inbred as gorillas. What good do they do? He wanted to hurt me and he really did. I gave him a good kick between the legs and that settled him. I made him pay me my full amount and left him to his blackened balls.'

'This happens . . . sometimes?'

'I won't put up with fools who enjoy hurting women. Let them go massacre one another in battlefields, I couldn't care less. With me they can play-act all they want but to really cause pain, ugh! Lately there's more of it. Like a pandemic. I don't know what sort of mood is travelling around the world.' Celeste lit her cigarette and lost all interest in the phenomenon. 'Then when I passed by they gave me Bruno's note. He'd moved on. I skipped here with wings on my feet – and nothing. I looked in your room, you were asleep. It's always interesting to watch the way a stranger sleeps, don't you think?'

No words would come. I could completely rewrite Domenico's manuscripts, but every time life gave me the chance to say something interesting I could conjure no words for myself.

Celeste said, 'You're uncomfortable with the conversation. Sometimes I talk like a soldier, I know. Or are you uncomfortable with all conversations?'

'Sometimes.'

'Apologies. I assumed a young man travelling with Bruno would be like Bruno.'

Celeste's accented use of the Italian language had a lightness of touch that made me want to hear more. It didn't matter if she used the language of a soldier or told me horrific stories of the life of a prostitute.

'It's not that I'm . . . uncomfortable,' I started, pushing myself to speak. 'It's just . . . I don't have a lot to say about things.'

'But you fill books!' She thought this over a moment then seemed content with what she came up with. 'Well, good. Most men talk too much and usually about themselves and their achievements, or to complain about their wives and no-good offspring. Such absolute shit, so dull. Silence is so much more exciting.'

She turned her eyes to me again, widening them slightly. Then she exhaled smoke and took a sip of her coffee.

'I should be quiet, I know, but you're exactly the boy in *Young Man* and the diametric opposite of the bastard in *Disappearances*.' Celeste let herself smile at the thought. 'At least on a first meeting.'

I didn't need to drop my eyes. I could meet her gaze, though my belly and chest felt tight.

'You were alone a long time if your book's to be believed,' she said, peering hard at me. 'Don't try to convince me that's not your direct story. It is and that's clear. Someone so shy usually has a few secrets worth investigating. I wonder if your books offer more clues?'

Everything around us seemed to stop. The air didn't move and the steam didn't rise out of our coffee mugs, and for me at least the world lost form. We simply continued to look at each other. Neither turned away.

And that was how Bruno Pasqua found us when he came into the apartment.

'What's this?' he asked, his tone gruff but good-natured.

'Getting to know each other over breakfast? I'm jealous as a caveman.'

He had bags under his eyes but seemed happy. From the way Celeste had spoken about him I expected her to jump to her feet with delight. Instead she turned towards him slowly, lost in thought. She glanced at me again, then brightened, or made herself brighten, and went to him. Celeste helped him off with his coat and wrapped him in an entwining embrace, one of her slender legs curling around his.

'I ran into Jean-Philippe Le Souef at the salon last night,' Bruno Pasqua said to me over Celeste's shoulder. 'I tell you, more business is done in brothels than boardrooms. Le Souef is the second publisher we were meant to see. Another fool who doesn't recognise your promise. At least we don't have to waste time with him. So we've got the day off.'

Then he held Celeste and kissed her and she returned the kiss without shame. I couldn't help overhearing what she whispered. It wasn't in the scandalised voice of a lover but neither was it the curious voice of a child.

'You smell of beautiful women,' Celeste murmured, as if she couldn't wait to taste him.

After that morning I could conjure Celeste and her eyes without trying. I wandered all day, then tossed and turned in my bed until it was Saturday and the goatherds were shepherding their flocks through rue du Roi de Sicile and the adjacent streets, Archives and Quatre Jeune filles.

Bruno and Celeste must have been walking with the goats, because they soon stumbled into the apartment, bringing the daylight with them, drunk and laughing. I waited until they locked themselves into the main bedroom. Then I made myself ready to go out. I couldn't stay in that apartment with them and I didn't have a clue how I would pass the weekend. If anything, I wished I was home in Catania with Signora Rosa; Paris was for people like Bruno Pasqua – and Celeste was for men like him, no matter what sort of longing I felt when I pictured her.

You smell of beautiful women.

You taste of beautiful women.

And her red robe and long hair falling.

Bruno Pasqua had told me there were others like her at *The Gilded Cage,* but from our visit there together, and the visit to that smaller brothel back in Catania, I already knew Celeste was Celeste, and to try and replace her with someone else would be like replacing gold dust with sulphur.

I'd heard about the markets in the rue Mouffetard and tried to make myself believe I wanted to visit them. I also tried to make myself believe that I wanted to walk slowly and thought-fully through the museums and galleries that I discovered after a leisurely breakfast taken in a small dining hall. In reality I barely saw a thing. Images of long-dead people, of meaningless items, of endless bronzes in their imitation of life. Then I was heading up toward the observatory and through little streets full of rundown buildings stinking of poverty, following the map to Mouffetard. Children played among broken-roofed homes and threw loose cobblestones at one another in re-enactments of battles their fathers and uncles must have told them about. The area where Bruno had his apartment was by no means wealthy, but these streets and alleys reeked of the lowest rungs of Parisian existence.

Before coming to the market quarter I was conscious of the stench of the nearby cesspools. They had to find a way to accom-modate all the shit and piss of these people until the tank wagons came by at night.

A boy leaning against a broken wall stared at me. I walked down the street and just after I passed him he stepped out and walked behind me, saying something in French. I didn't need to understand the language to know he was asking for money. Two other boys jumped a wire fence to quickly walk in step beside me. At the next corner they grabbed my shoulders and pushed me out of common view, and a group of little boys playing nearby immediately squalled with excitement and followed us at a run into this narrow alley.

My arms were pinned and a punch to the belly was meant to knock the breath and fight out of me. A fist struck my cheek and then a meatier hand gave me a stronger blow. They thought I was done. Doubled over, I was leaning with my back against a stone wall. Hands were already scrabbling in my pockets. I raised my head, gasping for breath. The dirty face of someone much older than any of these boys was in front of me. He took my hair in his fist and pulled me forward, then made me fall and pushed my face into the ground. The boys gathered around, itching to kick me.

I reached up and took him by the wrist and squeezed until he let go of my hair. I kept squeezing and now I was twisting his arm. As I found my feet I pushed his arm back around and up almost to his shoulder blade. He was heavier than me and still fighting my grip, but his mouth was open wide in a grimace of pain. None of the boys tried to intervene. Their eyes said they liked a fight even more than a straight beating. I put my hand on this man's face and shoved him backwards so that he slammed against the wall. He stood there, breathing hard, eyes wide – I would have left it at that, but he was both infuriated and humiliated. Gathering his nerve he came at me swinging, but I struck him first. He collapsed with his eyes rolled up in his head and what remained of his nose spread across one cheek.

Everyone backed away. I didn't check my pockets; I didn't care if anything was missing. The boys around me were panting. Their excitement was electric. They knew what they'd seen but they couldn't quite believe it. No one spoke and neither did I. A part of me wanted the boys to call for their fathers and elder brothers.

Why should there be only one man bleeding on the ground? Let's have a massacre. Even these boys, why shouldn't I start snapping them in two?

I forced myself to walk out of the alley and continue to Mouffetard. The dirty street children lingered behind. The good grace of the day was broken and I spent two hours in a hovel of a bar with the midmorning's drunk men and women, all of whom stank as if they'd bathed in old wine.

On the way back to the apartment I skirted the direct route and passed via Saint-Germain-des-Prés, where I could find out about trains to Italy. I was tired of this trip and if I saw Celeste again I'd push her against a wall and put my hand between her thighs. I wanted to taste her; I wanted to penetrate every part of her. I knew how boorish I was, how much like a spoiled brat. Yet the feeling wouldn't be controlled and I had no desire to rein it in. Why shouldn't I take a woman like that exactly the way I wanted?

There was a departure at six fifteen a.m. the next morning, Sunday, and if I could just endure the Saturday night ahead I'd be on it.

Now I felt a certain coldness towards Bruno Pasqua. He could put it down to the fact that I'd turned out to be a country bumpkin, a dumb backwoods' prude disgusted by his liberal ways. A fake who wrote like a libertine but who lived like a monk.

However my feelings only had to do with him in relation to Celeste. Bruno had a beautiful wife and family, and he had her. He had a successful business and great writers, and he had her. He bent as many women as he wanted to his pleasure, and he still had her. He was free to use her body as much as he pleased, and he also sent her manuscripts, and so he possessed both her flesh and her mind.

Some moments it seemed clear what to do: leave the country then secretly return to Paris after Pasqua was gone, find her at *The Gilded Cage* and give her enough money that I could take her to a locked room. Offer her cash to open her mouth and her legs and cry out my name.

Those moments of clarity were fleeting. In truth I didn't know what to do with my feelings. They were new and they frightened and excited me at the same time. Veronica had made me aware of my sexual appetite, but Celeste affected me in a different way. I longed for her body, yes, but a greater part of me wanted something else entirely. It was just as Domenico had said: *There's love and pain in equal measure, and people, they seem to be at their finest when they seek these things out.* When I thought of her, I thought I was a better man. Or that I could be better. Someone deeper, with truer feelings. And I wanted to touch more than her skin; I wanted her mind and heart.

Celeste should be reading *my* manuscripts; she should have *my* thoughts inside her head.

My words should be the ones to make her want to eat and to fuck and to dance.

My words to make her think of me.

They were concerned about the state of my face, but once I convinced them it wasn't all that bad Bruno stopped talking about a doctor and wanted to interest me in the evening's festivities. He didn't care if I looked like a boxer after a losing fight. He tried to apply an antiseptic medicament to my face but Celeste took over. She tended to me, and it was nothing like Signora Rosa's care or any of the other nurses I'd known. I'd never experienced a touch so velvety as Celeste's fingertips on my bruises and torn skin. I wished I'd been beaten worse, like some animal, so she'd have to give me even more attention. I wished Bruno Pasqua would go away. He was talking some tripe about a masked ball and now I saw him as an empty head who played the thrilling sexual adventurer. How pathetic he was. The disgust in my battered face must have been as clear as the bruises and lumps.

I barely heard what he said anyway. Celeste was just out of her bath and the red robe was loosely belted around her narrow waist. Inside her wide sleeves her white skin again seemed to me to be like snow, but not cold; she held the promise of warmth. Her knees; the barely visible, intricate tracing of veins at her wrists. Her hair was out and wet at the tips. Rosewater scent.

'None of this suits you Cesare, and if that's the way then all right,' Pasqua said, but not without a touch of sympathetic humour. 'With the masks there'd be nothing to stop you taking whoever you want. The only limitation would be your own energy. But if you don't want to join us, keep living like an aesthete.'

He was a satyr, a strange combination of artist, intellectual and peasant. Celeste left my bedside and was getting herself ready, but when she heard me tell Bruno Pasqua that I had a ticket for the morning train she returned to my door and said, 'And I can imagine you're not coming back. You hate it here don't you? You hate us all.'

This time my silence wasn't for being tongue-tied but for all the things I wanted to say and couldn't. There was a curious expression in her eyes. An even more curious expression came into Bruno Pasqua's face – but he was worldly enough to take stock and conceal it.

'What is it? Do you think he's hurt worse than it looks?'

Celeste searched for words that didn't come. Something was dawning inside her and I had no idea what it was.

'We've never met before . . .?'

'You read his books and I suppose they've stayed with you,' Bruno interrupted her. 'So you think you know him.'

He took her hand in a proprietorial grasp and now I knew that he understood my desire for his woman. What he didn't know was what thoughts were or weren't in her own mind.

'You really won't stay for our meetings, Cesare?' Bruno asked briskly. 'Monday and Tuesday. They'll be quick and then our work will be done. It *is* your future.'

I shook my head.

The man observed me for a moment, simply observed me. Then with that firm grip of ownership he led Celeste into their bedroom and shut the door. I heard their sounds. In all likelihood he wanted me to hear them. I imagined him stinking of other women and ravishing her with violence. The man was a king and I was a clown. My thoughts wouldn't let me be, and I dreamed of smashing down the door.

The rest of the apartment wasn't so much empty without Celeste as it was dead. I thought about a final walk around the city to do *something*, to occupy my mind, but once I'd eaten and packed my bag for the morning train the side of my head continued to throb and the lump on my cheek seemed to have a heartbeat. A quarter bottle of Bruno Pasqua's whisky didn't help, so I downed what was left in a flask of brandy.

I fell asleep thinking, *Thank God I'm leaving this place*, then I dreamed of stinking cesspools and drunken louse-ridden bodies singing wartime songs. An old street-witch with pendulous breasts said, 'You'll never have your own woman so why not give a *sou* for my cunt?' The me of milky skin and no face was standing behind her, fucking blindly and without passion, then he picked apart her spine and took out her heart, which was a dripping sack of wine.

Finally I was able to open my eyes. My pulse was racing. I wasn't alone. A naked woman in a gaudy theatrical mask of fake jewels and glitter was sitting on the bedside and she was gazing at me, as she'd been doing for some time.

It's always interesting to watch the way a stranger sleeps, don't you think?

There was no scent of perfume or soap, only of her skin, damp with perspiration. She didn't move closer. The moonlight entering the window was the only light she wanted. Slowly I discerned the shine of her eyes behind the slits of the ridiculous mask. Long hair was draped over one shoulder and fell over her white full breast. Her hips were slim; her skin had a honey glow and would taste the same.

Celeste didn't speak. I didn't know where Bruno Pasqua was. He could have been in the apartment or out fucking somewhere else. I didn't care. I didn't need to ask Celeste what she was doing here; her body spoke. For whatever reason I was in her mind as much as she was in mine. Not a time for talk, only for drinking her in. I could see that she liked the way I didn't let words intrude.

Silence is so much more exciting.

The rise and fall of Celeste's breast and the walls turn to vapour.

Celeste's skin glows but she only wants me to look into her hazel eyes.

She stops when she wants to stop then she's under me and I lift her mask.

I opened my eyes onto a grey morning of gorgeous rain, in a fifth floor flat on the rue Saint Louis en L'Ile, in a building that dated to the 1550s. I rolled over and pulled Celeste to me. This was how it had been for weeks.

Other than Celeste, Signora Rosa was the only person who knew that instead of taking the morning train to the French–Italian border that Sunday, I'd simply walked across the nearby bridge, Pont Marie, carrying my bag. I had an address that I was to find and a borrowed key that I could use. Two small rooms, a bath, a kitchen and a new water closet installed down the hall. The finery of a young woman. Clean plates and cutlery and glasses, flowers in vases, Peppermint tea. Bed linen and pillows touched by her skin and hair.

That Sunday, I put my head down and dreamed where she dreamed, but it wasn't enough.

That Sunday, hours and hours of sitting and waiting.

Books on her table, piled in corners, absently pushed under the bed. They were all in French except for something in Catalan. A night awake at every sound, still waiting.

Monday she turned up at noon, finally having escaped her paramour. She had to bathe before we could lie together, to get him off her, his touch, his spit, his semen. Hours spent lying in the bright afternoon sunshine of her rooms then she was gone again. Veronica was forgotten. Celeste, my second woman. No, my first. Veronica no longer existed.

She couldn't return until Pasqua's train had departed, then she ran — ran! — to me, breathless and excited, falling to her knees and devouring me as if she hadn't had a man in months or years. I was reborn, heartaches, troubles, loneliness, all gone. Only Celeste and her hands and her mouth and getting out of her clothes all at the same time.

These rooms were her private world. Bruno Pasqua had never been here, nor any man who'd paid for her. Once or twice there had been men she'd loved, but never to stay, to sleep.

'Then why me?'

Her eyes said, *Yes, why you, Cesare?*

It curbed my jealousy a little. Pasqua had never experienced life with her here. This was ours. He'd never slept in her bed or woken up sharing her pillow. One hundred other beds and one hundred other pillows, but not these.

'I'm not going back to work,' Celeste said.

'Good.'

'Maybe you won't want me for very long, because of Bruno and all the others.'

I brought her into her own living room. Sat her on the wooden dining table and parted her thighs. She wasn't acting when she shivered.

It was like this every day, punctuated by sleep, food and long trips into Parisian streets and quarters which no longer enervated me. Very little talk. We hadn't spoken that first night she'd come to my bed in her mask; we'd made our plans with so few words it was as if we read signals in our skin.

Celeste had Bruno Pasqua's collection of new manuscripts to work on. He liked to send her one or two a month. She wrote reports on good points and bad and suggested things that might be improved or reconsidered. It wasn't her job to do this with every book that passed through his hands, only those he was in two minds about. Mine had remained his pet projects; Celeste understood why. Ironic that our longest conversation so far was about him.

'He was a slave in that family of his. Love and hate between father and brothers. They sailed and fished; he dreamed. Love and hate also for the island and sea. He escaped like the boy in your book. Into the north. They hunted him and beat him and dragged him home. He escaped again and made his life the way he wanted it. Decades to reconcile. That's what he sees in what you write. Himself, his family, his homeland. That's why he goes back so often.'

'I won't,' I said. 'I'll never go back.'

'Never's too long.'

'Then what's next?'

'What do you think?'

'You and me,' I told her.

'How?'

'In whichever way you want.'

'What if I change my mind and decide I really do like to please men and be paid?'

'You worked in the salon and didn't need my permission, so why look for it now?'

'I can open myself to any man I want?'

'If you don't do what you want then who are you?'

'You'll stay if I do and you'll stay if I don't?'

'One or the other, yes. But I have an alternative to offer.'

We moved to the bed. She relaxed back. I gazed into those eyes, hazel with tiny motes you could see if you looked closely.

'Tell me about this alternative,' she said and she slid me into a beautiful place no one would pay for again.

'I'll tell you. Whenever I look at you there's no more world.'

'And?'

'And that's how we live. Inside a circle that's for us. Outside of it wars go on, men fight, politicians lie and all the good people of the world continue to be robbed blind.'

She was panting, urging me to go in harder. I moved more slowly.

Celeste squeezed her eyes shut and said, 'Women go on doing the bidding of men and slaves try to get free and promises last no longer than the time it takes to make them.'

'Except in our circle.'

'How will we eat?'

'My books might give us money.'

'And I've got savings,' she sighed. 'I can sell the jewellery my *amants* lavished on me.'

'No, give it away, burn everything, throw it all out, that'll be better.'

'Everything must go.'

'Yes. And we stay.'

'You and me.'

'You've got one man.'

'I'll have to dress in rags for him.'

'Why dress at all?'

Fools could sell their souls and give their fortunes for her but I'd only had to find a road out of hell. She gazed ahead into her own eyes in the mirror. The glass vibrated. She didn't want me to stop; I didn't want anything to be different to the way we were today, and didn't think to ask myself why.

Small cheques arrived from Bruno Pasqua's company, redirected to me by Rosa, but they weren't enough. The book wasn't selling and he hadn't been able to interest publishers in other countries, France included. I didn't care. I went and found myself work. It was an easy thing to get a common job for a week or a month, and make the most of the sun and air. No labour was going to hurt me, whether it was with the stonemasons or on construction sites, the marble cutters or the gravediggers. Some employers paid well and others were miserly as ticks. Some work offered good clean effort with sweat and exertion, and some like the grave-digging kept me ankle- and knee-deep in mud and bogs.

The cheques, Celeste's savings, the piecemeal odd jobs: we ate well enough and went out when we wanted, drinking wine in cafés and taverns, sitting in movie houses and watching all the latest pictures and newsreels. When it came to dances or glittering clubs Celeste wasn't interested. She went from taking a line of men in a single night, to me. Her friendships moved from lovely women and glamorous lesbians, to me. She was happy to forget fat wallets and expensive gifts and preferred to greet me as I was, caked in mud, sweat and grime, at the end of every working day.

I discovered she had no friends, no confidantes, no family. Her work had been her life, and her flat with its books and manuscripts, her sanctuary.

One evening as I was coming up the stairs a man I didn't know was coming down the other way. He was dressed well enough but I smelled the meat and black blood of him.

'What is it? Who was that man?'

'He said my vacation's gone on long enough. If I don't come back to work by Friday there'll be trouble.'

I took the spiral staircase two steps at a time and didn't catch up with him until I saw him crossing the street towards the back of Notre Dame. We were in the grounds and with the element of surprise I was able to push him away from passers-by and forward into a copse of trees. I slapped his piggish cheeks. His knife glinted but it was useless at his feet before it could do its job. His eyes bulged. I held him by his fat throat hard against the tree trunk, the dappled leaves like musical notes in the golden rays of the sun.

'She won't come back,' I whispered to his ear.

The man was passing into unconsciousness and I let him slide down. I crouched with him so that we remained face to face. As he gasped, his colour returned and he came back to life. I straightened his collar but loosened his tie, readjusted his vest and rebuttoned it where it had come open.

He started to take me in. I picked up his knife and opened his coat. A leather scabbard in his armpit. I slid in the thin, razor-sharp blade and clipped the handle in place. This man saw nothing but a dirty, grimy, sweaty boy. A boy of no standing. I could see what was in his eyes. It wasn't hatred, only the knowledge of what he was going to do.

'What's your name?' I asked him.

He wouldn't answer.

I spat in his face and left him sitting in the dust.

Celeste bathed and fed me and we held each other all the way through the night. In the morning I rose and stretched, but only to make coffee. I didn't get ready to go out to work. I wasn't going to leave her. We stayed in all day, then as evening fell went out to bars where we drank too much and forgot our troubles. Dinner was in a small kitchen full of the lonely and forgotten. Down by the Seine we strolled along the quays where prostitutes sucked and jerked their clients and more men came along looking for their relief. I wondered if this was where Celeste had her start. I didn't ask. We didn't talk. Silence was all we needed between us and it was right and the way we had to be.

When we slept I kept a small axe and a wood-handled machete by the bed. The door was locked and barricaded with a propped chair. I'd scattered crumpled newspaper pages around the floor so that any creeping footsteps would wake me. We knew that soon we would find a new home; this one was tainted. We'd go somewhere we'd never be found, into the provincial countryside maybe, think about settling in some picturesque little town. Maybe we ought to have left already, but in those days I had too much confidence in my abilities, I was too arrogant to be afraid of anyone.

Two or three times I snapped straight awake; later I dreamed I had no eyes. In my dream the man with the piggish cheeks and fat neck finally came calling, but I couldn't see him at all. He didn't arrive with other men and he didn't burst in through the door, but he was here as smoke which seeped through the cracks of the floors and the walls and the doors. He filled the stairwell and he passed into our rooms, running his fingers through our hair and lingering over Celeste's sleeping face. Let me see you, I told him. Then I was awake and choking in the dark and I grabbed Celeste by the arms and rolled her out of the bed onto the floor. That man had done his work – she lolled like a ragdoll and I found her face and slapped her but she only murmured and was very still again.

There was no light. I kept us low, but the floorboards were hot with the fire rising from below. It was black and acrid in these rooms and my eyes were burning, my chest already constricted. I couldn't see where to go or where anything was. Now the crackling and cooking filled my ears, and as the fire intensified it actually glowed through the smoke; finally I saw the outline of our front door in an aura of red, and that's how I knew where not to go, to not even try to get out that way.

I dragged Celeste with me, but the only thing I could do was to stand, and that was worse because now my head was enveloped in the dizzying smoke. I threw Celeste over my shoulder and ran towards the indistinct radiance of the windows and when I kicked the first set open there was an instant whoosh of thunder and storms and the rooms ignited.

We'd tumbled like fallen puppets to a lower adjoining roof where neighbours were already helping people through their windows, out of the blaze. Someone had quickly thrown an overcoat over Celeste's hair and put the fire out. Two people were dead: a forty-nine-year-old bachelor and a grandmother living alone. Both from floors below us.

When the doctors at the Pitié-Salpêtrière hospital continued their lung capacity tests, they found I'd regained normal functioning in only a matter of days. In fact, my lungs appeared to be better than normal. Incredulous, a group of doctors wanted to keep looking me over, discussing various elite athletes, professional Tour de France bicyclists whom they knew approached my capacity. I shied away for obvious reasons but there was something else too: the hospital made my skin crawl. In a whispery voice Celeste explained its name. In Pitié-Salpêtrière's original incarnation its buildings had been a gunpowder factory, then a prison for prostitutes. Twin revulsions for me.

The doctors would tap my chest and back and say things like:

'What a constitution!'; 'The development!'; 'Do you have any idea how lucky the both of you are?'

Celeste coughed up more black sputum than me and seemed to be in worse condition, but it wasn't very long before the doctors came to like Celeste's recuperative powers even more than mine. The words 'miracle' or 'miraculous' were used, then dropped. Instead I saw raw confusion, curiosity, and an acute concentration in their frequent ministrations. All of which set me to thinking.

Sometimes I'd watch Celeste carefully, looking for signs, but what signs could there be? I tried to remember everything that Domenico had told me.

Yes, Celeste said, she'd always been lucky, could barely remember more than two or three occasions of illness.

What was her background, what was her story? We spoke about it even though words between us remained mostly unnecessary.

Celeste only vaguely remembered parents, or the possibility of parents. At some indefinite age she was thrown into a family of drunkards in Montparnasse. Sexual abuse was a daily occurrence and she escaped to the street. Disease, bad pregnancies and winters took the girls she only knew by sight. Replacements would arrive to keep street corners and alleys well serviced. What saved her from this life was an older gentleman, a widower named Auger who took her home and kept her like a daughter – and a wife. His affection continued into her late teens, when she decided she didn't need a lover and a mentor and could strike out on her own. She wanted to work in the *maisons closes*. It was her choice.

Other girls had unwanted babies, abortions, miscarriages. Had she?

Not once. In fact, Celeste had decided long ago that there must be something wrong with her insides.

No words, but her face told me that she needed to know if her inability to bear children made me love her less.

I loved her more.

So were these the reasons our bond had come so fast and hard? Had we recognised one another without knowing it? Whatever the answer was, Domenico was a part of myself I'd lost, and now fortune had brought me Celeste Auger.

She still couldn't be moved, and lack of funds meant I had to take a box-shaped, windowless room in a fleapit hotel. The man who'd done this to us was Jean-Claude Batiste, proprietor of The Gilded Cage, part-owner of three more brothels, and personal friends with the type of powerful men who preferred to keep his friendship rather than see justice done. One day on my way to the hospital there was a blank space before my eyes and then I realised I was in a store looking at rags and tins of gasoline and tied packets of twigs and bundles of hardwood.

I slouched out and was by Celeste in her hard cot in minutes. We needed to get out of the hospital, move from Paris, start somewhere new. Time was confounding me and sometimes I felt I was being turned inside out. I remembered the dream I'd had when I'd taken Thunder up into the cold mountains, of the thing inside me boiling up with a rage that didn't want to be *kept down*. Celeste would look up at me with her grey eyes and her hair in tufts on her blistered skull: Where are you, Cesare? What are you doing?

Not me. It's the other.

I slept in my dismal room with him looking over me; often I'd close my eyes and dream by Celeste's cot; days and nights melted together and I was no longer sure if I was myself or the faceless thing walking in my shadow.

Then my eyes opened and Bruno Pasqua stepped forward from out of a corridor where he'd been speaking to one of Celeste's regular doctors. Without a word he put train tickets into my hands and leaned over the bed and kissed and touched Celeste's cheek. His hard palm hovered over her scalp, but didn't touch the ragged hair or ruined skin. His tenderness seemed to swell in a wave through him and I saw his face melt and his eyes glitter. In her dream Celeste murmured something. He turned to me.

'Half of me wants to let his friends finish you off. The other half, to inform the police.'

He took a folded daily from his overcoat and threw it at me. Amid world events was a photograph of The Gilded Cage's blackened remains. The proprietor Batiste's body had been found in the rubble with a butcher's knife in its neck.

'The lies. Stealing my Celeste. And to put your name on a dead man's work.' Bruno Pasqua nodded at me. 'I kept going to Signora Rosa until she let me see the room where you used to write. I perused your papers. I looked through the manuscripts by this gentleman Domenico Amati, rewritten by you. I'd been trying to find you to let you know the news. *Il Dio* has been awarded the best newcomer's award in the Alighieri Prize. In quick succession it was also recognised for best Italian fiction of the year. Two prestigious awards, and look at you. Who will go to collect these honours with his head held high, you with your artifice or me with my contempt for everything you stand for?'

He didn't like to look at me. He could only take in Celeste.

'What stops me from ruining you is her. She possesses more integrity than you'll ever understand. The young woman loves you, that much is clear. I won't break her heart for the sake of my own gratification. I'll keep your dirty secrets. But that means my obligation to you, Cesare Montenero, is through – and your books will turn to dust. To my last breath, I'll ensure they never see the light of day again.'

Celeste was returning, eyes fluttering.

I thrust the newspaper back at the man.

'Why show me this?'

Bruno Pasqua frowned for a moment. His eyes flicked to my hands. I followed his gaze. I smelled them. A last trace of gasoline.

Not me. It was that other self, the one holding all the rage, the one that —

And I saw the creature by the shadow of a wall as Bruno Pasqua bent and kissed Celeste one more time, before she was completely awake. Then Pasqua dusted his coat and the ashes of my books and life fell away from him.

Someone did attend the awards ceremonies, and proudly at that. Two small plaques now stood on Signora Rosa's mantelpiece. Two modest cheques were deposited into my bank account. I had this money wired to the chief accountant of Bruno Pasqua's firm, a small restitution.

There was a moment of newspaper and journal interest, but Bruno Pasqua wrote a heartfelt statement to explain that the esteemed young writer Cesare Montenero had returned to the *mezzogiorno* of his youth, due to sadly failing health. The worst was to be expected. Soon the matter was forgotten; the world had more important affairs at hand. The two awards created a spike of interest in bookstores and soon Bruno Pasqua's warehouse was finally cleared of titles by Cesare Montenero. These never appeared again; this man who I'd betrayed on every possible level kept his promise.

We passed through Catania. Rosa showed me a clipping of one of the award dinners. She was holding up the plaque for the camera.

'But they made a mistake, Cesare, look, they wrote that I'm your mother.'

'It wasn't a mistake,' I told her, and we finally held one another hard and found it difficult to let go.

Before Celeste and I left the city, Rosa asked where we'd go and what we'd do. I didn't have an answer. Celeste had recovered and her hair was growing back, but we had no money or prospects. Current events proved that the world itself seemed intent on destroying everyone's future.

'Then it's time I told you. Domenico mightn't have left a will, but he was no fool. When he sold the Amati property he created a bequest and made me the trustee. The government might have seized his country house and his financial accounts but this account has always been in your name, overseen by me. Investments have been favourable. His wish was that when the time was right I should hand it over. He wanted you to live first, to make your way. He wanted you to see what sort of a man you could be. I think now you know.'

I knew, all right.

I knew the man I was, and of course still am. One's sins and wickedness don't fade with time.

Signora Rosa passed me a fortune.

The Amati family sustaining Celeste and me into the future. I couldn't tell if this was an irony that ought to be repugnant or simply the most cynical turn possible. Then I remembered it, a moment just before Domenico died: *There's a lot of money, just waiting . . .*

I covered my face and cried. Celeste held me.

Around us the world had moved from a sort of crazed optimism into encroaching despair. Governments fell and economies crashed. Enmities between nations grew into flashpoints and, by the time German troops marched into Paris and the new premier Reynaud was entreating all free men to come to the aid of France, we were gone.

We travelled far from Europe. We were in Cuba, then Mexico. We were as lost as everyone else, but my Celeste found our way.

Black Book (ii)

I WATCHED MY WIFE WALK in her bare feet across the deep lawn as the sun finally began to sink into the orange horizon. She never overdressed for any occasion, but at every occasion she drew the eye. This evening she was in a new white silk dress, low-necked but not tawdry, sleeveless but not without elegance. It was her own party and she could be barefoot if she wanted to, even if this was scandalous to some of the region's older matriarchs. The younger ones, the wives in their twenties and thirties, even some in their late teens, implored their husbands with their usually complaisant eyes, wanting for once to rebel, and those who were allowed to shed their shoes as well, walking or dancing lightly over our lawns as if they'd been freed to expose the happiest part of their hearts.

These were our friends, or should I say they were Celeste's friends. In all the years nothing had changed and I suffered people and groups badly. If anything I was growing more into my old brother of the soul Don Domenico Amati than some genial middle-aged gentleman farmer. At least I'd learned the art of pretence. I endured these occasions and sometimes even created these occasions – such as the present party – not for my own benefit but for Celeste's. And these events always delighted her. The difference between us wasn't so much of literal age but that she seemed so unaffected by the passage of entire decades.

Though we were celebrating her fortieth birthday Celeste

could pass for ten years less. In her soul and with her smile, she made even the youngest farmers' wives seem positively ancient. Which, given their arduous lives and the number of children they bred and continued to breed, they already were. For ourselves, Domenico's words from so long ago proved true: we couldn't have offspring.

The country breeze was scented by pots and beds of wild herbs, by our great jacarandas, by hibiscus and silky oak trees and the flowering boabs. I took a fresh glass of champagne from a passing tray and the local state member was telling me and a group of not-so-interested husbands about his plans for a new bill to provide our region with covered roads. These roads would surely cause an influx of families and new businesses – boom days were ahead.

I listened without listening. Streams of multicoloured lights were strung among the trees, and the house was lit from within so that it resembled some kind of seductive pleasure palace. Swing music was being made by a twelve-piece orchestra on a specially constructed dais and Celeste danced over the deep green with an oafish farmer with a great belly. His suit had been purchased for him before the war and looked it. Celeste's hair swung. She managed to make the man seem just that little bit elegant of foot.

There was applause and some laughter as they finished. Ben Packard made a bow with his hand over his belly as if to keep it in. Everyone watched Celeste, a radiant star in this milieu of big-hearted, broad-backed, craggy-faced country folk.

Two of the six pillars of the land in this group glanced at me. One touched my elbow and said it was always such a pleasure to see how happy my wife was. I never had any doubts about the genuine quality of the warmth with which our neighbours and my fellow farmers treated me. They were country folk, and the men probably didn't feel any different to me when it came to social situations. They certainly looked uncomfortable in their church clothes and spit-polished shoes, their hair slicked back with oil. I'm sure they would rather have been riding a tractor or hoeing a field. Parties and gatherings and local hall dances were all well and good, and so were friendly one-set Sunday afternoon tennis matches, but these diversions served the interests of women and small children – not of men with the weight and worries of the world on their shoulders.

And this was how I was different to my neighbours. I had no concerns over money. I'd purchased extremely well almost twenty years back, and my holding of nine hundred acres was more profitable and productive than ever. The workers here received the best conditions in the region and I was very much like the Don Domenico of old, barely interested in the running of my land as long as I had good people to do it for me.

My fellow farmers, the heads of the largest families, weren't so lucky. Many of them had established or extended their acquisitions with too much credit and so were mortgaged to the hilt. It was hard to be so conspicuously privileged around these good folk, but the Montenero couple didn't wear their wealth or keep high profiles. Celeste with her friendship and willingness to always lend a hand tended to keep, I thought, any simmering envy at bay.

Tonight we had lights and burning torches set up in the gardens at the front and to the side of the house so that the party could continue through the night. The musicians and their leader – Jimmy Raven and His Fabulous Twelve Piece Orchestra – were booked till one a.m. They stayed making music until just after three. Some of our neighbours took things too far and we found them snoring under trees or on the verandah. Celeste circulated; then she found me and swayed with me to some playful Frank Sinatra tune. Dew had settled over the grass. Still no one wanted to leave. She nuzzled my ear lobe, and when she said, in Italian, 'Who would have thought it, Cesare?' I knew what she meant.

Such happiness between two people like us, such good times.

Yet when she fainted in my arms I immediately heard Domenico's voice again, and one more time he was telling me about the problems with the new people, why the program had failed: *There has been a predisposition towards cancers, though there have been other unexpected problems too.*

We learned it was in her pancreas. A week later we were informed that the disease had advanced through multiple organs.

Celeste spoke with a smile, 'I've worn out everything worthwhile, haven't I?'

Alone with me, her doctor said, 'She must have been in awful pain for a long time. How did she cope? Why wasn't your wife hospitalised?'

Domenico had hung on, Doctor Kristof Vliegan had endured his illness for years, but even I could see that Celeste was disappearing fast. I made furious calls all over the world, desperate for the first time to find the men who'd created our lives. It had never crossed my mind to do this before, to make contact with those who'd set us on this path and who'd then abandoned us to what we were. Someone would have to know how and where my wife could be restored to health. If she'd been stronger, if there'd been the hope that she wouldn't expire while I was away, I would have been on flights to research facilities in Europe, China, the Soviet Union.

But I couldn't even find them, identify them. What chance was there? I had the names of a few men long deceased: Vliegan, Bortolotti, even the Amatis – all gone. I didn't have a clue who or what I needed to be looking for.

Things turned worse and Celeste had to stay in the hospital. When I wasn't there I was in my home refusing to sleep, trying to find answers. Some solution, anything.

How? How?

Twenty telephone calls and four nights to find out that Signora

Rosa was still alive. That in itself didn't give me much hope, but I immediately rang the nursing home outside Florence that I'd tracked her down to. A staff member told me she was sitting up, her wheelchair facing a picture window.

'She's of very advanced years, sir, and feeling each of them.'

The line was clear enough to offer silence. Then her voice came, scratchy as a well-loved 78 RPM record.

'They say it's Cesare? No! Is it?'

An ancient woman's deafness wouldn't allow her to hear me. We couldn't speak properly. We needed an intermediary, a nurse who faithfully related information in both directions.

'Sir? She's crying. But it seems with happiness.'

'Let her know I'm happy too, to speak with her.'

'Sir? She's asking about someone named Celeste.'

And so I explained.

There was the silent air of eternity.

'Sir? I have to put down the telephone. She wants me to get something for you.'

The receiver was placed on some hard surface but I heard it being fumbled up. I imagined old Rosa taking it, pressing it to her ear and mouth.

'Cesare,' I heard her say, though she heard nothing in return. 'Nothing can help you or Celeste, but there's been contact, the thing's not dead, someone came to see me so you make what you can of it.'

'Are you still there, sir? I think it must be a telephone number. I'm not sure which country the prefix signifies. Or the city code. But are you ready?'

I wrote it down carefully.

'Tell Rosa that Cesare – tell Rosa that *her son* Cesare thanks her for every bit of life inside him. Tell it to her exactly as I said it. "Her son Cesare. Every bit of life inside him."'

I heard the nurse pass the message on. Spoken loudly and

beautifully in formal Italian. There was no return message though I heard a muffled weeping.

Then I hung up and dialled the number.

The woman who answered the call didn't announce the name of a business or company or family or person. There was simply a disconnected sort of 'Yes?' in English.

So I spoke English as well.

'Signora Rosa Bortolotti, who used to live in Catania, Sicilia, gave me this number to call. My name is Cesare Montenero and I'm a friend of Domenico Amati and the Amati family. I want to speak with someone please.'

'Repeat the names, thank you.'

I did.

'Which doctor would you like to speak with?'

'I don't know. What is this place, is it a hospital?'

'You don't have a specialist's name?'

'No but —' I thought it over quickly. 'The matter has to do with cancer.'

'Your name is Amati?'

'No. Montenero. Cesare Montenero.'

'You'll have to wait. It could be some time.'

It was as if she was about to transfer me but the line went dead. Absolutely dead.

When I tried the number again the bitch didn't reply. Every hour thereafter it rang out. No local or international operator service could or would tell me who or what the number related to. The only unassailable fact was that the code prefixes placed the number in Shanghai.

By the next day the number wasn't even ringing. There was only the heavy burr of a dead and disconnected line.

★

The spread and effect of the disease was cruel, the treatments worse, and after only a little time the doctors were saying the best they could offer Celeste was increased doses of medication to mask the pain. They remarked on her ability to deal with what in other people would have been unbearable agony. Imagining this my eyes were often shut, closing out the sights, the words, the terrors. In effect I could almost make myself insensate as a stone. Maybe this response was something ingrained into me: a way for soldiers in hopeless situations to deal with the inevitability of what came next. I had no way of knowing.

When Celeste returned home she was thin yet always exquisite. She wanted to make love, so we did. She slept a lot then passed away two days later, on a Tuesday, a nothing day, at a nothing time, just before eleven a.m. She was forty years of age. The sun was shining, and in the intense summer heat insects were legion. The dogs played but mostly they found shade and cool water to drink while the surrounding lands were in a state of fecund prosperity. I held Celeste's hand. It weighed nothing. She was in our bed and her eyes were closed and her mouth was a little open. I kissed her lips, which hadn't yet lost their warmth. Her skin was parched and her soft cheeks had hollowed. The way she lay there resembled a beautiful dress laid out on a bed, waiting to be filled. That was my Celeste, what was left of her.

'Where have you gone?' I asked, and a vision came to me.

Celeste was by the open French doors. She let her yellow dress fall, revealing her firm small breasts and her lithe body. She turned to show me her glorious ass but she had wings too, long, gorgeous wings, and she was about to leave.

'You have to take me with you. You can't leave without me.'

'Not this time,' she smiled, the devilment of old in her eyes, 'but come here and give me a kiss.'

I went to her and she wrapped me in her arms. She kissed my neck and I kissed her forehead.

'Don't be sad,' she said, her Italian always accented by her French. 'We're far from alone.'

She struggled a little against me because I wouldn't let her fly, then I had to give in, and I and the faceless man standing beside me both saw she was gone.

A nurse was downstairs, having arrived to perform her daily assessment of Celeste's vital signs and to help with her intake of nutrients and fluids. Before I called her up to the bedroom, I cut a large lock of Celeste's hair from layers underneath so it wouldn't be too noticeable.

What else?

I used the scissors to cut her toenails and stored them with the curl of hair in a small plastic container she'd used to hold her spare buttons.

And then?

Just a pinprick. I had to squeeze drops from her fingertip, all the while telling her I was sorry for doing this to her. I used a clean glass vial and stoppered it tightly.

Hair, toenails and a few drops of blood. The last of her and everything of her in the past and the now and in the future.

The literal meaning of words is always contentious, what their real intent is, what they're meant to say. *You'll have to wait. It could be some time.* That woman in Shanghai could have mentioned just how long the wait would be.

Several weeks after the cremation, my telephone rang and some premonition told me it wouldn't be a neighbour, or a real estate agent promising what price he could get me for my landholding.

'You know me as Kristof Vliegan, though I don't often use

that name, but Kristof Vliegan is who I am,' the voice said in Italian. Then he added with some humour, 'the third'.

I could hear the crackle and echo of an international telephone line.

'It must be seven in the morning where you are? Not too early?' he asked.

I assured him it wasn't.

'Here it's late and the end of another long day, but we don't stick to nine-to-five in this line of work.'

I suggested that there'd be no way I could know what the line of work he referred to might be.

'It's all right, Cesare, we can speak freely. This line is unencumbered. Of course I couldn't speak to you on that number you used. We have to be so careful. There's political espionage as well as industrial. Both, to be frank, stink to high heaven.'

I could hear the combined amusement and seriousness in his voice. This was a happy and motivated individual, a man in love with the world and his place in it, no doubt about it.

'You knew the previous version of me very well. I'm sure you remember. You also destroyed that poor beast he'd pinned some impossible hopes upon. Still, you never know what can happen. My originating Vliegan-self took his own life, but technology has marched on. Thankfully I've come back in a thoroughly better manner. This present incarnation is really very good.'

It couldn't have been more obvious exactly how good. 'You remember who you were?' I asked.

'Not at all. So I'm constantly reading about myself. The funny thing is, the first me was little more than a middle-level medical functionary, but I've moved myself quite a way up the ladder. You could even say I've become responsible for some significant tranches of our research and production. But let's not concern ourselves with any of that right now, we can discuss it one day when we meet.'

'We won't meet.'

'Why not?'

'I don't have any interest in this part of my life. Or yours.'

'We-ell,' Vliegan hummed, 'it would be a mistake to get too far ahead of ourselves. Now. I don't know anything about you other than what I've researched in the files and been briefed about. But this question of memory you brought up a moment ago is important. In fact, it's the next wave. We're working on ways to move memory and consciousness on, into future generations of new people. It may not be all that far away.'

'And then it'll be like living forever.'

'Absolutely. We don't care about the warring any more. We care about Life. That's where the market trended. But the raw material's got to be good or it all goes wrong. Take me as an example: fabulous as I might be right now, soon enough I will succumb to Vliegan's cancer, and probably at a highly accelerated rate. I can't tell you what general aches and pains do to my psyche, I'm aways expecting the worst.'

'Then what do you want?'

'Well, first things first. How are you, Cesare Montenero? Strong?'

'Strong enough.'

'And never ill?'

'I had hayfever for a couple of seasons, but that went away.'

There was silence. Maybe he was noting that down. Then Vliegan's voice returned, crackling over the line.

'Let me get to the point. Celeste Auger died of cancer, correct? Consumed by it. I've had the records.'

'Yes, that's true.'

'And it was her cancer that caused you to want to make contact?'

'Yes.'

'We couldn't have saved her, Cesare. That would have been an absolute impossibility.'

'So why are you calling?'

'We can't use her as a base for a future line, which – I know, I know – is a terrible pity. I've seen photographs and heard reports. An extraordinary woman. May I offer you our condolences, even so late in the day?'

He waited for a reply that never came.

'But, Cesare, I can offer something a little better too. And hence one reason for my call. We could bring her back for another short span. Maybe you can have her in a virtual sense. You agree to give us what we need of you, and maybe one day a future Cesare and a future Celeste can get together.'

'But I'm healthy and she wasn't.'

'Yes, it'll always be a tragedy in the making.'

'Could I have her now?'

'What do you mean, as a baby? A child? You're a little too old to take on the role of a single father, and, em, to be clear, we would never agree to place a child into a situation where she might be . . . vulnerable. We're not the monsters who started this research. Nowadays we stick to scrupulous ethics.'

'But —'

'*But,*' he interrupted me, forming an idea that might always have been in his head, 'we could introduce you to her one day, that's true . . . when she's old enough, and, of course, if you're still alive. We *do* think you might go on some significant time.'

'She won't know me?'

'That's correct. The technology's not there yet. She'd be a young woman approaching her prime, and you, well, you'd be much, much older. I think you understand what the situation would be.'

'Then she'll die?'

'General humanity has to run on death as much as it does on life so she'll be no different to anyone else, really, but yes – like me, she'll succumb to what went before. And possibly with an even worse process, I'm afraid to say.'

We were quiet. Then this 'Vliegan the Third' spoke for me.

'I suppose you wouldn't want to subject her to that again, though of course by the time that came it's highly likely you wouldn't be around. We're working on solutions to many, many unforeseen problems but this one, well, it's always going to be the toughest nut to crack.'

'Then leave her. Please leave her be.'

I felt myself breaking. No hope, all loss. No point from the start of my life to its very end. Born alone and bred to die alone. All my chances had come and gone and none were going to reappear. I had to be thankful for the span I'd been allowed with my Celeste, brief as it felt.

'I'll give you anything you want, Vliegan, if you'll just leave her be. That's my wish. Let Celeste sleep.'

'Well, we don't need much from you. There's no need to upset yourself.'

He wanted to discuss further details, but I wasn't interested in the plans and the failures. Or the hopes, for that matter. Kristof Vliegan knew he had to cut to the chase.

'So we'd like to use you as the basis of a new family tree. If one day we can get this issue of memory right, to pass from one incarnation to the next, then we're home. The next versions of you won't have any recollection of the Cesare Montenero of today, but there should come a time when your strand's later generations will start to know the one that went before. Memory and being, that's our Grail. We'll call that eternal life, or close enough. This will happen beyond your time and mine, unfortunately, but what are we if we don't pass all that's good on to our future children?'

It was almost amusing how he chose the word 'children' when neither he nor I would ever procreate – but I understood his meaning.

'One last question, then I'll ring off. I can send a representative to your home within the week, but it really would be so much more helpful if you'd come visit us. He can make the arrangements and accompany you. Flying's quite pleasant these days.'

'No, I won't travel. I won't come to China.'

'Oh, we're nowhere near China. Shanghai simply provides us with a clearing-space for telecommunications. Impossible to track and trace. We're not in Italy any more either, if that's what's bothering you. My particular branch is located outside Basle, and it's quite beautiful this time of year. Or you could choose from one of our facilities in Japan's San'in-San'y region, or near Leningrad . . .'

'I don't want any part of it.'

'The records in front of me suggest that's exactly what you would say. You would refuse. Well, we've certainly got your personality right, haven't we?' He waited a moment. 'Are you really so certain?'

'You can have what you want and then that's done and over and you leave me alone.'

'Our code of ethics requires me to accept your final answer . . .'

'And there's something I want to be certain about.'

'Yes?'

'You said no part of this serves a war machine. Is that the truth?'

'Yes, it is.'

'Your code of ethics won't let you lie to me?'

'Well, given fundamental parameters of secrecy,' Vliegan said, sounding genuine. 'The militaristic aspects of research died almost immediately, relatively speaking. Our forebears came to the conclusion that soldiering was never going to work. You probably know more about that from your own experience of your life, Cesare, than I ever will. The new men simply wouldn't operate the way that had been hoped. Yes, there were predispositions toward extraordinary bravery, and warring, and an almost complete rejection of social needs, but it was all so wrong that everyone gave up hope. The entire project shifted a long time ago. We're on the people's wavelength now. Everything these days is health and youth and longevity, and that's what we're looking to provide.'

'If that's what people really want.'

'Take it from me, they do. No one wants to be outlived by anything anymore. I more than anyone here can understand that. It's easier to face the prospect of simply going on forever than to contemplate terminal oblivion.' He drew a deep breath. 'Cesare, you could make your years, your entire life in fact, more worthwhile by coming here and helping our research. Your experience of being. There's so much we could learn from you. Unfortunately, you're rather the last of your kind.'

'Good.'

'And there might still be changes ahead. The project might not have quite played itself out in you. The future, so to speak, isn't quite written yet.'

'It is. I'm done.'

'I'm not so sure. But as you wish,' he sighed. 'I must reiterate, we're not criminals or standover merchants. No one's going to force you into anything you don't want. However, there is one last thing I would like to ask.'

'Silence? You're more than guaranteed that.'

'No.'

'Money?'

'Unless you have access to a few billion US dollars. No, what I want to ask is that you remember the philosophy we've adopted these days.'

'What is it? "Fill the world with useless egoists who'll never die"?'

'Our motto: *From this hand to the next.*'

That sat uncomfortably with me; in Vliegan's context it was a bastardised variation on what Domenico had believed.

I told him, 'It should be: *This hand* is *the next.*'

Kristof Vliegan laughed a little. 'I'll pass it on to the troops, that's very funny.'

'It wasn't meant to be.'

'You know, the temperament you display is something of the tenor of things we've worked very hard to rid our new people of.'

'Then you should be very careful what you do with what you take from me.'

He laughed a little more. 'It's an idea, at that. But we're somewhat contrapuntal here, for want of a better term. We usually learn by doing the opposite of what's come before.'

There was a silence. It was the longest conversation I could remember having in entire decades.

'I want to ask you something, Cesare. One of the biggest problems we've always had to deal with is that of strange visions or fantasies brought on by pressure and tension. Have you experienced that?'

'Sometimes, but not enough to worry me. My friend Domenico suffered with it much more. He saw flying women.'

'Naked, I'll wager. That would be repressed sexuality, of course.'

'And a faceless milk-skinned man.'

'Really? How incredibly literal. The clay he was moulded from pushing its way to the fore.' The line was silent as Vliegan seemed to think about it. 'Well, what I wanted to say is, take care you don't let yourself come to believe in such things, Cesare. Their origins are simple. And we think it starts with the Amatis being not quite right.'

'Was Celeste from that family?'

'Oh, I don't know that and I wouldn't want to tell you if I did. I suspect, though, she was much later.'

Again there was silence. The time for talk was over. All I felt was an even greater loss; I couldn't help wishing that Celeste was still with me.

'You're still there, Cesare?'

'Yes.'

'I hope you take comfort from the fact that you've had a hand in giving the world a future that's never been brighter.'

'Goodbye, Doctor Vliegan. I'd prefer not to hear from you again.'

There was a momentary pause, a held breath. It was like the shroud of disappointment that had covered me so long ago, when I'd been the small rejected boy named Sette.

Then Kristof Vliegan said, 'Godspeed, Cesare,' and the line started to burr.

I could have made moved anywhere, of course, travelled far and wide, but what I decided to do was to stay where I was. My objective was to minimise human contact, hurt no one and forget everything and anything about my antecedents, not to mention entrepreneurial do-gooders like the new Kristof Vliegan.

As the doctor promised, a man came to visit me within a week of that telephone conversation. He was surprisingly young and arrived at the house without fanfare.

'Blackmore,' he introduced himself. 'Justin Blackmore. So pleased to meet you, sir.'

The boy was in a white hired sedan and he was neither tall nor short, light nor dark. Simply a neat young man without any particularly distinguishing characteristics, who might pass unremarked and unnoticed by customs agents and through airport terminals. His accent was neutral: he could have been German, Italian, British or North American.

With a new syringe he bled me of two vials of blood, sealed them, labelled them and packed them in ice. Then he produced a pair of scissors and helped himself to substantial cuttings of my hair. Finally he took out a razor-sharp scalpel and plenty of cotton gauze and disinfectant. To make the job easier I cut a nice piece of meat out of my palm for him, from the fleshy part of my left hand. Justin Blackmore placed the bloody lump into a small glass container and sealed, labelled and packed it away into a snap-lock valise.

'I hope I'll get to meet you again, Mr Montenero,' he said.

That brief visit so long ago caused me to do two things.

The first was that I went to the refrigerator and took out the small airtight plastic tub that contained Celeste's lock of hair, her nail cuttings and the vial of blood. I had an overwhelming desire to kiss the cold plastic, and so I did. A feeling of warmth flooded through me; it was undeniable, as if Celeste's essence had remained, something of her that was greater than these sad contents so carefully sealed away. I kissed it again and again, then, holding the tub up to the light, I saw how the strands of gold still shone.

I also saw that the drops of blood had of course long-since dried. I wondered if that rendered them useless. Her ashes had been scattered among the trees of our patch of forest out back, and this in my hand was all that physically remained of my wife. Doctor Vliegan and his associates would never have it, they would never have *her*, so now what could I do? Put the container in the trash, bury it in the dirt?

I replaced her remains lovingly in my refrigerator.

Despite what I'd said to Doctor Vliegan, one never can tell what might still lie ahead, isn't that correct?

The second thing is that from this point I took up a pen and tried to write again. It was the first time since Bruno Pasqua had taken me to Paris with him. Maybe I did it to try to fight loneliness;

maybe I was trying to rediscover my worth. It only struck me later, far into the neverending process, that I was writing to the line that would come later.

To you, and for you, whomever you might be.

It was what Vliegan the Third had suggested I not forget, their motto: *From one hand to the next.*

It strikes me now that if the new Kristof Vliegan is to be believed, the present fixation is on such profitable attributes as longevity, looks and health, but once these are conquered then surely there must come the next steps: how to make people wiser, or more artistic, or more mathematical, or more benevolent, or more industrious, or calmer, or more musical, or quieter – and, if so required in order to cull the chaff of inevitable failures, how to make the discards and the misfits better resiled to their mortality.

The possibilities are, of course, endless.

So here is my memory, my consciousness, for whatever good it might do the next new people.

For whatever heart it might give you, friend.

Godspeed.

Epilogue

PAIN WOKE HIM. EITHER PAIN or something else, something out-side. Maybe both. The pain was in his belly, to one side, and it travelled down into his groin. Yet when he opened his eyes the hurt disappeared and some remnant of a nightmare he couldn't recall still clung to him. At first he was confused, but he knew exactly where he was; at first he was uncertain, but the living room was quiet and unthreatening; at first he was unsure of his own name, but beneath his breath he said: *I am who I am and nothing else.*

He listened to the house. Silence. Or silent steps.

Still curled up in the deep sofa where he'd fallen asleep, Mark's eyes were open even though he couldn't bring himself to move. Montenero's books had settled inside him. He'd fallen into a deep slumber with the great fire blazing and now all the lumps of firewood were down to embers. The light of day was in the sky. Friday? Saturday? It felt as if weeks or months had passed.

Mark stayed where he was, dazed, disbelieving, relieved. All at the same time.

The ramblings of a crazy old man or the road into himself. Mark didn't know which he'd found. So many of those words and sentences written in blue ink continued to sing through his mind that he couldn't seem to separate his own thoughts from Montenero's. This morning the ghostly old mansion enveloped him; so did the old writer's story.

Mark glanced toward the coffee table by the sofa. The diaries were strewn across the polished oak. Two black covers, then blue, green, turquoise, more. He pushed himself into a sitting position, his spine and neck rebelling because of the cramped position he'd been in. He stretched one arm then the other. His clothes were filthy from the digging. He'd scrubbed his hands but there was soil beneath his fingernails. The last diary was still open and there was its last word: *Godspeed*.

He put his hands to his face and wept. Only a moment. When he pulled himself together he flicked those last pages with his wet fingers, scanning random sentences. His eyes lingered on that one there: *Despite what I'd said to Doctor Vliegan, one never can tell what might still lie ahead, isn't that correct?*

Was *he* supposed to be what might lie ahead?

The old writer had written those words in the context of Celeste. Mark thought about that, then he wondered if he could find out fast just how much of this tale Montenero had dreamed up. He made himself get to his feet and stood shivering even though the morning wasn't all that cold. He found himself wishing that the three dogs hadn't been whisked away. It would have been good to have their untroubled companionship.

The kitchen. The place to try first.

It was dazzlingly bright with sunshine that flooded in far too directly. More than motes of dust hung in the air, it was a veritable storm. His eyes flinched from the glare and the sheen of the shiny surfaces and he had to turn his back from the window. Then he opened the refrigerator and freezer, digging around carefully, investigating, feeling slightly foolish, only discovering the sorts of things one man without very much appetite might want to eat.

What about the pantry, that older, second refrigerator?

He opened the door to the pantry, switched on the light, went inside. Scents of condiments and spice and loose onions in a bowl. He studied the full-size appliance quietly humming in a corner. Something about it was odd: in a moment Mark worked out what. He checked again. The main refrigerator in the kitchen was plugged into a normal mains socket but the second one was plugged into a small electronic board on the floor. Mark crouched down. He could see it was an automatic switching device. One light, currently illuminated green, was marked 'Mains'. The second light, which was unlit, read 'Generator'. There must have been an auxiliary generator somewhere on the property, probably in one of the tool sheds near the house. If mains power went out, it took over.

What made it so important for the second refrigerator to have access to an uninterrupted power supply?

Inside, there was a packet of rice flour that looked a hundred years old. Also a quarter-full bottle of eyedrops and a small sealed pail marked 'arborio rice'. Nothing else. He closed the main door and opened the freezer, which was overcrowded. There was all the frozen dog meat he'd seen the day before. Dog bones too, plus plastic containers of what might have been frozen stews and soups.

Mark shook his head. The old man had only wanted to protect important perishables such as meats and future dinners. Shifting things around a little more, he saw there was one mid-sized tub with contents he couldn't quite identify.

Mark took it into the brighter light of the kitchen. He held the tub to the sunshine. Indefinite. He prised open the cold lid, flakes of ice and frost falling away. So that was why he hadn't been able to tell what was inside: it held a smaller, airtight plastic container. With the edges of his shirt he gently wiped off the plastic and held the container up to the streaming light by the window. That pure sun brought its contents alive. He shook the container a little, holding it up.

My God.

Nail clippings.

A small cloudy vial of brown dots.

Strands of gold hair that could still shimmer.

They shouldn't have meant anything; they could have meant anything; just a small memento of an absent wife that a loving husband might have treasured – but with a flood of warmth running through him Mark Alter kissed the iced plastic. Kissed and kissed it because the essence of Celeste was there, was still alive.

His heart lifted. It had no right to. This was an old man's pleasure, a forgotten husband's tenderness. Not his own, but he felt it anyway.

And, feeling it, he knew every word in Cesare Montenero's diaries was true.

Mark Alter fell to his knees.

The great Amati mansion is crumbling, but it houses itinerants, passing travellers, pigeons and locals mammals seeking shelter. The roof has caved in at any number of places and the western wing's main wall has collapsed, a lot of it falling inward, some outward. Weather and time have had their way. Even though the first sight of the old mansion had as much effect on him as staring at a dead dog in a ditch, he liked looking around at the abandoned pastures, liked imagining the young Cesare Montenero running with a ball and learning how to play with other children.

The huge landholding itself hasn't been completely abandoned, however. Mark sees that there are small stone homes with smoke whispering from their chimneys, and several hoed fields where asparagus, corn and maize crops prosper. Up above, the volcano is in one of its regular dormant phases. Like the nearby chimneys, only a breath of smoke floats into the sky. He decides that before returning home, he'll make an expedition, maybe hope to see the magical smoke rings he'd read about.

He walks down to the broken houses with his backpack over

one shoulder, drinking water from his flask. Though he knows the direction and has planned out almost every step on his Michelin map, he wants to ask one of the younger workers if he knows the way to the country house of the people who used to live here.

Mark consults his phrasebook and tries to get the words to make sense.

The teenage boy in front of him interrupts his stammering and says, in accented English, 'Which the ones you want to know?' He's chewing a mouthful of bread and cheese, hands large and hard, face dirty and sunburned. 'The Amatis was first, then this bunch a *bastardi* called "Westenholz". *A famiglia Westenholz* from Denmark. They gone broke. They just load their cars and drive away, 1953, 1954. Dunno. We call *il abbannunamentu,* you know?'

'It's the Amati family I'm interested in,' Mark tells him.

The boy sniffs hard. 'Good. Amati. I ask.'

He turns around and shouts something in Sicilian. Mark recognises the words 'Nonna' and 'casa' and 'Amati' and nothing else.

Soon a very small, very old woman emerges. Dressed in black, with a shawl, ninety-nine years of age if a day. She looks at her grandson, sniffs, and sucks her few remaining teeth as she considers the question. Then she looks more closely at Mark Alter.

And looks again.

Gradually it dawns on her. She has cloudy eyes but she sees the Amati in front of her as clearly as she sees her own grandson. She spits at Mark's feet.

'*Amati,*' she says with a sneer. '*Domenico Amati. Tuo padre?*'

'*Gesù,*' the grandson says with some feeling. 'Nonna wants to know if some bastard name of Domenico is your fudder? So you better fuck off before we start remembering the bad days, okay?'

Mark makes the trek in his own time, at the pace he likes. He can't see any need to rush. The days are mild, turning warm.

There might be no need to hurry, but he can't really stop the excitement that continues to build inside.

For the most part the terrain is easy to traverse and he takes every opportunity to climb slopes that look interesting and might offer better views of the dense forests surrounding him. Most of all, he likes seeing different aspects of the volcano's slopes.

One night he sleeps by a pond being fed by a running stream of water so cold it gives him a thrill to take off his clothes and wash himself down. As dawn breaks he stokes the small fire he'd built up for the night and surveys the silent forest landscape. He thinks it's as gentle and untouched as it must have been on the first day. He imagines he's been here before, done all of these things in earlier times, but maybe Cesare Montenero's neat sentences in blue ink simply refuse to stop moving through him.

Rabbits bound into a meadow. Clouds move across a foreign sky. He wants one more balmy night to sleep in the clear, clean open.

He does it.

Then there's the long straight road into the grounds of the country house. He sees the place and it seems as familiar to him as his old shack at Prospect Point or Montenero's mansion back in Godbless. He knows that if he rode a horse or drove a car he would be raising enough dust to alert anyone in that distant property that a visitor is coming, but he's sure he now approaches unseen, and certainly unexpected.

The excitement turns a little, becomes a small twisting of fear. All these days of wanting to find himself, now there's that secluded country manor ahead.

Mark Alter moves to the side of the dusty road and sits on a rock. He slings his backpack off his shoulders and takes out the diary he's been keeping. More than two hundred pages have already been filled, and he finds room for one small annotation, perhaps the last:

There's a lot of things that have stayed in my mind, questions that went begging, answers that only seemed like they filled half a story. Where's Vliegan; what's Blackmore got to do with all this; why did Cesare Montenero send his dogs away for six months then tell that man the answer to what he needed to do would become clear?

I feel like there's more for me in this. Cesare Montenero's last word was Godspeed. *He didn't write* The End. *So maybe the end hasn't arrived yet. Maybe it never will.*

But those are all small things. I don't let them bother me.

The major thing to think about is the ongoing effect of what we are, of what we were meant for. I look like Domenico Amati. I get that now. But I think like myself. I like to be alone but I don't have crazy dreams. I get a little pain every now and then. It doesn't lead to anything. Then there's all of this: the Don Domenico Amati of old could shoot two men as cleanly as if he'd been a trained marksman; Cesare Montenero could strangle a poor creature and put it into a fire; he could even take out his bloody revenge on a man named Batiste. And me, I could dream such horrors upon the world and its people. I proved that with what I twisted the creature No-Face into, in my screenplay.

I know what I am.

I don't know that I have complete faith in the promise of renewal.

Then again, maybe the facts are just ahead, right in front of me.

The young man is stripped to the waist, working in a tomato patch, setting up trestles for the running vines, a cloth turned around his head like a turban. He looks up and sees Mark approaching, the surprise in his long face slowly dawning into disbelief. His garden fork drops from his hands.

A woman is coming out the front door of the place that was once Don Domenico's isolated country retreat. She has a plate of sandwiches and a pitcher of cold water to bring to her man. She's in a yellow dress and her long blonde hair is tied back. Strands of gold catch the sun. He waves her over.

'Look. Come here, see who's visiting.'

She goes to him, presses close to his wiry, perspiring frame. He takes the plate and the pitcher and lays them onto the deep-green grass. She's wary, doesn't know Mark Alter or even Domenico Amati; neither does the baby in Celeste's belly, a beautiful round belly as ripe to burst as any of Cesare Montenero's fat fruit, or his rows and rows of sun-filled vegetables.

Acknowledgments

I'D LIKE TO THANK THE Literature Board of the Australia Council for its assistance in helping me complete this novel. Sincere thanks must also go to the State Library of Queensland, which in 2005 endowed me with its inaugural John Oxley Library Fellowship.

Kate Cornfoot worked as my assistant and researcher and will always have my appreciation.

The quote in 'White Book' is taken from the preface to Casanova's *Histoire de ma Vie*.

Warm thanks to Fiona Inglis, Madonna Duffy, Bettina Keil, Jim McCarthy, Giovanni Messina and most especially freelance editor Lindsey Moore.

To the memory of Angelina Armanno, 1935–2008.

THE DIRTY BEAT
Venero Armanno

Rock and jazz drummer Max is dead.

Now, in his coffin as his friends prepare to bury him, Max is surrounded by the ghosts of his life and the dreams that never faded. All the old music is back too – from raw seventies rock-and-roll to the type of cool jazz that made legends of John Coltrane and Miles Davis.

In this sea of memory, Max recalls the tragedies, people and relationships that defined his life. From his first love, Maree Kilmister, he learned about sex; from his great love, Debbie Canova, he learned about loss; and from the enigmatic Laetecia Sparks, he learned about hope. As the players in his life gather for his funeral, he has one last chance to relive his past and see it for what it was.

Driven by music and passion, *The Dirty Beat* shimmers with an electric intensity.

PRAISE FOR *THE DIRTY BEAT*

'One of the most versatile and daring of Australian novelists . . . An exhilarating, hectic, ultimately poignant journey.'

Bulletin

'*The Dirty Beat* is a bold, original and moving reckoning of a life in those final post-mortem moments with which Max – at least – has been blessed.'

Age

'A lovely rocking rolling swoop of a novel about a muso with a penchant for self-destruction, but in the most engaging way.'

Good Reading

'The book goes off like a shot, fast and furious and dirty and seeking a target that, in the end, explodes with a surprise, bittersweet ending that leaves you reeling.'

Sunday Mail

ISBN 978 07022 3690 7

UQP